PRAISE FOR SHIRLEY HAILSTOCK

The Secret

"Compelling characters drive the story in a satisfying, intricately plotted tale that involves issues of abandonment, trust, and the true meaning of family."

—*Library Journal*

You Made Me Love You

"Hailstock pens a strong, moving drama. Tension fills nearly every page . . . pacing is fast, and the intrigue and danger are just as intense as the love that develops . . ."

—*Romantic Times*

"Ms. Hailstock always comes through with good details, plotting, and a sense of adventure."

—*Affaire de Coeur*

HIS 1-800 WIFE

Selected by the Black Expressions Book Club

"Shirley Hailstock is an exceptional writer. This is a departure from her usual romantic suspense novel, but it is an incredibly successful one."

—*Romantic Times*

"This book really took me by surprise. While Ms. Hailstock's last book [*More Than Gold*] was full of danger and intrigue, this one is very up close and personal. I love the journey her characters take as they realize and examine their mutual love for each other. A very moving story by an accomplished author."

—*Old Book Barn Gazette*

Whispers of Love

Winner of the HOLT Medallion

"[Ms. Hailstock's] . . . plots are over the top of the world."

—*New York Times*

". . . as sensual as a Sandra Brown romance, as riveting as a Clive Cussler thriller. Love and espionage at its best."

—Michael Lee West, Author of *Crazy Ladies*

"A perfect love is shattered in this emotionally-charged roller-coaster of espionage, intrigue and romance. Not to be missed."

—Joanne Pence, Author of *Too Many Cooks*

More Than Gold
Winner of the Booksellers Best Award

"This is a fast-paced story . . . with the protagonists constantly on the run, staying just one step ahead and outwitting their pursuers. Miss Hailstock's painstaking care with detail and research does not go unnoticed. With many twists and revelations this well-plotted story is worthy of being made into a movie. I hope the BET producers are paying attention."

—*Affaire de Coeur*

"*More Than Gold* is just that—a treasure . . . *More Than Gold* explodes with action and sensuality. Its twists and turns leave you breathless for more. Your heart pounds as Morgan and Jack escape death and destruction while they learn to trust each other and fall in love. Ms. Hailstock is a master of suspense."

—*Bridges Magazine*

Legacy
Winner of the Waldenbooks Award
Chosen as one of the 100 Best Romance Novels
of the 20th Century

"[*Legacy*] . . . will put the reader through an emotional roller coaster. From a deep and abiding love, to spine-chilling suspense, *Legacy* has it all."

—Dinah McCall, Author of *Jackson Rule*

"Beautifully drawn characters and a riveting story combine for a marvelous read! Exciting, sensuous *and* suspenseful. What more could you want?"

—Suzanne Forster, Author of *Angel Face*

"Legacy is a riveting drama that blends the best elements of romance and suspense to create a quality literary liqueur too smooth and too lush not to be addictive!"

—Romantic Times Magazine

White Diamonds

Glamour Magazine "Fall in Love Again" List

"White Diamonds is a fast-paced romantic suspense that entices readers to finish in one sitting. . . . The audience will shout 'Hail, hail,' to Shirley Hailstock for a great story."

—Affaire de Couer, 4+

"Gripping. A powerful drama—a powerful love story."

—Stella Cameron, Author of *Glass Houses*

"Shirley Hailstock has once again raised the ordinary to extraordinary, the sublime to exquisite, and bathed it in an exotic romantic fantasy."

—Romantic Times, 4 1/2 (Excellent)

Opposites Attract

National Reader's Choice Award Finalist

". . . Hailstock thoroughly explores the emotional conflicts of her characters . . ."

—Publishers Weekly

"Opposites Attract is a complex, emotional love story with ribbons of poignancy pulling the romance together in a treat that is just too good to resist."

—Romantic Times

ON MY TERMS

SHIRLEY HAILSTOCK

Kensington Publishing Corp.
http://www.kensingtonbooks.com

DAFINA BOOKS are published by

Kensington Publishing Corp.
850 Third Avenue
New York, NY 10022

ISBN-13: 978-0-7582-1351-8
ISBN-10: 0-7582-1351-4

First mass market printing: January 2008

10 9 8 7 6 5 4 3 2 1

Printed in the United States of America

To Mary Lou Frank, Gail Freeman, and Lois Rosenthal. These ladies, cloistered in my car on the way to and from the Long Island Romance Writers' Annual Luncheon, played the "what if" game as we plotted this book.

Chapter 1

Theresa Ramsey gripped the wheel of the vintage Mustang as she sped along the mountain road. Sunlight winked in and out of the trees like strobe lights star-bursting through the dense thickness. Squinting at the intermittent blindness, she lifted her chin and the wind snatched her hair, streaking it out behind her, the sun warming her face and arms. It was the kind of day when Theresa itched to throw the car into third gear and test the way the tires gripped S curves and hairpin turns, luxuriate in the way it responded to the slightest nudge of the steering wheel. A day when the exhilaration of being alive and carefree would open not only the road, but her spirit as well. However, today wasn't that day, and it hadn't been for years.

Theresa slipped her sunglasses up into her hair to hold it back and to take in the natural beauty of the day. She breathed deeply, wishing she were anyplace else except on the road to Collingswood.

It was ironic how a place can hold years of happy memories: birthday parties, Christmases, hide and seek played in the summer sun, afternoon teas in the backyard. You only need to call it to mind for the wonderful times to roll like a movie projector. And then something terrible happens and they are wiped away as if the good times never happened.

That's how it was with Collingswood, the house in Royce, New York where she had been born.

Theresa couldn't think of a single reason from her experience why anyone would want to go home again. She certainly didn't want to return. But she had no place else to take her seven-year-old withdrawn cousin. Circumstances and lack of money had made the decision for her.

The '67 Mustang's engine purred as Theresa took one curve after another. Actually, it wasn't her car. Well it was, but it didn't have her name on the registration. It had been her cousin Meghan's car. And Meghan was dead. The car was the one thing about the entire situation that brought a smile to her lips.

Glancing at her cousin's daughter, she noticed the child had not moved. Chelsea sat quietly, staring through the front window, focused on some point that was out of reach. She'd done this for the last three hundred miles, since they'd left the house in Buffalo, New York and headed east. Theresa hadn't been able to get her interested in anything for the last few months. Instinctively, Chelsea must have known the end was near for Meghan, and Chelsea died a little, too. Even her favorite sport, gymnastics, couldn't get her excited enough to attend her weekly lesson.

Slowing down, Theresa rounded the last turn. She was tired, weary from travel, and hungry. Abruptly, she hit the brake. In front of the gates was a crowd of people.

"What's this?" she muttered under her breath. Cars straggled over the road and the shoulder. Crowds of people blocked the entrance. She pressed the horn for several short beeps. They looked at her but didn't move. Again she blew the horn, then moved the car inch by inch, forcing them to divide into a path wide enough for her to reach the wrought iron gates that were the last barrier between her and a hot shower.

Chelsea shrank in her seat. It was the most reaction Theresa had seen from her since they had left Buffalo that morning. Yet she wished the child didn't have to do it. She also wished she had put the top up when they had stopped at the grocery store a few miles before they started up the mountain.

"Who are you?" someone called.

"Are you part of the crew?" another voice asked.

"Can you get us in?"

Theresa rolled to the gates. A guard stood there. "Sorry, ma'am, no one except the crew is allowed in, and they are all accounted for." He gave her a friendly smile and glanced at Chelsea.

"Who are you?" Theresa asked, confused.

"Name's John Willis. Security Protection. Hired for the duration." He flashed her a smile that should have been on a billboard.

"Duration of what?"

In the background, Theresa heard someone say, "Aw, she's nobody." The crowd ignored her then, and most moved away, taking up their previous positions along the fence. Several stragglers stayed close in case there was more to the situation than appeared on the surface.

"Just the duration," he said. Obviously, whatever had brought this crowd here wasn't going to be told to her.

"Mr. Willis, my name is Theresa Ramsey. I own this house."

"I have no information about that, ma'am."

His smile was getting on her nerves. The crowd behind her moved in again. They must have sensed something was going on. Theresa glanced at them and through the fence. Then it dawned on her, security, groupies. That film company couldn't still be here. Her agreement with them ended a week ago.

Anger surged through her. "Did you hear me?" She tried to keep her voice calm. She'd been doing that since she'd come back from England to care of her dying cousin. She'd done it for Chelsea's sake, but at this moment, she wanted to shout at this man.

"Yes, ma'am. I heard you, but I have orders . . ."

"Mister," she interrupted. "Here's my driver's license. It has my name and my photo on it. You can see I am Theresa Ramsey. This is my house. I've driven three hundred miles today with a child who really needs to rest. And I am going through this gate."

"Is there a problem here?" Another security guard arrived. He was older than the first, but his body was just as hard. His face was set in a no-nonsense expression.

"No."

"Yes." She and the first officer spoke at the same time. "I am the owner of this property, and I'm coming in."

"We don't know anything about . . ."

Theresa rolled her eyes. "I don't give a—" She stopped, remembering Chelsea. "How many guards are here?"

"What?"

"Are there enough to control this crowd?"

The two officers looked at each other but said nothing.

"Call them," she ordered.

"Ma'am." Obviously, the second guy had more authority. He was going to try to reason with her, but Theresa was beyond reasoning.

"Call them!" Although her voice was soft, there was no doubting her seriousness. "I have a remote control here." She snatched it from the visor and put her hand on the button. "If I push this button, that gate will retract." She looked around. "Do you think the two of you can control this crowd, or will they surge through in the wake of dust I'll leave behind?"

Seconds later, several men the size of linebackers came surging toward the gate. If Theresa wasn't so tired, she'd laugh. The way they came running, you'd have thought she was holding her finger on a nuclear bomb instead of a gate release. Theresa didn't wait for them to give her clearance. She pressed the button, and just as it had the last time she'd entered Collingswood five years ago, the gate retracted. Only this time, the squeak of the chain wasn't so apparent. Someone had oiled it.

As soon as there was enough room for the car, she hit the gas and flew through the opening, hoping she kicked up enough dust to blind the guards. The road was paved, but it had been left untended for years and nature had tried to reclaim it. She winged the vintage Mustang around the curve and came to a sharp stop in front of the house.

Theresa had expected the place to look as it had five years ago, or worse. It was a fieldstone-covered structure with huge white pillars supporting a double level porch. The paint on the porch had once been white, but last time she saw it, it had turned a dingy gray. Two of the steps had needed replacing. Vines had grown along the east side in an unruly tangle that had reminded her of Jack's beanstalk. But what she saw was different. The place had been repaired. The paint gleamed in the afternoon light. The vines had been cut back, and the trees manicured. The place had been restored to the way it had looked when Theresa lived here as a child. Before her father disappeared. And before her mother committed suicide.

She blinked, feeling she was looking at an illusion, that things would fall back into place, into the disrepair she expected. But nothing had changed when she opened her eyes.

"We're here," Theresa told Chelsea. The little girl said nothing. She didn't move either. Theresa got out of the car and pulled the bag of groceries out. She'd get everything else later. Right now, feeding Chelsea and letting her rest was paramount in her mind. Then Theresa would let these intruders know that they were trespassing and that she wanted them gone.

After Theresa opened Chelsea's door, the little girl got out. "Are you hungry?" Theresa asked. Chelsea looked up at her with big, sad eyes. She said nothing. Theresa thought of those velvet paintings with bright colors that people sold on the highway or at gas stations. Usually, they were of horses with their front legs in the air or a beautiful child with one tear rolling down her cheek. That child could have been Chelsea's twin. Theresa hated those paintings. Why should children cry?

Why should they be sad? Children were born to be loved, and their childhood should be filled with pleasant days and the promise of more to come. As they went up the now repaired steps, Theresa remembered her childhood and that of her brother had been nothing like the fantasy she'd just created.

The porch was large. Wicker chairs had been arranged in conversation groupings on both sides of the front door. Theresa dropped Chelsea's hand and turned the knob before she remembered the key was still in her purse. The door swung open on silent hinges.

Lights suddenly glared in her eyes, and she raised her hand to shield them.

"Cut!" a voice boomed. "Who the hell opened that door?"

Startled, Theresa dropped the bag and pulled Chelsea to her. The bright lights came from everywhere. She glanced in one direction after another, but everywhere, there were lights blinding her. Her heart raced. She could see nothing.

"Who the hell are you?" the same voice shouted at her. He was closer this time.

Theresa looked in the direction of the voice. A dark-skinned man with braided hair came toward her. A shock wave ran through her. He was striking, with long braids tied back with a leather band and light brown, angry eyes now boring into her. Theresa felt her stomach drop as if she were on a roller coaster that had just plunged down the first drop.

Squaring her shoulders but keeping hold of Chelsea, she shot back. "Who are you? And what is going on here?"

"How did you get past the guards? Get her out of here," he said, apparently to no one in particular, but a large man standing nearby moved toward her.

"I wouldn't touch me," she told him in a voice as deep and menacing as if she held a gun. The man stopped.

"Am I ever going to get this scene done?" The first man spoke. "Lady, whoever you are, please leave. We're trying to work here."

"I'm not leaving, you are," she told him.

"Why would I leave?"

"Are you in charge here?" she asked.

"I'm in charge," the light-eyed guy with braids said. "This is my house."

"Your house?"

"That's right. This is my house. And I'll thank you to vacate it this very minute."

She reached down and picked up the bag she'd dropped, retrieving and replacing the items that had fallen out. Taking Theresa's hand, she moved through what obviously was the movie set, staring down anyone who deigned to look at her, and went to the kitchen. Placing the bag on the counter, she pulled a chair out and pushed Chelsea into it.

"Are you all right?" she asked in a low voice.

Chelsea nodded.

"Do you want something to eat?"

Again, she nodded.

"I'll fix us some omelets. You just sit still."

Quickly, she removed the things from the bag. Finding stuff in the refrigerator of dubious dating, she shoved it aside and put in fresh milk and the eggs that hadn't broken when she dropped the bag. She had already whipped up the eggs and was pouring an omelet into the frying pan when the man she had spoken to earlier came through the door.

He was tall and good-looking and carried a sheaf of papers in his hand. "Are you Theresa Ramsey?"

She looked at him and nodded.

"Dean Clayton." He offered his hand.

"Sorry." She looked at the frying pan and spatula she was using to turn the eggs.

He turned and looked at Chelsea. "Hello."

Chelsea said nothing. She stared at Theresa, her eyes full of fear.

"It's all right, honey," Theresa assured her.

"Are you the silent type?" Dean asked her. "We need your type in the movies." He smiled at her. She stared blankly at him.

He smiled warmly, but Chelsea did not respond. Turning back to Theresa, he said, "I have an agreement here signed by Jamison Taylor as your agent for the use of this property."

"You're supposed to be using the guest house and the out-buildings." Theresa flipped the eggs onto a plate. The toast popped up, and she grabbed the pieces and slid them onto the plate.

"At the last minute, that was changed."

"And you were supposed to be gone last week."

"We're running a little behind schedule."

"That's not my problem, Mr. Clayton. This is my house, and I want it."

She put the plate in front of Chelsea. Then she opened a new container of strawberry jam and spread some on the toast. After Theresa had added a glass of milk to the side of the plate, Chelsea leaned forward, almost brushing her nose in the food, and began to eat.

"Do you think we could talk somewhere in private?" Dean asked, glancing at the child, who ate methodically and appeared disinterested in their conversation. Theresa relented, giving him a small amount of credit for considering the insecurity that could be instilled in children who witnessed arguments.

She bent down and looked into Chelsea's soft brown eyes. "I have to speak to this gentleman," she said. "We're going to go out there on the porch." Theresa pointed toward the back porch. It was an enclosed space with French doors and windows that brightened the kitchen. Theresa's father had had it built for her mother. "You'll be able to see me through the windows," she continued, ending with, "Eat your food, and I'll be right back." She kissed Chelsea's cheek and stood up.

Dean Clayton stared at her with a soft and approving look

in his eyes. Theresa turned away from him and strutted to the porch. No approving look was going to soften her resolve. The people in her house were trespassing, and she wanted them out.

"We seem to be in a sort of dilemma here," he began.

"Only on your part. I am perfectly aware of my rights in the situation."

She watched as his face darkened. He stood up straighter, exuding power that grew as she watched him. Theresa felt intimidated but refused to show it.

"I have a contract here for the use of this house signed by your duly appointed agent."

She was shaking her head as he continued.

"Mr. Taylor agreed to an extension of three months. We'll be done by the end of the summer."

"Not worth the paper it's printed on." She folded her arms and stood her ground.

"What do you mean?"

"I mean, Mr. Clayton—"

"Dean," he interrupted her. "I have a large number of brothers and sisters. Calling me Mr. Clayton makes me want to look around for one of them."

"All right, Dean it is. I'm Theresa. But first names don't change things. Your contract expired five days ago. Mr. Taylor had only the right to act as my agent for that period. After that, I'd have to sign for it to be legal." She raised her hands, palms out. "And I didn't sign anything." Her smile was sardonic.

"I'm sure we can work things out. It's only for three months."

"Three months is a lifetime, Mr. . . . Dean," she corrected herself. As you can see, I have a child to consider." She glanced at Chelsea through the window. The child ate her food with the precise movements of a robot programmed for repetitive actions.

"She's been through a trauma," Dean said. His voice was low and concerned, as if he was speaking to himself.

"You're very perceptive," Theresa said. Most people who had met Chelsea recently thought she was retarded or autistic.

"What was the trauma, if you don't mind my asking?"

Theresa moved closer and stared at her second cousin.

"Her mother died last week. We buried her three days ago. Chelsea thinks it's her fault. Her father died in Iraq, she's lost the only parent she ever knew, been uprooted from her home and driven six hours away from her friends."

"I'm sorry. I understand some of what she's going through." He turned back to face Theresa. She was sorry she had moved closer to the window. It had brought her close enough to Dean to feel the heat of his body, smell his aftershave. "You must be tired, too. You should get some sleep. We can talk about it in the morning."

"No, you should be gone in the morning."

"Please, Theresa. There are a lot of people here that you'd put out of work."

"In case you haven't noticed, I have a child to take care of. She's lost her mother; she's grieving and needs loving care at the moment." Theresa's voice nearly broke. She swallowed hard and continued, "We don't need a lot of people running around. I doubt we could get any rest at all with the noise going on here."

"At least give it a try. It's been an awful day. This scene hasn't gone right once. I've sunk everything I have into this project. Please," he ended.

He looked as if he'd had a harried day. Her day had been the pits, too. But he was right—she should get a good night's rest before making a decision. After all, she was broke.

After a long moment with the two of them staring at each other, she said, "I don't know why I'm doing this. Let's just say that I have a headache the size of this room. I'm tired from the long drive. I'm hungry enough to eat a steak the size of Texas. And Chelsea's welfare is more important to me than either you or your film."

Theresa woke disoriented. It was dark, and the room was unfamiliar. Where was she? Quickly, she sat up in bed, searching for Chelsea. Then she remembered. She was back at Collingswood in the carriage house. Getting up, she nearly ran to the adjoining room. Throwing open the door, she found Chelsea, peacefully asleep. Theresa took a deep breath. Her shoulders dropped in relief.

Closing the door, she padded barefoot to the bedroom door. Thirst sent her to the kitchen in search of water. Dean stood up the moment she opened the kitchen door.

"Oh, I didn't know you were here," she said, squinting at the sudden light.

"I often work in here after finishing the day's shooting and viewing the dailies." He sat back down.

"I was just looking for some water."

"Here, let me get it."

"I'll do it." Theresa went to the fridge and grabbed a bottle of water. She hadn't been in this building for years. The last time she'd seen it, it had looked much like the rest of the property, run-down and in need of repair. Now it looked lived in, freshly painted and occupied.

"What do you and the crew do for food?"

"We have caterers. Food is prepared three times a day and snacks are always available."

Theresa took a chair opposite him. "I see," she said.

"We didn't expect you to return. Mr. Taylor said you hadn't been back here in five years and that you weren't expected."

Theresa took a long drink of her water. "That's right. But things change, and I had to come back."

"You say that like you didn't want to come."

There was that perception again.

"Did it go well after we left?" She changed the subject.

He leaned back in his chair. The kitchen table was covered with papers. His cell phone lay next to the stack.

He sighed. "We finally got the scene done. But things aren't going well overall."

"Why is that?"

"I don't know." Putting the papers he was holding down, he looked intently at her. "I look at the dailies, and I can tell something is wrong, missing. I don't know if it's chemistry or something else. I just feel we haven't reached or found what I think we should for this film."

"Are you telling me this because you think I'll change my mind?"

He smiled at her. Theresa felt something happen to her. Her stomach tightened, even though Dean seemed to relax.

He shook his head. "Have you changed your mind?"

"No." She took a drink from the water bottle to hide any visible expression of her feelings. She somehow felt his smile was used more than the scowl she'd witnessed earlier today. He was tall, an inch or two over six feet, from what she'd noticed earlier, and his skin was smooth, a dark, dark brown. He had a generous amount of long, dark hair braided into strands the size of her little finger. It cascaded down his back, although earlier he'd had it gathered in a rubber band. The hair was striking, but even more so were his noticeably long eyelashes fringing eyes so light brown Theresa thought sunlight could pass right through them. His eyes alone probably got him a second glance from every woman walking the planet. Or at least all those beautiful California women he must meet as a film director. He was the best-looking man Theresa had ever seen. And from the way her stomach fluttered, well, he was getting a second look from her, too.

"Is there anything I can do to make you change it?"

The question snapped her back to the issue at hand. "Let's let it rest until morning."

He nodded. "I'm really sorry about your cousin and Chelsea. She seems like a nice little girl."

"Thank you. Chelsea just needs rest and time to grieve."

"And you?"

The question threw her. No one seemed to have any concern for her plight. All the focus had been on Chelsea. Including Theresa's. She was an adult and should be better able to understand the cycle of life and death, even when it took a twenty-nine-year-old mother. Chelsea was only seven years old, so she thought she had done something wrong.

"I'll be all right," Theresa answered him. "I came home from England after she got too ill to take care of herself and took care of her for two years before she died."

"Is that why you have an accent that is fading?"

She smiled then. "Meghan, my cousin, used to talk about the accent. I lived in England for a long time."

"It's beautiful," he said. "I like the sound of it."

Theresa felt heat pour into her face. She was glad she wasn't as light-skinned as Dean, or he'd see how much his comment affected her. It had been a long time since a man had noticed her. Taking care of her cousin and Chelsea had left her no time for a personal life.

"What's the movie about?" Theresa asked, directing the conversation away from her. She sat down at the table, curled her feet up in the chair, and looked directly at him.

"I'm wondering if I even know," he muttered more to himself than to her. Then he looked at her and said, "A boy is separated from his parents, and is trying to reach them while trying to avoid those who would murder him."

"That's it?"

He looked at her. "In a nutshell," he replied.

"Is that it?" She pointed to the sheaf of papers on the kitchen table.

He nodded.

"May I read it?" she asked. She noticed his slight hesitation.

"I've never seen a script before." He passed it to her, but she noticed the reluctance. "I suppose around Hollywood these things are top secret."

"Not at this stage, but we don't pass them around like candy."

"I won't be going anywhere with it. With that mob outside the gate, I doubt I can get in and out for food."

"You won't need to if you let me stay."

"I didn't come back to be cloistered inside these walls."

"I apologize. I'm feeling lousy today. I didn't mean to imply that you did."

Theresa stood up. "I'd better take Chelsea and go up to the house."

Dean stood up, too. With the lower ceiling of the carriage house, he appeared even taller than she'd remembered.

"I brought your stuff in." He glanced toward the front door. Theresa couldn't see it from where she stood.

"You don't expect me to move in here and give you my house?"

"No," he said, raising his hands as if to ward her off. "I just thought for tonight. Chelsea is already asleep, and it seems a shame to wake her. Also, from what I've seen of the rooms in the house, they need cleaning. I can have a crew do it for you in the morning."

Theresa could see he was trying to help her, and that he was trying not to blow off some steam. She wasn't used to being helped. She'd always been the caregiver. No one had ever put her needs ahead of their own. She didn't fault Meghan. Her cousin couldn't help what had happened. And she'd been Theresa's best friend all her life. If it hadn't been for Meghan, Theresa didn't know how she would have lived with her aunt after her father's disappearance and her mother's death.

"That was very nice of you," Theresa said.

"You can stay in the room you were in. I'll join one of the actors in the trailers."

"Oh, I won't put you out," she interrupted. "As long as you're willing to share, and there is plenty of room here, we can manage to stay out of each other's way for one night."

"Are you sure?"

She nodded. Dean Clayton was not what he had been made out to be in the fanzines, e-zines and news reports. Based on those, she would have thought he would care nothing about her comfort and think little of spending the night with a strange woman and her child. Didn't all Hollywood stars bed-hop all the time? Yet he'd offered to give up his space and move in with someone else.

"I think I'll turn in, then." She looked at the script in her arms. "I'll do some reading before going to sleep." She turned toward the bedroom, then back at him. "Maybe you should take a walk along the river."

He looked at her questioningly.

"It used to relax me when I was younger. I'd work out my problems down by the water."

"Maybe I'll do that." The two of them looked at each other for a moment. Theresa felt reluctant to leave him. Somehow, she wanted to delve into his personality and see who he really was.

"You . . . you want to go with me?"

Yes. She nearly said it out loud. The thrill at the thought of spending more time with him was strong, stronger than she had felt about a man in a very long time. Then she thought of Chelsea sleeping down the hall. She glanced at the doorway to the bedrooms.

"Chelsea," she said.

"Oh yeah."

It wasn't unusual for people without children to forget them. If Chelsea hadn't been exhibiting unusual behavior, she could have left her for a few minutes, but Theresa needed to be close to the child in case anything happened.

"Well, good night," he said.

"Good night," she echoed.

Theresa went back to the bedroom she'd slept in and looked in on Chelsea. She was still asleep. Theresa smiled and adjusted her covers. She pushed the child's hair back from her face and whispered, "We're home, baby. We're back."

Chelsea hadn't been sleeping well. She had nightmares and walked in her sleep now. Maybe being here, away from the memories and the house she had shared with her mother, would help her mend and live a normal childhood. Theresa hoped so, even though Collingswood had not been a happy childhood for her.

Several minutes later, she got their luggage from the entryway and changed into her nightgown. Then she crawled into bed and began reading. Moments later, she heard the door open and close. Dean had taken her advice and gone for a walk.

He'd impressed her. It was his vulnerability that she liked. It was under the surface, and she wasn't sure he let many people see it. But she'd seen it. There was something about him that spoke to her, spoke deeply to her heart.

She looked at the script. *The Homecoming, by Dean Clayton.* She shivered. With all that had happened to her, this seemed like a weird prophecy.

Chapter 2

The night was soft and quiet except for the singing of the crickets. Dean could hear no music or muffled conversation coming from the scattered trailers. The generators that provided electricity for air conditioning and all the comforts of a Hollywood home on wheels faded to a low hum as he headed toward the river.

On a night that was dark and moonless, everything around him was still. The water appeared black and secretive. It was just as well, Dean thought. The water reflected his feelings. Theresa had said the river helped her think, work out her problems. He supposed you had to know what your problem was before you could work it out.

The problem was in the script. He just didn't know where. When he'd presented it to the producers, some had been enthusiastic. Others had reviewed it with as much enthusiasm as they would have for a piece of cold toast. That's where the family had stepped in. His sister Rosa had come to his rescue with money. And behind his back, she'd told the family. He had enough money to get the story in the can. He could do it. He'd helped do it before, more than once. But not with one of his own scripts. And not with money that meant so much to him. He wouldn't bankrupt any of the Claytons if the cost wasn't recouped at the box office, but he needed to prove to himself, to his family, to the powers in Hollywood, that he was one of them. That he had that spark. Had the gall, gumption, and talent it took to translate a script to the screen and make it something the public hungered to see.

Dean sat down on a bench and held his head up with his elbows on his knees. He stared out at the dark water, wondering what it was hiding under the surface. Would it be the well that bubbled the answer? Was what he needed to know hovering below the sleek calm of the surface?

He thought about Theresa. She was sleek on the surface, too. But there was something under her surface. He'd felt it the moment he'd confronted her in the doorway of the house. He was now a director. In Hollywood, he'd been an assistant director. His name appeared on the opening screen of five pictures, and his reputation was growing. Women usually fell all over him. Most wanted him to cast them or put in a word with the casting director for a picture. A few had acted as if they were truly interested in him, and not as a director, but that had proved untrue.

He leaned back and laughed. If he were like his brothers, especially Owen, he'd be off women for good. Well, maybe for years. Owen had found his perfect match last year, and he was a changed man. Dean didn't put women on the "quantity is better than quality" list, but he was wary when they approached him. Theresa was different. She was removed from the world of make-believe, and she didn't appear enthralled by it the way the fans outside the gate did. Her concerns were more for Chelsea than anyone else.

She'd refused to walk with him because of the child. He admired that in her. It reminded him of Erin, his brother Digger's wife. She ran a nursery school and had adopted a child who had lost her parents.

Dean envisioned Theresa in the darkness. Her eyes were deep brown, but as dark as the water. They had a mysterious pith to them that bore into his mind as if she could read his thoughts. He set her age at about twenty-seven, fair-skinned with yellow-red undertones. She had thick black hair that had been wind-combed when she barged onto the set this afternoon. It had been more disheveled when she came out of the bedroom, but she hadn't even thought of her appearance. Hadn't put on lipstick or made sure she presented her best side the way women usually did in his presence. Yet he found her beautiful. Her head came up to his chin, but the legs she had tucked under her as she sat in the kitchen chair were as long as the Golden Gate Bridge. Her breasts, although only of medium fullness, were the right size to show a hint of cleavage or provide the half-moon promise in a strapless gown.

And she was the last thing he needed.

He had the script driving him mad. The lead actress couldn't remember her lines. There was no chemistry between the two leads, and they hated each other. The set was plagued by noise, malfunctioning equipment, the weather, and every other conceivable inconvenience. And now, here he was, distracted by a landlady threatening to throw him off the property, yet she made his body tremble.

What else could happen?

Jamison Taylor's office was as neat and clean as any Philadelphia lawyer's. Huge and spacious, the dark paneling and cases of law books showed not a speck of dust. Jamison sat behind a massive desk before two huge windows that looked out on Main Street.

"Were you out of your mind?" Theresa asked him. "How could you extend the rental of my property without authority? You're a lawyer. Isn't that illegal or something?"

"Theresa, please sit down and let's discuss this calmly."

"I don't want to sit down." She paced back and forth behind the two wingback chairs that faced this desk. When she'd awakened this morning, Dean was gone. There was a fresh pot of coffee in the kitchen with a note telling her that breakfast was in the dining room of the main house. And would she please use the north entrance.

She'd dumped the coffee down the drain and balled the paper between her hands before throwing it at the trash receptacle. She missed. Chelsea came in saying she was hungry. There was nothing for breakfast in the refrigerator, and for some unknown reason, Theresa became angry at Dean. She helped Chelsea dress, and they drove out, stopping for breakfast at the first fast food place they came to. Then Theresa drove to Jamison's office, storming in with all the anger that had been building since she had arrived at her property yesterday.

"You had no authority past a week ago. So why is Dean Clayton and a full film crew still on my property? I want them gone."

Jamison got up and came around the desk. She knew he liked to sit behind it. The vastness of it made him look like a king, and the people in front of him his subjects. She'd known him when they were children, but she had only been in his office once before. He'd contacted her in Buffalo when the film scouts had first discovered her property. She'd executed all the papers he'd sent her to allow the crew to use the property, including a document giving him power of attorney, but there was a time limit to it, and that time had come and gone.

"Theresa, no one expected you to return."

"That is beside the point. The house is mine, and you had no right to lease it to anyone, for any period, without my permission. I could have you before the Law Review Board over this."

"Let's not get hasty." He covered his nervousness with a laugh, but Theresa heard it.

"Jamison, I have a child in that waiting room." She pointed toward the door. "She needs somewhere calm to grow up."

"Then why'd you bring her here?"

Theresa leveled him a stare that could have withered plastic plants.

"I'm sorry. I shouldn't have said that." He took a step toward her. Theresa wanted to step back but stopped herself. "They pay a lot of money for the property, Theresa. The people in town are making a fortune from the things they need out there. Nobody is going to like it if you toss them out."

"Especially you," she replied. "They're a week past their last *legal* date. You didn't bother to call and let me know, and you certainly never wired anything to my bank. If I hadn't shown up, unexpected and unannounced, when would I get my share of any of this money?"

"Of course I was going to tell you. We're just a little busy right now. I'm shorthanded and—"

"Save it, Jamison. You're a shyster if I ever saw one."

Jamison stepped back as if she'd hit him.

"Let me tell you what we're going to do," Theresa said, moving forward. *"You* are going to write a letter telling Mr. Clayton that you had no authority to rent my property. *You* are going to return every cent that company paid you for the time for which you had no authority. And *you* are going to do it today. I will deal directly with Dean Clayton or whoever is in charge out there. And I am going to put my trust in another lawyer."

Theresa gathered her purse and slipped the strap over her shoulder in preparation for leaving. She looked Jamison directly in the eye. "Now, I suggest you phone Mr. Clayton and get your secretary to draw up a check. It better be for every penny he paid you, no deductions for legal expenses, since we both know there was nothing legal about this."

She went to the door and opened it. "I'll be back in an hour. Have it ready. I'll return it in person. That should suit you since it saves you from having to look a *man* in the eye."

She let the implication hang in the air as she took Chelsea's hand and marched out of the office. Outside, she took a deep breath. The air felt cleaner, and she felt as if she needed to wash her hands.

Dean met her as she drove through the secure gates. Theresa stopped. “Get in,” she said.

“What’s going on?” he asked. “I got a call from your lawyer.”

“He’s no longer my lawyer.”

Theresa drove toward the house where she’d parked yesterday.

“Go to the carriage house please,” Dean instructed. “The crew is eating lunch, and I’d like to discuss this without them hearing.”

Theresa turned off the main drive and onto the alternate road. They needed to get their luggage, and she wanted to put Chelsea someplace where she wouldn’t hear the discussion. Inside, she found lunch set up in the kitchen. Theresa looked at Dean.

“I thought you might be hungry,” Dean said. Then he dropped down to Chelsea’s level and spoke to her. “Are you hungry?”

She stared at him, then looked up at Theresa. Since Meghan had died, Chelsea had said very little. She’d whimpered in her sleep and screamed when she had nightmares, but she didn’t speak like a normal seven-year-old.

Theresa nodded to her. She looked back at Dean but said nothing.

“Well, I thought you might like a hamburger and french fries.” He got up and popped the food in the microwave. Moments later, he’d fixed her a plate and offered her a chair. Chelsea clung to Theresa’s hand and made no move.

“It’s all right, honey. You can eat it.” She looked at Dean. “It was very thoughtful of you.” Theresa smiled. Again she was feeling that strangeness that made her body go warm and tingle in his presence.

Theresa helped Chelsea to her chair.

"Be careful," Dean cautioned her. "The french fries are very hot. Do you like catsup or vinegar on them?"

Chelsea pointed to the vinegar.

"From what I've read about you, I thought you were from Texas?" Theresa asked.

"Dallas, but I thought I'd lost most of my drawl."

"I have a keen ear. And I'm sure they don't serve french fries with vinegar in Texas."

"I've been here for several months."

Theresa nodded. "You've developed a taste for them?" She reached over and grabbed one of Chelsea's. The child didn't react.

"Chelsea, I need to talk to your cousin in the other room. Is that all right?" Chelsea said nothing. She looked at Theresa.

"Like yesterday. It'll only take a few minutes, and we'll come back and eat with you."

Theresa noticed how clean the living room was. Last night papers had been scattered about, interspersed with empty water bottles. Theresa opened her purse and pulled out the rescinded contract and check. She handed them to him.

Dean read the letter and looked at the check. "This means we're out."

Theresa sat down. She gestured for Dean to take a seat. "You're not out. You're just no longer dealing with Jamison Taylor."

"Then why . . ." He lifted the check and the contract.

"They're not legal. And I noticed the amount of the check is almost three times as much as the original contract."

"He said because we were beyond our time limit, the amount was higher."

"He was rooking you."

"I know that, but I had no choice. We couldn't start over. We were already here, and if we closed up, the process would start again from scratch, and this film would never make it to completion."

"Well, here are my terms."

Dean drew in a breath and held it.

"You can make your movie here."

He let out the breath.

"Don't relax too quickly," she cautioned. "There are conditions."

"Go ahead," he said.

"My one and only concern is that little girl in the other room." While she kept her gaze trained on Dean, she pointed toward the kitchen.

"I understand that. And I commend you for putting her first."

Theresa kept her face businesslike. "The rental amount is the same as it was originally. I don't believe in taking advantage of people, not even rich Hollywood people."

"I am by no means rich," he said.

"Nevertheless, you can continue paying the original rental amount, prorated for the remaining time. I will stay out of your crew's way, and they'll do the same. I understand that the house is being used. We'll occupy the back upstairs bedrooms and the kitchen. You will provide me with a schedule of dates, rooms, and times if you need any room that we are occupying. While you're filming, we'll make sure we don't disturb you. I hope we can count on you to do the same when filming is over."

His head bobbed up and down. "Of course, you're welcome to eat with us. There is always plenty of food."

"You'll do something about that crowd outside the gates." She went on as if he hadn't spoken. "Position a checkpoint at the entrance to the road. It's a private road. Anyone turning onto the property without permission is trespassing."

He nodded.

"And do something about those trailers. They are all over the place. Station them in one area."

"Anything else?"

"That's it."

"Should I have an agreement drawn up, or will a hand-shake do?"

Theresa offered her hand. Dean leaned forward and took it. She expected it to be warm and strong. However, when he touched her, she felt as if a bullet had gone up her arm. She already knew there was chemistry between Dean and herself. Theresa recognized chemistry. But she was unprepared for the charge that ran up her arm.

Theresa had no place in her life for Dean or anyone like him. She had to focus on Chelsea and no one else. Once Dean learned of her mother and father, he'd be running in the opposite direction.

"I'm so relieved," Dean said. "The entire crew will be relieved when I tell them. Thank you." Theresa felt embarrassed. She didn't know why. What did she have to be embarrassed about?

Dean didn't let go of her hand. He pulled her to her feet and gave her a bright smile. "I'm famished," he said. "Let's go join Chelsea for some lunch."

The suitcase hit the floor in the bedroom Theresa had occupied as a child. It was nearly the same as it had been the last time she'd seen it. The furniture had been rearranged, and the bed was made. The rose-colored spread had been replaced with a blue one that had airplanes all over it. The shelves were empty of the stuffed animals she'd left behind when her aunt had driven her away with her two suitcases and her pillow. The wallpaper was gone, and the walls were painted a light tan. Curtains that matched the bedspread hung at windows that faced the river. It was a little boy's room.

"Mine," Chelsea stated. Theresa looked at her. The little

girl probably thought she'd brought her to the room she would sleep in.

"Sure," she said. "If you like it." Chelsea dropped Theresa's hand and walked to the windows. She looked out, then turned around and opened the closet door. The other door led to a bathroom. "Mine?" she asked.

Theresa nodded. "All yours. I'll sleep across the hall." She glanced at that room. It had been unoccupied when her family lived here, a guest room that was rarely used as they had few guests. It was directly next to her parents' room. The room her mother had died in.

Stepping into the hall, Theresa meant to look into the guest room, but her feet started toward the closed door of her parents' room. The double doors she'd run through too many times to count stood before her.

"Everything all right?" Dean asked, coming up the stairs.

Theresa stopped, jumping at his sudden appearance. Her reaction was more about breaking a grip on the past than about Dean's appearance.

"Have you changed things up here?"

"Some things. We had to redo some rooms to fit in with the story."

"What about this one?" She indicated the double doors.

"It was tempting," he said. "It's a beautiful room, but it reminded me too much of my parents' room." He grabbed the door handles and pushed the doors open. "I couldn't change it, but we reproduced it on the set."

"Set?"

"Some of the scenes are filmed back in the studio."

Theresa stepped into the room. It was like walking back in time. Nothing in here had been disturbed.

"You had it cleaned."

"It was this way when we got here."

Theresa stared at him. "How?"

"I assumed Mr. Taylor had it cleaned."

Theresa nodded. She'd sent him the keys. It was logical that he'd come out and look over the property. When she'd left, she'd locked the door. Her aunt considered the place a pink elephant and wanted nothing to do with it. As Theresa's mother's will had left the property to her and her brother, her aunt could do nothing without their consent. Her brother hated the house and had signed it over to Theresa as soon as he was legally able to do so. Theresa had let it sit, visiting infrequently, until Jamison contacted her with Dean's offer. She'd been in a particularly vulnerable moment when the call had come.

Meghan had had a harrowing episode the night before. Her heart was weak due to a rare condition she'd contracted during her teen years. Childbirth aggravated it and weakened it more. She was in the hospital with tubes running from her to the machines that were keeping her alive. Chelsea was plagued with nightmares, and Theresa was running out of money. Jamison's call had seemed like a godsend.

"Is it all right?" Dean's voice brought her back to the present.

"It's fine," she said, her voice sounding small and distant.

"Are you all right?"

Theresa looked down. Then she walked further into the room. She needed to get away from Dean. She had wanted to be alone when she entered this room for the first time. She opened the drapes and let in the light, but she knew what had happened in this room. In her head, she could hear the screams. Loud. Raw with horror and disbelief. And complete helplessness.

"Do you want your things in here? I'll get them for you."

Theresa turned around and looked at him. She couldn't sleep in here. She'd done it on nights when it rained and the lightning scared her. She'd crawl in bed with her mother, and they would talk away the fear. She smiled. It was one of those good memories that had eluded her, that she'd filed away in a locked room in her heart and never brought out. The by-product was too painful.

"Theresa?"

"Yes," she said. "Bring my things here."

"Can't we go in the house?" Chelsea whined. Theresa winced as the comb the little girl was using to play in Theresa's hair caught a snag.

"Not so hard, sweetie," she said, reaching up and grabbing her hair.

"I'm tired of being out here."

"The water is so pretty. Doesn't it make you feel calm to watch it?"

"No."

Theresa laughed at the honesty of children. It had been a week since Theresa and Dean had agreed to the terms of use for the property, and she and Chelsea had been outside since breakfast. Filming was going on in the house, and they couldn't go in.

The truth was, Theresa was glad to be outside. Memories were coming back to her, things she'd repressed, put in the back of her mind behind a door that was never to be opened again. Yet cracks of light were bursting through it.

"Come sit next to me." Theresa took Chelsea's hand and guided her around to sit on the bench next to her. Placing her arm around Chelsea, she pulled her to her side and hugged her. "I'm glad you're talking more." She felt the little girl stiffen against her. "It's good. But you have to talk to more people than just me." She smiled and kissed Chelsea's freshly combed hair. "It's what Mommy would want."

"Do you think she can see me?" Chelsea looked up. Between the trees was a small patch of blue sky.

"Who can see you?" Dean came up behind them. Chelsea gasped when she heard his voice. If Theresa hadn't been hugging her, she was sure Chelsea would have scooted away. She looked down at her, nodding that it was all right for her to answer. Chelsea looked down. It was her method of crawling into herself.

"We were talking about Chelsea talking more."

Dean came around and hunched down before her. "Well, why don't you start with one person?" He smiled at her. "Hello."

Chelsea looked for so long Theresa didn't think she was going to speak. Then she whispered, "Hello."

"Thank you," Dean said. He moved to sit next to her on the bench but avoided touching her. "I'm glad I was the one you chose to say your first word to." He stopped, giving her time to let his words sink in. "You know, Robbie wishes you'd talk to him, too. You're the only person here close to his age."

It had been a week. Dean had made good on the handshake. He'd organized the trailers on the opposite side of the carriage house. From the house, Theresa couldn't see them at all. The groupies were no longer outside the fence, and she felt comfortable walking around the property with Chelsea.

The little girl hadn't come out of her shell completely, but that single word spoken to Dean was a major break in the routine she'd set for herself.

"Hungry?" Dean looked at Theresa. "Do you want to come have lunch with us?"

She nodded. So far they had not mixed with the cast and crew, although she'd smiled and waved at a few of the people from a distance.

"I don't think we're ready," she said. "Taking Chelsea into a room with that many people could be scary."

"Would you like to have lunch with us?" Dean asked Chelsea. "Up at the house?"

Chelsea shrank closer to Theresa. She buried her head on Theresa's stomach and shook her head.

"It's all right, Chelsea," Dean said. "When you're ready, you have an open invitation to lunch with me and the cast."

Chelsea nodded.

Theresa looked over the child's head. Silently, she mouthed the words "thank you." Dean placed his hand on hers, and she felt the shock that accompanied it. This time, it wasn't a jolt, but a warm, familiar homecoming.

"I read your script," Theresa said. "Did you figure out what's wrong with it?"

He shook his head. "I made some changes to it last night. In fact, I've changed it every night for the last week. The cast is ready to lynch me." He paused and looked at her under hooded eyes. "Usually, I don't ask for feedback, but what did you think?"

"I'm no judge. Yours was the first script I've ever seen."

"You've seen movies before. If there is a hole in the story, the public picks up on it right away. So be Mrs. John Q. Public and tell me what you think?"

The story was about a little boy finding danger everywhere he turned. Separated from his parents, he was alone in his quest to reach them before someone killed him.

"It's a wonderful story. I like the action—"

"You don't have to spare my feelings." Dean interrupted her. "What do you think it needs?"

"I don't know," she said. "I'm not a good judge, but it doesn't seem to have a clear focus. There is a lot going on, car chases, explosions, but nothing is pulling everything together, giving it the thread it needs to grip the audience and make them a part of the child's plight."

Dean looked pensive, thoughtful. Theresa couldn't tell how her comment had been received. She wondered if she'd gone too far.

"I don't mean to—"

He stopped her. "It's fine. I'm trying to see it in my head.

I understand a little of what you mean, but it isn't clear there, either."

He looked out at the river, his body relaxed as he sat back against the bench. For a long moment he was quiet.

"Would you do me a favor?"

Theresa said nothing. She wouldn't commit herself without knowing what she was doing.

"Would you come to the set and watch?"

"Me? Why?"

"I don't know. You're an audience."

"Is this normal? I thought sets were closed."

"They are. But it isn't unheard of to have visitors on site. There are parents, writers, teachers, and any number of people who have no acting or technical responsibilities."

"They have a purpose in being there. I'd be an audience and nothing more. Plus, I have Chelsea to think of." She stroked the little girl's hair.

"As quiet as she is, she can come too."

"There are some scenes that . . ."

"The set is closed for those. Necessary personnel only."

Theresa thought about it. She was basically the landlady here. She didn't want to get involved with the film people. She wasn't starstruck. She loved the movies, but she only occasionally read fan magazines or watched programs about stars. She liked her screen personas, but seeing them outside of that arena could destroy her image of them.

"What will the actors think when we sit around and watch?"

Dean grunted a laugh. "You really have never been on a set. The actors wouldn't care if the U.S. Army Band was sitting behind the cameras as long as they stayed quiet and didn't walk through their shots."

The Homecoming starred Lance Hunt and Opal Cooper, two stars on the rise. Theresa had been surprised to find their names on the script when Dean had given it to her. She'd seen them walking about the estate and driving through the gates to go into town, but she hadn't gotten close enough to speak to them.

"Aren't you interested in how movies are made?"

"No . . . yes." Theresa hid her smile by looking at the water.

"How about you come a few times and see how you like it. If you find it too boring, you don't have to come back. I would really like your opinion on what you see."

Theresa couldn't think why. She was so far removed from someone who knew what they would be seeing. She was an economics professor. She was more equipped to explain the demand for theater seats in major metropolitan areas of the United States than she was to evaluate a script or actors moving around a stage.

"Is she asleep?"

Chelsea immediately sat up when she heard the young voice. All three of them looked around at the sound. Robbie Abbott, the actor playing the young boy, stood behind them with a half-eaten banana in his hand.

"Hi," he said to Chelsea. "Do you wanna go get some ice cream?"

Chelsea looked up at Theresa. Theresa had gotten used to reading her eyes and determining what she was thinking. Right now, her eyes said no.

"You like ice cream, Chelsea," Theresa stated. "Wouldn't you like to get some?"

"You come." Her normal voice was now a raspy whisper.

"I know where it is. I'm Robbie. I work on the picture. I can show you around." Quickly, he looked at Dean to make sure it was all right.

Dean nodded. "Just be careful. Don't break anything."

"I won't." He looked back at Chelsea as if everything had been decided. "Come on."

Chelsea still hesitated.

"Why don't we all go up to the house, Chelsea," Dean suggested. "Maybe I can persuade your aunt to have some lunch."

Robbie took hold of Chelsea's arm, giving her a little pull to get her started. She snatched it away as if he'd burned her. The two started walking. Theresa and Dean fell into step behind them. Robbie didn't seem put out by the affront. He chatted jovially as they made their way to the north entrance.

"Is Robbie the only child on the set?"

"Yes. I think he was glad to see Chelsea. When you were that age, didn't you always want someone your own age around to talk to?"

Theresa nodded. "What about a double?"

"You mean a stunt man. Robbie has a stunt man. He's four feet tall and thirty years old. He often does the stunts for child actors."

"This is all so new to me. My thoughts on movie making are exactly what I see on the screen."

"What you think you see," Dean corrected. "Why don't you come by the set and observe?"

"How can I refuse," she said, glancing at him, "now that Chelsea has a friend?"

Chelsea wasn't the only one. Thoughts of Dean at work, directing the making of a movie that would be seen by people around the world, were one reason Theresa agreed. But the other reason was the man himself. She didn't know what it was about him, but when he was around, she couldn't get enough of him. There was something underlying his demeanor. It seemed to attract Theresa like the red flag in front of a bull. She found it frightening and exciting at the same time.

Theresa's eyes snapped open as the scream pierced the quiet night. As she flailed with the bedcovers, adrenaline poured into her system, giving her an instant headache. Chelsea was the first thought in her head. Springing out of the bed like a popped up jack-in-the-box, she ran barefoot to the room across the hall, threw the door open, and went to the bed.

Short hiccups came from the crying child sitting up in the bed, her arms banded around her legs, rocking back and forth.

"It was just a dream," Theresa whispered as she sat down and pulled Chelsea into her arms. "I'm here. It's all right. You're safe." She continued to say soothing things to her second cousin. Over and over, she repeated that it was only a dream and that Chelsea was safe.

Theresa leaned against the headboard and drew Chelsea against her. She pulled the sheet over them both and cradled the child, gently rubbing her back until her sobs stopped and she settled into a comfortable sleep. It didn't take long. In fact, the periods of time for her to calm down and return to sleep were shorter and shorter. The dreams were less frequent than they had been. Theresa had hoped moving away from the house in Buffalo would completely eradicate them. That's what the psychologist had told her might be possible. Obviously, he'd been wrong. Yet this was the first time Chelsea had had the dream since they had come here.

Slipping out from under the covers, Theresa adjusted the sheet around Chelsea. Straightening up, she stretched, massaging her temples. The headache persisted. With a last look to make sure Chelsea was asleep, Theresa returned to her own room. Her new room. It was dark. She had rearranged the furniture, moving the bed and dressers and using left-behind linens to replace the colors and fabrics on every surface and at the windows. She'd updated the room to her own tastes, removed the image of her mother, although it was harder to wash it away from her mind.

Turning around, Theresa went downstairs to the kitchen. Maybe warm milk would relieve her headache and allow her to get back to sleep. Warm milk and chocolate, she amended. She hated plain milk when you heated it, but hot chocolate was different. The house was quiet compared to the activity during the day. The cameras in the front rooms were dark now. Miles of cables snaking across both tiled and hardwood floors led to equipment standing like silent ghosts.

Theresa poured the warmed milk into a mug filled with chocolate powder. Stirring it, she went to the kitchen door and looked through the window. Cicadas played their music to the silent trees. Pushing open the door, she stepped onto the porch. The river lay beyond, quiet and shadowed. Theresa went down the steps. Her bare feet touched the damp grass. She jerked when its coolness shocked her. Chocolate spilled over the side of the mug, and she jumped back to keep it from hitting her feet.

Shaking her hand where the hot liquid had run over it, she let the night air cool it. The river gurgled softly around the rocks that obstructed its smooth flow. Theresa took a seat on the bench where she'd been when Dean found her earlier. She glanced around at the carriage house. A light burned in the bedroom where he slept. He must be awake, she thought. And with that thought came a sudden tightening of her body in places she didn't know it remembered. Her nipples pointed, and her stomach clinched. The cup in her hand shook for the second time in as many minutes. It almost took her attention off her reason for being here at this time of night.

Chelsea's scream had awakened her, but it coincided with another, further away scream. One that had happened decades ago, yet still echoed in her mind. It was horrible, full of disbelief and rage. Her own voice. Her scream. And it was the real reason she been driven out to the river. The room was closing in on her. The memories of what had happened there, of finding . . .

"Theresa?"

She stood up, jerking around at the sudden and unexpected sound of her name. Dean stood a few feet away. This time, the cup she was holding dropped from her hand. The chocolate, which had cooled, spilled down her gown, plastering it to her in places she'd rather keep hidden. Dean sprang forward, brushing the liquid away and replacing it with his own brand of fire.

"It's all right," she said, moving back, stepping away from the fire his hands created.

"I'm sorry. I didn't mean to frighten you," he said. "I saw you from the house and wondered if everything was all right."

"Just a little case of sleeplessness." She grinned. "Chelsea had a nightmare. I got some hot chocolate to help me get back to sleep." She looked down at the chocolate covering her pink nightgown. "I came out here to drink it."

"I'm sorry," Dean said, glancing up at the house.

"It's all right." She sat back down, more to cover her clinging gown than to keep talking to Dean, although she was drawn to him.

"Does she have them often?" Dean sat down, but far enough away from her that she didn't feel the air electrify, skittering over her skin like tiny needles. He looked out at the water.

Theresa nodded. "Not as often as she used to."

"When I was younger, I had nightmares," Dean explained.

"I thought bringing her here, changing her surroundings, would make the nightmares go away. We'd seen a psychologist in Buffalo. But Chelsea . . ." Theresa left the sentence hanging.

Dean glanced toward the house. All the windows were dark, except the kitchen. When he looked back at her, Theresa felt a little self-conscious. She had nothing on except her nightgown. But Dean wasn't trying to make her uncomfortable. And he hadn't made a pass at her, either, even though she knew there was something between them. It had been there from the first, from the moment he'd shouted at her the first day she'd arrived at Collingswood.

"What were your nightmares about?" Theresa asked.

"I don't remember." He looked down at his hands. "I'd wake up with one of my parents' arms around me. I'd be fighting and screaming. They'd hold me, dry my tears, and tell me it was only a dream."

Theresa nodded in the darkness. "Did it help?"

He looked at her. "It did. I was less lonely. Less afraid."

"But you still sleep with the light on," she stated.

His head came up suddenly. For a charged moment, he stared at her. Then his body relaxed. "How did you know?"

"I can see the carriage house from my window. The light is always on."

"Are you always this observant?" Dean asked.

She thought of her decision to return to Royce and what had prompted it. If she'd been observant, she would have known that her aunt had taken out second and third mortgages on the house in Buffalo. Meghan had taken them over when her mother died. Theresa had been in England, studying, teaching, glad to be away from the verbal abuse her aunt had subjected her to until she boarded the airplane and flew away.

But Meghan was her savior, her friend. They were like sisters, even if her *mother* treated one as a princess and the other as the pauper she was. The bond between Theresa and Meghan had grown. When Meghan took ill, she'd called for Theresa, who'd come home, but it wasn't until the will was read that Theresa found out Chelsea had received nothing. That the bank owned the house. Theresa had no job, only the money from the rental of Collingswood to the film company and the house behind her that she'd never wanted to return to.

"Theresa, where are you?" Dean's voice snapped her back to the present.

"Unfortunately, I'm not that observant." She finally answered his question. She heard the controlled softness in her own voice.

"Want to explain?"

Theresa looked down at her lap. She shook her head. Dean slid closer to her. He took her hand and held it. The contact was unexpected, and she nearly jumped when his fingers covered hers. His hand was warm, his palm soft. He reacted like someone who didn't mind jumping into the ditch and picking up a shovel to get the job done. It scared Theresa. She was usually in the ditch alone. No one ever helped her. She had to dig her own ditches.

"I think I'd better go in. I need to check on Chelsea." Pulling her hand free, she picked up the mug, holding it to her breasts as if it were her protector.

"She's a full-time job, isn't she?"

"I can handle it. She'll get better. It just takes time."

"Yeah," he sighed. "Time."

His tone of voice prompted Theresa to search his face. She had the feeling he didn't mean what he'd said. Dean still leaned forward, looking out at the dark lake as if the answer to something was out there.

After a moment, he sat back and looked at her. The air changed with his movement. Theresa felt it tingle against her face. Dean's eyes were dark pools, yet Theresa felt them connect and hold her as if creating a bond between them. Her nipples contracted again. Her stomach became a butterfly, fluttering and nervous. And further down in the core of her being, her arousal was so pronounced she didn't think she could stand up.

Dean got up first. He looked down at her and offered his hand. She took it, pulling her sticky nightgown away from her body. He kept hold of her hand. Theresa looked at their entwined fingers, then up at him. This had to be a movie, she thought. His head bowed toward hers. Hers came up to meet him.

"You're not going to kiss me, are you?" she asked in a voice as light as air.

"That's my intention."

Theresa's free hand came up and touched his cheek. She needed to balance herself, and she needed to touch him.

"Why?" she asked, looking straight into his eyes.

"Why?" His eyebrows went up.

"From what I've seen of the cast and crew, there are some beautiful women here. More than one of them has her eye on you. All you need to do is look up, and they'll come running. I'm not nearly as pretty as they are. I don't understand the film business. Why me?"

His took the hand on his jaw and pulled it down to his waist. "You don't think you're beautiful?"

"With the right makeup, the right dress, I can turn a head now and then, but I'm no Barbie doll."

"Barbie dolls are plastic," he whispered. "Dressed up in perfect clothes and shoes and for display purposes only."

"How do you know I don't aspire to be one?" Her voice was low but stronger than her insides, which were slowly melting.

"Here, I'll show you."

Dean's tug on her hand pulled her off balance. She took the final step that brought her up against him. His mouth didn't immediately take hers as she expected. He looked at her features from a distance so close he could see the imperfections in her skin. Theresa endured the scrutiny. She should be uncomfortable with him so close, but what she felt was anticipation, an expectancy that something wonderful was about to happen.

Since she'd returned from England, her life had been one crisis after another, one set of bad news on top of another. With Dean, there was a promise of something better, something special. She moved in, running her arms around his waist and pressing her mouth to his.

Something burst inside her when she touched him. And it was mutual. Dean's arms cradled her, threading through her hair and holding her head at the precise angle to fit the tilt of his. She'd never thought about how perfect she fit with a man. In fact, she'd never thought of life with a man. The marriages she'd seen had ended in divorce or something worse. Yet with Dean, she knew she'd found something she didn't know she'd been looking for.

His mouth tantalized hers, softly lifting and repositioning. Theresa felt herself shimmering, leaning into him, stepping into that infinitesimal space that separated them. Raising her head, she opened her mouth, and Dean deepened the kiss. Her arms tightened around him. She moved them up as Dean's moved down, and they traded positions.

As his hands circled her waist and their bodies aligned as man and woman, heat unfurled from her toes to cover her whole body. Dean's mouth worked magic on hers. Theresa felt oddly reticent, even scared. It had been a long time since a man had held her. She was the caregiver, the nurturer. She'd taken care of Meghan and now Chelsea. No one took care of her. No one wrapped her in his arms when she felt lonely. No one asked her what she thought or how she felt. And no one gave her this body-ringing feeling. This feeling of being *alive.*

The minute the thought entered her head, it scared her. She broke the kiss and stepped out of Dean's reach.

"What's wrong?" he asked.

"I think I'd better go in." Theresa forced herself not to stumble over the words, but she couldn't help the nervous way her fingers twisted together. The memory of her last disastrous love affair came unbidden to her mind. Meghan's call to come home had given her the escape she needed. Having to take care of Meghan had left Theresa no time for her own miseries, and she'd quickly gotten over Frank Walley, the man everyone had told her she'd find eternal happiness with. But Frank was also seeking happiness with Carol Simmons and Sylvia Blake and Tina Winslow and Gabriella Hilton, and she was sure there were others. The fact that the university hadn't fired him for sleeping with his students was no endorsement. As Frank had told her, they were all consenting adults.

"I'm sorry," Theresa said, unsure of how to exit gracefully. "I really need to check on Chelsea."

Dean made a gesture. She was unsure of what it meant—did he agree with her, or was he just consenting to her story? She backed away, then turned around to retrieve the mug that had thudded to the ground the moment Dean had reached for her.

She reached the steps and backed onto the porch. Dean watched her, but didn't move. Their gazes locked and their eyes searched each other's, but neither raised a hand in salute. They moved further and further away as if some receding camera was panning backward, pulling in more of the background and making their presence less and less distinct.

Theresa opened the door and turned around. She went through the kitchen door and closed it. Leaning against it, she said, "I'm not going there again."

Chapter 3

The little town of Swanson was only an hour's ride from Royce. Theresa and Chelsea got in the car early the next morning and went through the checkpoint that made her feel she was leaving a walled city.

She knew she was avoiding Dean. He'd asked her to come and watch the filming, but she was unsure whether she could concentrate on anything other than his hard body and those braids that made her hands want to brush down them in long, even strokes.

She hadn't seen her brother Kevin in five years. Today was perfect for letting him know she was back in the area.

His small grocery store had grown larger since the last time she'd seen it. The china shop that had been next door was gone, and he'd expanded into that space and added onto the end.

Theresa's smile when she got out of the car was as wide as a saucer. No one ever gave Kevin credit for anything, especially not for being a success at something, but from the looks of the store, he'd proven them wrong.

"Are we going to buy food?" Chelsea asked.

"We're going to see your other cousin. Kevin."

"Here?" Chelsea twisted her face into a frown. She hadn't

mentioned the dream of last night or the sleepwalking episode that Theresa had interrupted as she retreated from Dean's kiss.

She'd found Chelsea in the hall outside her room walking toward the back of the house. Ignoring the old wives' tales warning against touching a sleepwalker, Theresa had gently placed her hand on Chelsea's back and coaxed her back to her room.

"Kevin owns this store."

"He does?" She looked a little impressed. Theresa took her hand, and they started for the entrance, while looking around. The town was a little busier, as was Royce. And being here was having a positive effect on Chelsea, barring the nighttime escapades. Despite how Theresa felt about the place, returning to Royce had been the right thing to do.

Suddenly, Dean's face appeared in her mind, and she stumbled. Catching herself before she fell, she found Chelsea's hand gripping hers.

"Sorry," she said.

Inside, the store was bright and clean with a layout that was easy to maneuver through. It was also busy. Theresa had to move out of the way several times as she headed for customer service and the office behind it.

"Is Kevin Ramsey around?" Theresa asked the clerk, who couldn't be more than seventeen years old.

"He's in the back. May I help you with something?"

"He's my brother. I just wanted to see him."

The young man with blond hair that tended toward the greasy side smiled. "If you wait a minute, I'll call him."

"I think she knows the way." Someone spoke from behind her.

Theresa turned around. "Donna!"

A short, squat woman with a flawless complexion and perfect hair grabbed her and hugged her tightly.

"How have you been?" Donna asked, releasing Theresa and stepping back to look at her. "You've lost weight. And

I've found it." With a laugh, she slapped her hands on her hips. The two were the same age, and they had been in some classes together in Royce before Theresa had left for Buffalo.

"Donna, you look great."

Donna frowned. "That's a lie, but it's well intentioned." Her tone held no censure. "And who is this?" She looked down at Chelsea, who took a step behind Theresa and clung to her as if Donna might take her away.

"You remember my cousin Meghan? This is her daughter, Chelsea." Theresa wouldn't go into Meghan's death in front of Chelsea.

"Hello, Chelsea. It's good to meet you. When Meghan used to come down here, the thing I remember about her is that she loved chocolate bars. Maybe she passed that gene on to you." Donna pulled a Snickers bar from her pocket and offered it to the little girl.

"My mother liked chocolate?" she asked in a small voice.

"She couldn't get enough of it," Donna told her.

Chelsea hesitated a moment, then reached out and took the candy. "Thank you," she said.

Donna smiled at her. Straightening up, she looked at Theresa. "Are you back for a while?"

"I'm not sure yet." She glanced at Chelsea, signaling to Donna that she couldn't talk in front of the child.

"Well, Kevin's opening boxes in the back."

"Thanks, we'll see you later."

Few people got to see the back of a grocery store, and if they did, they probably wouldn't want to eat again. So many different food aromas were mingled together, but unlike a warm kitchen filled with baking and cooking smells, here they merged together in a discordant odor. Outdated and over-ripe foods, systematically removed from the shelves, had to be disposed of and separated from incoming perishables.

Theresa and Chelsea negotiated the pallets of stacked canned goods and dry goods such as flour and cereals to find

Kevin. Her brother was six feet tall and looked like a bodybuilder even though he rarely exercised. He said he got all the exercise he needed keeping the store stocked.

"Kevin," Theresa called.

His body went stiff the instant she called his name. He turned to see her, and they raced across the floor to hug each other. Who would ever think that this hunky guy had spent more than ten years in and out of mental institutions? Both Theresa and Kevin knew there was nothing wrong with him, but her aunt didn't want him around and she was happy to allow the state to maintain his residence.

When Theresa turned eighteen, she took over his guardianship and sprung him. He went from working in a small delicatessen to owning it, expanding it, and finally, turning it into the grocery business. She was proud of him.

"Well, this is a surprise." He kissed her on the cheek and hugged her again. "When did you blow into town?"

"I'm back in Royce." Her voice was flat.

Kevin stiffened like a man turning into a statue. "What do you want there?"

Theresa stretched her hand out, and Chelsea came and took it.

"Is this Chelsea?" He dropped down on one knee and offered the little girl his hand. "You are so beautiful." It took Chelsea a moment, but she eventually accepted his hand. "You don't remember me, but I saw you when you were only three years old. You must be four by now."

"I'm seven," she asserted.

"As old as that?" He raised his eyebrows in mock surprise. "My, my, you'll be marrying soon. Got a boyfriend?"

"No," she blushed.

"Well, give the boys time. They'll be falling all over you." Chelsea took a bite of her candy bar and stared at him. "I have to go back to my boxes. How would you like to sit up high on the top of them?" Kevin stood up and looked at Theresa for permission. They walked over to the pallet of boxes he'd been slitting the tops off of, and he hoisted Chelsea to the top.

"Business looks good," Theresa said. "I see you've expanded."

"So, what are you doing back at the house?" Kevin never beat around the bush. At least not anymore.

"I had nowhere else to go," she explained. "I had a little savings when I came back from England. Meghan kept up the bills, and while she was . . ." She stopped. She found it hard to discuss her cousin's fatal illness. "When Meghan was dying and no longer able to do anything, she gave me power of attorney to use her funds to pay expenses. The only one I didn't pay was the mortgage. That had been automatically set up as an electronic transfer. I was so busy with Meghan and Chelsea, I never thought about it."

Theresa took a deep breath. She'd been careful with Meghan's money, knowing that Chelsea needed a legacy when her mother died. The attorney who was taking care of the settlement had commended her on her record of expenditures. It was better than most accountant records he had to review.

"After she died and the will was read, I discovered that Aunt Patty had taken out a second mortgage on the house, and there was no equity left. In order to live, we had to sell the house. And come back here."

Kevin put his arm around her shoulders. "I'm sorry. I'll help you any way I can."

"I'm not here for a handout." She hugged him. "But thank you for the offer." Releasing him, she took a step away. "Right now, there is a movie company using the house." She explained how they were at the house when she got there and the contract she'd agreed to. "Chelsea seems to be coming out of her shell, and it gives us some income until I find a job."

"That's a big house, and the grounds will need a small army to keep them in order. Winters are harsh. How are you going to survive there on a teacher's salary?"

"I'm a college professor." Anger flashed through her.

"I know, Theresa. You're very smart. You wouldn't have been a Rhodes Scholar unless you were better than smart. And since you excelled in economics, you can calculate how much it costs to maintain Collingswood."

"I don't have to worry about it for at least a year," she told him. "It will give me time to decide what to do next."

"Why don't you sell the house?"

This wasn't the first time Kevin had asked her that question. When she was spending a thousand dollars a year on state and local taxes, he'd asked her time and time again to sell the place.

"I'll decide that later," she said.

"You always say that. This time, tell me the real reason."

She stared at him. Her eyes filled with tears, but she kept them from falling. "I hope someday . . ." She stopped.

"What?" Kevin prompted. "What do you hope?"

"That he'll come home." After Theresa said the words, it was like the air had been sucked out of the room. Since they were children, they had spent many hours talking about the night their father had left them. Kevin had spent years in and out of therapy over the events of that one summer.

"Theresa, you know he's not coming back."

"I know, I know," she said. "But I wonder. I want to know what happened, why he left us."

"Selling that white elephant doesn't mean you won't know that he comes back. You know how small Royce is. If Dad came back, it would be all over town before breakfast could be served."

"Well, I'll think about it."

"You won't," he stated. "So, if you need my help, let me know."

"Thanks," she whispered. "Now, how about taking me and a hungry little girl to lunch, where you can explain to me why you haven't given Donna Wheaton a wedding ring yet?"

* * *

Theresa drove through the crowd of groupies that had been moved from the front gates to the beginning of the private road.

"John," she greeted. The security guard she'd had the altercation with her first day back had become a friend. Built like a Chippendale dancer, his uniform highlighted his physique, outlining every muscle in his shoulders and thighs.

"Afternoon, Ms. Ramsey."

"By now, you should be able to call me Theresa. This isn't medieval times."

"How's Chelsea today?" he asked instead of using her first name. Chelsea looked at him. Although she offered no smile, she blushed and turned away.

John Willis opened the new gate, and she drove through it. Dean was the first person she saw when she got to the house. There was no set schedule for filming. They went as long as the actors could stand it or the director forced them, except for Robbie, who as a child was limited by the laws regarding child abuse and working conditions.

Since Theresa's purpose for leaving this morning had been twofold—to avoid Dean and to see her brother—she was perturbed at having the object of her avoidance thrust at her immediately on her return.

He approached the car and opened her door. "I thought I'd see you today."

"I had some errands to run. And I didn't say I'd come."

"You let me believe you would be there."

He was angry. She wondered why. And then thought, what right did he have to be angry? He was here by her good graces and nothing more.

"Is the filming over?"

"We're on a break right now. The lights needed to be rigged for another scene."

She nodded. “Is it all right for us to go in?”

“Sure.”

At that moment, Robbie came bounding out the front door, and Chelsea appeared to come to life. “Hey, where have you been?” he hollered. The two ran off together.

Theresa turned to go inside.

“Is it the kiss?” Dean asked.

She stopped with one foot on the top step. He remained on the ground. She’d driven one hundred miles to avoid it, but Dean had cut through all the mist and gone straight to the heart of the matter.

She turned back, her confidence in place. “It was only a kiss, Dean. No one made any commitments.” She turned around and hoped she made a graceful exit. Her insides were shaking as they had the previous night when he’d held her in his arms and the magic of the moonless night and the water had set the scene for a love story.

But this wasn’t a story. This was her life, and she didn’t need it complicated by a man who looked better than she did.

Watching actors make a movie, you had to use the same muscles you would having your portrait painted. For the first hour, Theresa was enthralled. She smiled at everyone, watched intently what they did, how they spoke, how they looked at each other. The second hour, her body ached from sitting still so long. By the third hour, she was too bored to care. Chelsea, however, looked more alive than she had in months. Maybe it was meeting Robbie. The two spent time together within eyesight of Theresa. Several times, Chelsea had glanced back to see if she was still in view. Other than that, she only said a few words to Robbie, but he was by far the major conversation holder.

Today, Theresa watched them running and rerunning the same scene, feeling as if there was a movie clip on a continuous loop. She could feel the tenseness on the set. Dean wasn't satisfied with what the actors were doing. And the actors were obviously tired of covering the same territory. Earlier, there had been a discussion over the script that verged on explosion. Theresa felt she should leave, but one of the crew members told her it was always like this and not to worry.

She couldn't avoid looking at Dean. He looked even better this morning than he had two nights ago. After their kiss, she wanted nothing more than to have him do it again, but that wasn't going to happen. Yet thoughts of him kept drifting in and out of her mind.

Theresa had brought paper and pen with her. As a teacher, it was second nature for her to have them at hand. Chelsea watched the action with a child's fascination. Extremely quiet, Theresa lifted her pen and started making notes. They had nothing to do with the scene. Instead, they concerned her future. Theresa had told Kevin the truth. She and Chelsea would be all right if she managed their finances carefully, but she had to work. She wrote a cover letter to the local university. Later, she would type it and send it with her resume for a teaching position.

She also made a tentative budget of services she would need after Dean and his crew packed up and left. The more numbers she added to the page, the deeper the frown on her face. Looking at the final total was crushing. Her shoulders dropped in defeat. She doubted she could get a job that would cover the heating bills this winter, let alone food and clothing for Chelsea. Dean's company had done a lot of repairs, but the house still needed some updating. It would have to wait, she thought.

"Cut!"

The word jarred her out of her reverie. Theresa sat up straight in the chair, blinking her eyes as if to adjust them to the light.

"Lunch," someone called.

Robbie, who had been in this scene, immediately came over and got Chelsea. "Wow, that looked like fun," Chelsea said. "Do you think I can try it later?"

"Chelsea," Theresa called her name. "I don't think you better try those things. Robbie's been trained."

Chelsea's face fell. Theresa hated to refuse her something. She needed things in her life that made her smile, but she also needed to be protected from things that could hurt or injure her. Then Robbie took her hand, and Chelsea began smiling and ran off toward the dining room with him.

Dean came over and took the seat Chelsea had vacated. "Taking notes?" he asked. He took the pad from her before she could stop him. Perusing it for a moment, he handed it back.

"It's a budget. I need to get a job and figure out how Chelsea and I are going to live." She paused, but she didn't want his sympathy, so she went on. "That reminds me. I'd like to use your computer to write some cover letters, if that's all right. My stuff hasn't arrived yet. I expect it soon."

"Several big boxes?"

"Yes, why?"

"They're here. They were delivered to me."

"Why?"

"I suppose we get so many deliveries that the UPS guy just brought everything to the carriage house." He glanced at her, noticing her harnessed anger. "Don't worry. I didn't open them. I intended to tell you about them yesterday, but you were a little distant."

Theresa looked away. The room was quiet and dark. While they filmed the scene, racks of lights were on. Turning them off made the natural light of day seem dark and foreboding.

"Dean, I can't get involved with you."

"I didn't ask you to."

Theresa recognized the defenses in his voice.

"You didn't ask with your voice, but your mouth spoke another language." He started to say something, but she stopped him. "We're both adults, and we both have things to do. You're here for a short time to get your film made. I have a child to care for and a future to determine. We're only crossing paths. You'll be gone soon, and I'll be here. Let's act like adults and forget that kiss ever happened."

She waited for him to agree with her. For a moment he stared at her, weighing her words. Theresa couldn't breathe. She wanted him to agree with her, but some part of her wanted him to stand up, pull her into his arms, and kiss her silly.

"All right," he said. "We'll play it your way."

Dean slammed the door behind him. It had been hours since he talked to Theresa and he was still smarting from her comments. The woman had been there for barely four days, and already, she was driving him crazy. Dean paced up and down the living room. What was wrong with him? He couldn't remember the last time a woman had gotten under his skin. And this quickly.

Going to the kitchen, he snatched open the refrigerator door and grabbed a bottle of water. He really wanted a beer, but there was none.

Snapping the top off, he drank the entire bottle in one long gulp. It didn't make him feel any better. The feelings he was having weren't entirely unfamiliar, but they were unwanted.

Theresa Ramsey was a beautiful woman. But she was single-minded. Everything she thought and did revolved around Chelsea. Even the budget he'd picked out of her hands had things Chelsea needed before she put in taxes on the house and maintenance of the property.

Dean understood she had a lot on her plate and knew she needed money, yet she'd returned his substantial rental fee.

He admired her for her honesty and her loyalty to Chelsea. But from a practical basis, she should have taken the money.

Dean threw the empty water bottle in the trash can and headed back toward the living room. He'd thought of some changes to the script and needed to get them written. And maybe work would take his mind off Theresa Ramsey. Then he remembered Theresa had asked to use his computer. He had a backup machine he could loan her. He'd run it over to the house later. Right now, he was in no mood to see her or her vulnerable eyes and kissable mouth.

Going to the bedroom, Dean avoided looking at the bed where she'd slept her first night here. In the bathroom, he turned on the shower and adjusted the water to a tepid stream. Dropping his clothes where they fell, he stepped under the flow and let the water slice over him. He'd only been in the shower long enough to soap himself before he heard someone banging at the door.

"I'm coming," he muttered, grabbing a huge bath towel and wrapping it around his middle. He'd had one altercation after another with the actors. Which one was it now? With the banging on the door incessant, he hurried to reach it despite the water still running down his body. Yanking the door inward, his heart lurched when he saw Theresa standing there. The light from the porch lamp illuminated her hair, which she'd pulled back into a long ponytail. The Mustang convertible sat several feet away.

On seeing him, her eyes opened wider, and she sucked in a breath. "I can come back," she stammered.

"No!" Dean's reaction was instinctive. She looked him up and down. "Give me a minute."

He left the door open for her as he disappeared into the bedroom and quickly dried himself. Pulling on a T-shirt and shorts, he went back into the living room. His heart was beating fast. He hadn't expected to see her again today, and while he knew it wasn't good to run down the path his body was taking him, he didn't seem to have enough control to stop it.

"Why have these been opened?" Theresa accosted him the moment he entered the room. She was standing in the midst of the boxes that had arrived for her.

"My assistant opens everything."

"But these are addressed to me. Surely she could see they have nothing to do with your production company."

He spread his hands. "I apologize, Theresa. We get a lot of deliveries. Some of them are addressed to different people. It was an honest mistake."

She picked up a box and started for the door.

"Here, let me take that." He reached for the box, but she tugged it and refused to let go. Dean stepped back. "We don't need to argue over them. I was only trying to help."

"I don't need your help." She went to the door and used her foot to push it open.

By the time she returned, Dean had stacked three of the heaviest boxes on a hand truck. "I understand you're very self-sufficient, but this will make it easier and you can't get all the boxes in that car at one time. You may as well let me help you. I'm going to whether you like it or not."

He could tell she didn't want to, but she let her stubbornness give way to logic. After a moment, she stepped aside, and he wheeled the boxes out the door. As Dean unloaded the hand truck, Theresa came out carrying a single box.

"That's all that will fit," Dean said. Theresa said nothing. She continued to hold the box in her arms. He walked around the car and opened the passenger's door. Once inside, he reached for the box she was holding. She only hesitated a moment before giving it to him.

Silently, she got inside and turned the key. The engine fired as if it were brand new.

"This is a beautiful car. I've been meaning to ask you about it."

She said nothing.

"What is it? A '65? '66?

"'67," she said. "It belonged to my cousin. She was a classic car fanatic."

"What about you?"

"For me, it's transportation. It gets me where I need to be. That's all I ask of a car."

Dean had the feeling her words had a double meaning, but he ignored it.

"I have three brothers and two sisters. You'd think at least one of us would have taken an interest in cars."

"Let me think, doctor, lawyer, Indian chief, filmmaker."

She was talking to him. A thrill went through him that lightened his mood like no shower could. "Doctor, architect, carpenter, filmmaker. My sisters work in child psychology and modeling. No lawyer, no Indian chief."

She smiled. At least, the shadow of a smile curved her lips.

"I saw it," he said.

"What?"

"The smile. It was there. So you're not angry with me anymore."

"I'm not angry," she said. "It's just the stress of so many changes happening at once and Chelsea being so fragile."

The drive was short, and they were already at the main house, but neither of them moved to get out of the car.

"I know you worry about her a lot, but she seems to be doing fine. She's alert and interested. It's you who needs some down time."

"Down time? What are you talking about?"

"You need to take some time for yourself."

"I'm afraid I don't have time for that."

Dean looked her directly in the eye. "Make some time," he said. "I'm sure Robbie's mom will watch her for a couple of hours while you go shopping, get a massage, or do something for yourself."

"Maybe I will."

Dean knew she didn't mean it. Her agreement was a way to get him to stop probing. He allowed it. For now. Opening the door, he angled himself and the box out of the car. Using the hand truck and the side ramp they had installed to get the cameras and equipment inside, he ran the boxes up to the front door and inside.

"Where do you want these?"

"Right there is fine. I'll open them and put them in the right room."

"Let's not do this again," he said. "I'm not leaving until you tell me where they go."

She directed him around the house, and he put the boxes in the rooms she indicated. There were still three boxes sitting by the stairs. "Where do these go?"

"Upstairs, but I can take them."

"It's not a problem." Dean picked up one of the boxes. It was very heavy.

"I don't want to wake Chelsea."

"I'll be very quiet." He started up the wide staircase, leaving her no option but to follow. "What's in this?"

"Some clothes, photographs, books."

Two trips later, everything had been moved to its proper room. All except Chelsea's things. Those were stacked outside her door.

They came down the stairs after putting the final box in Theresa's bedroom. "There are still three more boxes. If they show up, please let me know."

"I will."

"Thanks for helping me. How about something to drink?" She headed toward the kitchen.

"I'd really like a beer."

Theresa stopped. "You're out of luck. The strongest thing we have here is pineapple juice and cola."

"Come with me," he said impulsively. "We'll drive into town and get a beer."

Theresa took a step back. "I can't," she said. "Chelsea."

"I'll call Mrs. Abbott, Robbie's mother."

"You have an early call in the morning."

She was putting up obstacles. Dean recognized it and should have let it go, but he didn't want to.

"How long has it been since you've gone out?"

"You mean on a date?" she frowned.

He nodded.

"You're asking me out on a date?"

"No, I'm asking how long it's been since you were on one. You took care of your cousin for two years, and now you're here with Chelsea. How long has it been?"

She looked down and fiddled with her hands. "A long time."

Dean moved closer to her. "So come have a beer with me."

She looked up at him, and he held his breath, willing her to say she'd go. "Should I call this a date?"

This was a fool's errand, Theresa thought as Dean drove through the security checkpoint. She had offered him the keys knowing he was itching to get behind the wheel. Men were like that. Automobiles were part of who they were. Even if Dean had said no one in his family had taken to cars, she knew how excited men got over the combination of steel and glass in a sleek configuration. Vintage automobiles made them drool, and Dean was no exception. Guys would even pull up next to her at stop lights and immediately begin conversations over the car.

It was a short drive to Marv's Tavern and Grill. Although Theresa had never been inside it, she was familiar with it because she had gone to school with Nancy, Marv's daughter, before she had moved away. She remembered Marv was short for Marsella Evans.

Inwardly, she wondered what the town would say when they saw her. After so many years, Theresa hoped no one would recognize her. She didn't look the same as she had at twelve, but she'd been here five years ago and she had changed little since then. Oh, she was thinner and her hair was straighter, but other than that, she was the same. No doubt Dean would turn a head or elicit a stare, however, when they walked in.

Theresa wasn't disappointed. His long hair and body caused a gasp from more than one female when they came through the door. Dean didn't seem to notice. Theresa was glad he was the object of beauty. Less people to scrutinize her.

The bar, which did serve whiskey by the shot with a jukebox in the corner, also had a collection of small round tables in the center and booths along two walls. The bar, taking up the back wall, was shiny and polished. The jukebox was playing loud music along a side wall, but the wood plank floor was empty.

As all the booths were occupied, Theresa went toward an empty table in the shadows. She deliberately sat with her back to the room and was happy when she didn't recognize the woman who immediately came by and took their order. The waitress smiled at Dean, ignoring Theresa. None of the other patrons seemed to take any notice of her, but she knew if she said her name, they would all remember.

Dean poured his beer down the side of his glass, minimizing the head.

"I suppose this is not the kind of place you're used to," Theresa began. She wondered what his world was really like. She'd seen him directing, seen the glamorous people in his film, but this wasn't his everyday life.

Dean looked around, then took a sip of his beer. The look on his face said it was the best thing he'd ever drank. He set the glass on the table but held it between two hands. "That's the glorified version of the job you're imagining. I've been in places where you wouldn't want to drink anything they had. This is a paradise compared to some places."

"It's a small town." She glanced around.

"Small town mentality?"

Theresa took a drink of her beer. She hadn't meant to give anything away, but the way the town had treated her five years ago, her venom must shine through. She didn't have any friends here, and she was not going to explain why to a short-timer. Him knowing wouldn't help anything.

"Sometimes. I suppose it's a consequence of not having enough going on—you tend to get into everyone else's business."

"That's not limited to small towns."

"True, but let's not talk about the town. What happened today to drive you to drink?" She glanced at the beer, hoping the change in subject would keep him from talking about the town and her.

"You were there for most of it. You saw how awful things were. Let's not talk about it. Most of it is my fault anyway."

"Have you told the crew that?"

His head came up, and he stared at her. "What do you mean?"

"They're working as hard as you. If you explained your frustration, maybe they could help you."

His stare was blank. For a moment, Theresa wasn't sure he'd heard her. Then slowly, a smile creased his face.

"What are you thinking?"

"That the solution is so simple—why didn't I think of it?"

"Glad I could be of help."

He saluted her with his beer glass and took a long swallow.

"You mentioned that you had a lot of family. How many brothers and sisters again?"

"There are six of us, including me. Two sisters, three brothers."

"Do they all live in Texas?"

He shook his head and smiled. "One brother lives in Philadelphia, a sister in New York City. The others live in Texas."

"What's the smile for?"

"Nothing really. I thought of something funny one of them said the last time we had a meeting."

"You have meetings?"

"Family meetings," he nodded. He rolled the beer glass between both hands, then looked her directly in the eye. He looked as if he were deciding if he wanted to continue. After a moment he said, "We were adopted by our foster parents when we were children, and even though we're pretty spread out over Texas and the States, we get together in person for important things or we telecommunicate when that isn't possible."

"You mean you can see each other on television screens?"

"TV or computer. Any electronic viewing screen."

"That's wonderful." A sudden chill ran through her. "I wish Meghan and I had had that." She shrugged, pushing off the threatening tears. "We kept in touch through e-mail. She got sick, yet her messages said nothing about her condition until she needed me to come home. If I could have seen her on a screen, I would have known she wasn't doing that well."

Dean reached across the table and touched her hand. "You couldn't have done anything about it. She knew you had a job to do and didn't want to worry you."

Theresa laughed to cover her need to cry. "That's what she said."

"It's true."

Theresa pulled her hand free of Dean's and drank from her glass. His hand was making her body warm, and she could feel the effect of his nearness going up her arm, into her shoulder.

"So what did you think of that was funny?" she asked, again changing the subject.

"In the last three years, we've had three weddings in our family. My brother Owen married last fall. Prior to him finding and marrying Stephanie, he was a ladies' man. "Quantity over quality" was his motto. Then Stephanie came along, and he fell."

"Hard, I suppose."

"Like a sack of potatoes out of a jumbo jet. He was completely shattered by the emotions that took root in him. At the reception, he kept introducing her to us, saying, 'Have you met my wife.'"

Theresa smiled. She knew it was something that you needed to be there to understand, but Dean seemed in a mood to talk family.

"You miss them." It was a statement.

He nodded. "They're the best family a man could ask for, and we're only together by happenstance."

Theresa frowned. She took a drink of her beer, hoping he would explain. When he didn't, she said, "I don't understand."

"We're all adopted. Most of us were what was called 'the unadoptable.' If it weren't for our parents taking a real interest in us, we'd never have turned out so well, and we wouldn't be brothers and sisters."

Theresa suddenly envied him. When he spoke of his family, he showed a tenderness that she would not have imagined he possessed.

The jukebox had gone quiet while they were talking. Suddenly, it began playing again. Dean looked up as Gladys Knight's sultry voice told the story of the "Midnight Train to Georgia."

"Let's dance," he said. "This is one of my favorite songs."

"Dean, no one else is dancing. This is strictly a beer and whiskey place. Although if you want a greasy burger and some fries, they can probably scare some up in the back."

He stood up and reached for her hand.

"Dean, no one dances in here." Theresa repeated herself.

"We will."

He didn't leave her much choice. He was pulling her from her chair and drawing her into his arms. Gently, they began to sway from side to side, turning slowly in a tight circle. Theresa felt the stares from the other customers.

"Relax," Dean coaxed. His voice was deep and hoarse, whispery in her ear. His warm breath fanned her neck. Her concentration dissolved although she tried to focus on where she was, what was going on. When she breathed in his scent, she remembered him opening the carriage house door, his body still wet from his shower, and everything receded except him. She felt his arms holding her, aware only of the two of them, the music, and the sure way he held her against him.

Her arm slipped around his neck, combing through the heavy sheaf of hair that cascaded down his back. She inhaled fully, taking in the clean scent of his hair and the raw maleness talking to her in a language older than the hills. He pulled her closer. Somewhere in the back of her mind, she heard muted voices and shuffling sounds. But she ignored everything except the sound of his heart beating against her ear. They swirled about the empty floor, incognizant of the rest of the room.

Both her arms were now around his neck, pushing under the braids. She loved the way his hair slid over his shoulders, down his arms. She loved the coarseness against her bare arms sending tiny firecrackers through her. Sensation sweet, hot, and jolting. His eyes, half-closed, with a drowsy kind of sexiness that made her throat go dry and her limbs grow weak, stared into hers.

Their mouths were close enough to taste each other's breath. She could taste the beer, anticipate the feel of his mouth on hers. Theresa was drowning. She knew it, knew she should move her head from his shoulder. She should stop listening to the strong beat of his heart. She should step on his toe or do *something* to break the invisible connection that drew her to him, that made her press her body into his, that seemed to link them with the threads of a lifetime of need.

She wanted him. She could not deny that, and he wanted her. She could feel it in the erection forming against her belly. The music ended, but she didn't want it to. She willed the song to go on, willed him to keep his arms around her, to keep this warm, safe, cocooned feeling that held her in its magic.

It didn't.

Dean stepped back. Theresa was unsure whether propriety or Dean's realization of the enormity of what was happening prompted him to move away. Theresa noticed other couples had joined them on the dance floor. She'd been so involved in her feelings that she hadn't realized that shuffling noise she'd heard was other feet, other dancers.

A woman smiled at her. She smiled back and moved toward their table.

"Theresa, is that you?"

The question cleared her mind as effectively as jumping into a lake before the water temperature had risen enough for comfort. Even the aura induced by Dean's arms couldn't stop the fissure of remembered pain from pushing past all her other emotions.

Turning back, she saw it was the woman who'd smiled at her. Squinting, she tried to determine how they knew each other. The woman, who was about Theresa's age, was wearing tight jeans and heels high enough to break an ankle. Her hair was pulled up in a ponytail, with curls dropping to the nape of her neck.

"It's me, Nancy . . . from the fifth grade."

Theresa's face relaxed, and she smiled. She was just about to say something when Nancy spoke again. "Hey, everybody, you remember Theresa Ramsey."

The other conversations that had been going on stopped with the mention of her name. Theresa felt claustrophobic, as if a tightly woven blanket had been dropped over her and all the air was being sucked from under it. In the silence, she heard the accusation against her mother, the unanswered questions about her father's disappearance.

She'd known this would happen. It was why she would rather have gone to any place on earth except here, if she could have afforded it. But Aunt Patricia had taken that option away from her when she took out a second mortgage, leaving no equity in the house in Buffalo. Meghan's death hadn't discharged the debt, only passed the responsibility on to Chelsea and ultimately to Theresa. She'd had to sell to satisfy it, and selling meant one thing—returning to Collingswood and the chance of resurrecting the old secrets.

Dean stepped up behind her. Their fingers touched, hands clasping. She knew he was letting her know he had her back even though he didn't know why she needed it. It was the first time since she was twelve years old that anyone had come to her aid, had stood with her against the silent accusations of the town.

Chapter 4

How they got out of the bar, Theresa didn't remember. Dean was driving along the road, but they weren't headed for Collingswood. She really didn't know where they were. Around them were only mountains and trees and darkness.

"Where are we going?"

"Nowhere," he said. "I thought you needed some air."

The top was down on the Mustang, but she knew that wasn't what he meant.

"Wanna tell me what that was all about back there?"

"I'd rather not." Theresa did not want to revisit the story. She wanted one person in her life that didn't know the rumor and conjecture, didn't know about her family and the skeletons that held secrets, even from her.

Dean didn't press her for an answer. He continued driving for another few minutes, then stopped the car. Getting out, he came around to the passenger side and opened her door.

"Let's walk," he said. Dean offered his hand to help her out.

Theresa took it. The wind was cold, and she put her arms around herself. Dean took a jacket she had left in the back seat, and she pushed her arms into it. As they turned to walk, he caught her fingers and threaded them through his.

"This is Lookout Point," she said, recognizing the place. "It used to be the local Lover's Lane."

"You've been here before?" There was a little mischievousness in the question, but Theresa heard the serious undertone.

"I was twelve when I left. At that age, no boy I knew could drive, and most of them wouldn't even look at me."

"They must have been crazy."

She didn't say anything. She was remembering how much they had stared after her father's disappearance, and then, after her mother had committed suicide. Then, she had wished no one would look at her.

"What stopped it from being a Lover's Lane?" he asked. They had fallen into step, walking toward the clearing where people used to park to look at the sky and make out. Tonight, the stars were as beautiful as always. Here she could see more of them, feel closer to them. Even in the immense sky, tonight Theresa felt she could reach out and touch them.

"There was an accident one night. From what the newspapers reported a couple of cars drove too close to the edge and both went over. Four teenagers were killed. It traumatized a lot of people in the area. After that, the police would patrol and roust anyone who came up here." She walked over to a large tree. "A makeshift cross was placed here with flowers and candles. It felt more like a graveyard than a place for lovers. People stopped coming."

"Did they find another Lover's Lane?"

Theresa walked away from the spot and leaned against a huge rock. "I suppose they did. Teenagers are very resourceful. Before I left, I never learned of another location, though."

She wasn't going into the fact that there was a lot more on her mind at the time than where people were hanging out and making out.

She looked up at the sky. It was so calming. Theresa slid down the rock where she had perched and sat on the ground. She looked up at the heavens. Dean crouched next to her. The heat from his body warmed her side. The change his presence effected in hers removed any calm she might have derived from the stars.

"You like looking at the stars."

She nodded, not turning to look at him. She could tell from the corner of her eye he was looking at her. "When Meghan was dying . . ." she stopped. It was the first time she'd used the phrase, and it felt heavy on her tongue. "When I was taking care of her, I had little time for anything else. I used to go outside while she slept and look at the sky. It made me feel better, better about knowing she wouldn't be with us for much longer and better about knowing there was a divine order, a God if you will, that would make it all right."

"You would talk to the stars."

"Sometimes," she admitted. "I didn't speak out loud," she said. "I figured they could hear me think." Then she looked at him. He could only understand if he'd been in a similar situation. "Why did you do it?"

"I was very young. There was no one else to talk to. This was before I was adopted. So I talked to the sky."

She wondered at the coincidence that the two of them, coming from such different places, would do the same thing. Dean took her hand in his and held it. She laid her head on his shoulder and closed her eyes. She felt peaceful, more so than she had in a long time.

The house was quiet when Theresa entered. There was the soft hum of the television in a distant room, but other than that, the place was silent. Yet it had a softness to it. Theresa couldn't remember the last time she felt content when entering this house. She knew her feelings had been influenced by Dean. She hadn't wanted to go to the bar for fear of being recognized, and it hadn't proved as bad as she expected. But the visit to Lover's Lane and being close to Dean had changed the night for her.

She wondered if he had known this was what she had needed. She felt he had. No other man have ever understood her needs so quickly. It must be because he worked with eccentric people all the time, prima donnas who needed his assistance or his compassion. Whatever the reason, it had worked.

Going down the hall toward the sound, Theresa found Mrs. Abbott sprawled out on the sofa, the television on. She smiled, deciding not to disturb her. Robbie was in one of the empty rooms upstairs. Theresa slipped the afghan lying on an empty chair over Mrs. Abbott before turning off the television. She left the lamp burning in case she woke and didn't remember where she was.

Upstairs, she looked in the first guest room. It was empty. In the second one, Robbie slept innocently. Crossing the hall, she opened Chelsea's door and went inside. A cold fear gripped her when she looked at the bed.

It was empty.

Chelsea was sleepwalking again, Theresa thought. She had done this before, but no matter how often it happened, the fear that something bad might happen to her coursed through Theresa, with cold panic, followed by a hot streak of concern. Forcing the panic down, Theresa rushed into the bathroom. The white tile gleamed, and the towels hung from their proper handles, but the room was devoid of a child.

"Chelsea," she called. Switching on the overhead light, she looked in the closet and under the bed. Running to her own room, she followed the same routine. Nowhere she looked did she find her niece.

"What's going on?" Robbie said, rubbing his eyes as he came out of the guest room.

"Have you seen Chelsea?"

"She's asleep," he said.

"She's not in her room."

"Where'd she go?" Robbie was fully awake now.

"I don't know. She walks in her sleep."

"She does?"

Theresa was getting frustrated with his questions. Her heart was beating fast, and her throat was dry. She was shaking inside.

"You search the rest of the rooms on this floor. I'll look downstairs."

"Okay," he said without argument. "Chelsea." He was calling her name as she ran to the next room.

Theresa flew down the stairs, her feet loud on the wooden steps. Skipping the last three, she jumped to the floor and headed for the kitchen.

"Chelsea, where are you?"

No answer. Theresa swung the kitchen door inward and stepped inside, snapping on the light. Chelsea was not there. Still, she checked under the furniture and in every crevice large enough to hide a child. She ran from room to room, calling Chelsea's name and snapping lights on.

"Theresa, what's wrong?" Mrs. Abbott called from behind her as Theresa checked the back porch.

"Chelsea's gone. When did you last check on her?" she asked.

"What?" the woman said. Her hand went to her breast, and she stepped back as if she'd been hit.

"She sleepwalks, and she's missing."

"I didn't know."

Theresa realized that Mrs. Abbott might think she was being blamed for Chelsea's disappearance. "Forgive me, Mrs. Abbott." She ran a hand through her hair. "I'm not blaming you. Would you help me find her?"

"Sure."

Robbie walked in at that moment. "She's not upstairs."

"Robbie, did you hear anything from her room?" Mrs. Abbott asked her son.

"I was asleep. I only woke up when she started shouting." He pointed to Theresa.

Leaving them, Theresa went to the other rooms. She checked the basement, the front hallway, and finally, deciding the child was not in the house, she went outside. Racing to the garage, she found it empty except for the ticking engine of the cooling car, which Dean had parked in its usual space.

"Chelsea," she called out again, and again received no response. Sweat was pouring off Theresa now, yet her hands were ice cold. Where could Chelsea be? Was she hurt? How long had she been gone? Theresa turned around in a full circle, her eyes darting in every corner. In Buffalo, the house had been small, but Chelsea had never gone outside. Here the property was vast, but there was a lake at the back of it. Had she gone there?

Running around the house, Theresa scanned the water. She screamed the child's name again. Robbie and his mother joined her.

"What about the bubble?" Robbie asked.

"We'll check it," his mother answered, already pulling Robbie in that direction.

Theresa needed more help. Dean's face flashed in her mind. Without thinking, she headed for the small house where he was staying. Her steps pounded on the path. Still she kept looking around, hoping to get a glimpse of Chelsea's pink nightgown. Only the dark shadows of trees and bushes stared back at her. At Dean's door, she banged on the wood. It opened almost immediately, and she fell inside. His arms came out and caught her.

"Sh-h-h," he whispered in her ear.

Theresa looked up. She knew she looked frantic, but she didn't care. "Dean," she whispered.

"She's here."

Theresa stopped. For a moment, she had no idea who he meant. Her only concern was for Chelsea. She didn't care about anyone else. Dean didn't know that, though, unless he'd heard them calling her name. However, the generator providing the electricity to the array of trailers on the side of the property was close to the carriage house, so he might not have heard them above the hum of the engine.

"Chelsea is missing," Theresa said breathlessly. "I need yo—"

"Sh-h-h," he interrupted her. "She's here."

Theresa stared stupidly. "Here?" she repeated.

Dean took her arm and led her to the bedroom door. "I was calling a couple of my brothers when I noticed the door was open. I was just going to call you."

Theresa looked at the sleeping child, curled on her side, her body relaxed and innocent.

Relief jerked through her, and Theresa gasped. Suddenly the adrenaline that had been pumping triple time through her blood shut off like a faucet. Her knees went weak, and the room turned black with streaks of gold. Theresa bent over, trying to remain conscious.

"Oh-h-h," Dean said, pushing her into a chair. "Keep your head down." He put his hand on it to make sure she complied with his command.

Theresa took deep breaths and willed herself to be calm. Dean left her a moment. When he returned, she heard him twist the top off a bottle and pour something into a glass. He pushed it into her hand, and she took a gulp of cold water. Then he pressed a wet cloth against her forehead.

"You'll be all right in a moment." His voice was soothing, and Theresa felt like closing her eyes and drifting off into quiet sleep like Chelsea.

"Why would she come here?" Theresa asked after a moment.

"I don't know."

She hadn't really been asking Dean. She wondered why Chelsea would choose Dean's house as a safe haven.

"Mrs. Abbott!" she suddenly remembered. She looked up, trying to sit up straight. Dean kept her head down.

"What about her?" he asked.

"She and Robbie are still looking for Chelsea."

"Stay here. I'll find them and let them know." He left her then. Theresa drank more of the water. The sensation that threatened to topple her passed, and she felt herself returning to normal. Sitting back in the chair, she noticed the walls were no longer black and gold, but the soft white they had always been. Her head didn't feel light, either. Getting up, she walked to the bedroom door and checked on Chelsea again.

Theresa had to make sure Chelsea was there. Her niece had begun walking in her sleep the month before Meghan died. Each time Theresa found her gone, her heart dropped to the depths of a dark canyon.

Why had she come to Dean? Did he feel like safety to her? Theresa closed the door and turned around. Did she think of him that way, too? He'd understood her needs tonight at the bar, and he was the first person she'd thought of when she needed help. The security guards were on site, yet neither she nor Chelsea had gone to them. They both had come to Dean.

Theresa heard a muffled voice. She listened. It wasn't Dean's. It sounded like a television was in another room.

"Excuse me."

Theresa heard the muffled voice again. She looked around, expecting to see a television show. The television was on. But instead of the normal picture, there were three squares with people in them, a woman and two men. Had they said something to her?

"Excuse me," the woman said. Theresa jumped back. The woman was beautiful, and she also looked familiar. Maybe she was an actress. The men were also good-looking, better than good-looking. She'd certainly take notice of them if she was watching a movie.

"I'm talking to you," the woman spoke again. "Would you come over here?"

Theresa looked around for who the woman was talking to. Then she felt like an idiot in a horror film. She knew she was alone. Who else could the woman be talking to?

She walked toward the television.

"Hello," the woman said. "We haven't heard about you. Are you one of the actresses?"

Theresa sat down in the chair.

"No," Theresa said curiously. "Who are you?" Theresa had heard about this type of technology, but she'd never seen it.

"We're part of Dean's family," one of the men said. He had no smile and a serious look on his face. The other man wore an easy smile. The woman's classic features were relaxed. "I'm Owen, Dean's oldest brother. These other two are my brother Brad and my sister Rosa. We saw you come in," he continued.

Theresa remembered her hysterical entrance. Her hands went to her hair, smoothing some of the wildness out of it.

"I'm sorry for that. My little cousin was missing."

At that moment, Dean came through the door. Theresa started as if she'd done something wrong. "They called me over," she said by way of explanation.

"I'm sure Rosa did," he said. "I found Mrs. Abbott. She's a little upset, but I let her know everything is all right."

"It wasn't her fault. I should go to her."

"She's fine now."

"Then I'll take Chelsea and go back to the house." She glanced at the screen. It felt strange having an audience to their conversation. Then Theresa thought about them seeing her with her head between her legs.

"You can't carry her all that way." Dean said before

turning back to the screen. "Why don't I call you back tomorrow?" he said to them.

"Same time, same station," the smiling one said.

"And you can tell us about her," the woman said.

With a series of good nights, the squares went black and disappeared.

"They said they were your sister and brothers."

"They are," he said. "They're also busybodies, especially Rosa. She's the youngest, but she bullies us whenever she can."

Dean moved toward the bedroom. He scooped Chelsea into his arms. She curved her small body around him as if she trusted him. A pang of jealousy went through Theresa, but she didn't have time to dwell on it. Dean was already striding toward the front door.

Theresa followed him. The night air was cool, and with all the trees around, there was a slight mist in the air. "Did we interrupt anything important?" she asked as they walked toward the house.

He looked at her, confused. "The television? Your family?" She glanced over her shoulder at his house. The lights were on in several rooms.

"No, we talk frequently. I'll call them back tomorrow."

"They asked who I was."

"Rosa asked?"

"Yes," she said.

"She isn't being nosy, just protective maybe, but she's got a good heart."

"And she's beyond beautiful."

"She's a model."

"So that's where I've seen her. I thought she was an actress. Your brothers, too. They're good-looking enough to star in movies."

Dean chuckled. "They'll like that when I tell them." Then he looked serious. "Feeling better?"

"A lot." Theresa moved away from him. Dean looked at her

as if he were a doctor assessing her symptoms and making sure she was fit. Theresa withstood his scrutiny until it morphed into that indefinable presence between them that electrified the air.

Theresa stepped back. Dean broke his scrutiny and secured the blanket around Chelsea, and the two of them walked toward the house.

"Does she do this often?" he asked.

"Sometimes. I'd hoped moving from Buffalo would stop her night walks. With new surroundings and Robbie as a new friend, she seemed on the road to being her old self. And she is in every way, except when she's asleep."

When they reached the house and opened the door, the sudden light made Chelsea squint. Quickly, Theresa rushed to the switch and extinguished it. During her mad rush to find Chelsea, she'd turned on every room light.

"I can take her from here." She reached for Chelsea, but Dean started up the steps.

"She's all right," he said. Together, they went upstairs. After Dean laid her in bed and Theresa pulled the covers over her, she smoothed the child's hair back and turned to go. She didn't know Dean was directly behind her, so she bumped into him.

Ready to apologize, the words caught in her throat as she saw the way he was looking at her. As lightly as he had at Lover's Lane, he took her hand and led her from the room. Theresa looked back at Chelsea. Leaving her door ajar, the two went down the steps.

"It's been a very interesting day," Dean said as they reached the front door.

She nodded, committing herself to not telling him anything more about the night's activities.

He stepped outside the door.

"Dean." Theresa stopped him.

He looked back at her.

"Thank you," she said. "Not just for Chelsea, but for . . . tonight."

He said nothing, only stared down at her. Theresa looked at him. Silhouetted in the light of the doorway, his eyes were dark, yet the way they looked intently at her made her want to move closer to him. But she couldn't move. That connection between them was back, the invisible string holding the two of them in place. Dean's hand went around her waist, and his nearness did strange things to her. Her world changed. She could feel the splay of his fingers through her blouse. Time seemed to slow down or stop altogether. She didn't know which. Dean pulled her forward. She moved slowly, flowing toward him as if her body was a semisolid jelly. His features grew sharper and sharper, and the heat between them roared hotter. His mouth approached hers, and Theresa felt her entire body tingle at the anticipation of his kiss.

It didn't disappoint. His other arm slid around her waist, and he pulled her to his body. His mouth hovered over hers, but he didn't touch her lips. Theresa tried to keep her breathing normal, but it was an effort. Her eyes focused on his lips. She wet hers and swallowed, forcing her lungs to expand and contract. Dean's hand came up and slid through her hair. He angled her head and settled his mouth over hers. The kiss was tender yet wildly erotic. He held her lightly. If she had wanted to move, she could have. But she felt like Chelsea must have, cradled in Dean's arms, safe, loved.

She pushed her arms around his waist and aligned her body with his. The heat between them exploded, and Dean lifted his mouth only to resettle it on hers and deepen the kiss. Theresa dissolved in his arms, fitting herself to him as if they were made from the same mold. His mouth tugged at her lips as his tongue dipped and tangled with hers.

His hand, still in her hair, moved to her neck. Shivers skittered along her spine. As the hand moved lower on her body, sensation swept through her to every area Dean favored with his touch. Sound ceased around them, dropping them in a world devoid of anything except their need for each other.

The need to breathe forced Theresa's mouth free of Dean's. Weakly, she clung to him, taking in huge gulps of air. Theresa rested her head on Dean's shoulder. His heart beat strong and steady under her ear. When he leaned her back to look at her, she felt the strength of the connection joining them. And like an addict, she never wanted to lose the plane of euphoria on which they currently floated.

Chapter 5

Theresa didn't sleep after watching Dean retreat down the driveway and around the bend to the carriage house he occupied. She couldn't see the trailers from her bedroom, but she thought of them and the people who occupied them. She knew there was a fair amount of attraction between the cast and crew, and that many of the people working on the film had paired off, even if their time together ended when the film was canned.

Hollywood love affairs were notorious. So far she had not taken Dean to her bed, but the inevitable would happen. As long as the two of them were within proximity of each other, the chemistry between them was undeniable.

She didn't want an affair. She hadn't thought about what she did want. Her life had been on hold since she'd returned to the United States. Now, taking care of Chelsea, she hadn't given herself time to consider what was best for her, but with Dean entering her life, she needed to know what was happening, what she could expect, and if she should continue this path. Was it only leading to heartache and destruction when the film was done and he packed up and moved on? From the way he'd held her tonight, the way he kissed her, she thought the answer would be different. But was it because she wanted to think that way?

She luxuriated in her bed, pressing herself into the mattress as warmth spread through her at the memory of Dean's mouth on hers, the feel of his body pressing into hers. She'd wanted him to continue. She hadn't wanted him to stop when he lifted his head, had wanted him to take her to his bed. Yet Chelsea was in the house, and she could not leave the child alone. Theresa was not sure that Chelsea wouldn't come looking for her in the night if she'd led Dean into her bedroom.

Life was very complicated, she thought. Turning over, she grabbed the pillow and hugged it as a surrogate for the tall, dark, and handsome man she wished was with her. With a smile on her lips, she closed her eyes.

Morning came like a bad hangover. The sun shone, and she squinted, bringing her hand up to stop the stabbing pain in her eyes. Memories of her frantic search for Chelsea and Dean's devastating kisses flooded her mind. Like lightning, she was out of bed and rushing to her cousin's room. Chelsea sat up with a smile the moment Theresa pushed the door fully open.

"Can we have waffles for breakfast?" she asked.

Often, she didn't remember her nocturnal walks. Theresa usually didn't make a big deal of them. She was safe, and the trauma was over.

"Sure," Theresa said.

"With lots of syrup and some eggs too?"

"All you can eat."

"Okay," she said.

"After we eat, I have an errand to run. Would you mind staying with Mrs. Abbott again?"

"Will Robbie be there?"

"I think Robbie may be on the set, but I'm sure Mrs. Abbott will take you to watch."

"Okay." Pushing the sheets back, she climbed out of bed. "Where are you going?"

Other than last night when Theresa had gone to have a beer with Dean, she and Chelsea had not been separated. Chelsea had clung to her after Meghan died. Her "okay" wasn't a jump for joy reply. It was a baby step, but it was a step in the right direction. Theresa knew the child feared she would lose the only other person she knew. But she was doing better. Today would be the first time Theresa left her alone.

"Chelsea, I'll be back," she told her. "You know I'll be here with you for always."

Chelsea's head bobbed up and down. "Where are you going?"

Theresa thought of Dean and how good she'd felt in his arms, but she knew he wasn't her future. While the two might eventually, *would* eventually make love, when his job here was over, so would their time together. Unlike Chelsea, who was adjusting to life at Collingswood, Theresa would have a new adjustment to make when they were well and truly alone.

When that day came, she needed to be ready for it. This was why she was going into town this morning.

"I'm going to look for a job." Her voice was strong and sure, although inside, she was fearful. Anywhere else in the world, she wouldn't feel like she was breaking through thick glass, but in Royce, the shadow cast over her family was dark and ominous. But she had no place else to go and she had to find a means of supporting them once the money from renting the house to Dean was gone.

Theresa twisted her hands, evenly distributing the lotion on the front and back and each individual finger. Today was the day, she told herself. Checking her reflection in the rearview mirror, she pressed her lips together to assure herself that her lipstick was on right. Her hair shone from long brush strokes, and her makeup was flawless. In any other town, she would barely have checked it or even tried to improve upon what nature had given her, but today, or any day she ventured into Royce, she would be on display.

But not for her beauty.

She knew people pointed at her and whispered in their hands when she passed. Getting out of the Mustang, she adjusted her skirt and walked to the curb. Her feet, unused to high heels, scraped against the pavement. Already, she could feel her blood pressure rising. She lifted her chin and tossed her hair back. Remembering she needed to support herself and Chelsea, she swallowed any pride that might have changed the direction of her steps.

She needed a job.

She'd been trained as a professor. She'd taught in England when she lived there. Stepping onto the campus gave her a rush of belonging. It was the first time she'd ever felt like that in Royce since leaving Collingswood fourteen years ago. Without giving herself time to think, she found the office of the Department of Economics and walked through the door. She'd taught economics at Oxford, and her credentials were exemplary.

"Theresa!" The same woman who had announced her name to the crowd at the bar got up from a desk and came toward her. There was no counter preventing students, teachers, or guests from strolling through the room and entering the offices beyond or going to sit at one of the three desks that shared the anteroom.

"Nancy, what are you doing here?"

Nancy Evans had been Theresa's best friend. After Theresa had left, the two had lost touch. She'd seen her for the first time at the bar the other night.

"I work here. I teach calculus over in the mathematics department. I just came over to drop something off for Jane here." She turned and acknowledged the other woman. "Jane Greene, meet Theresa Ramsey. She used to live in these parts."

Theresa cringed when Nancy said that. But Jane only stood and offered her hand. She showed no trace of knowing anything about Theresa's past. Theresa shook her hand and returned her warm smile.

"It's nice to meet you. I teach Econ I and II."

"In addition to running this department," Nancy added.

"You're the dean?" Theresa asked.

She nodded.

"Hey, Theresa, I'm sorry about the other night," Nancy started.

"It's all right," Theresa interrupted her. She wanted to forget it, and she didn't want Jane to hear the story if she didn't already know it.

"What are you doing here? Are you enrolling?" Nancy asked.

"Actually, I was hoping to fill out an application for a teaching position."

Nancy smiled. "Great! Jane is the perfect person to talk to." She gestured toward Jane as if she were introducing a talk show guest. "I hate to run," Nancy said. "But I have a class in twenty minutes. Why don't you call me, and we'll get together for lunch or something."

Nancy pushed her hand inside a purse large enough to be a small suitcase and came out with a bent business card. She brushed it off before handing it over.

Addressing Jane, she said, "Jane, I'll vouch for Theresa. If you have a job, give it to her." Then she hugged Theresa and rushed out.

Theresa was stunned. Only a few minutes ago, butterflies were fluttering in her stomach, and now she had a friendly recommendation for a job.

If only the rest of Royce, despite what they knew about her family, was as friendly.

Theresa's mind was screaming for joy when she bounded across campus on her way to her car. She knew exactly what it felt like to be a kid again. She had a job. Come September, she would be employed. In the past, she'd needed employment, but nothing to the extent of putting a roof over her and Chelsea's heads and food on their table.

The Economics Department still needed to check her credentials, and she had to have a physical and drug test, which she would pass without a doubt. Other than that, she could begin teaching Introduction to Economics this fall.

If she was careful with her finances, they would be all right. Theresa's feet were barely touching the ground by the time she got to the car. Her face held a huge smile that had students staring at her. She greeted them as if they were old friends. And soon they would be.

She loved teaching. At Oxford, it had been both her source of income and her first love. Theresa was still grinning when she left the campus. Driving through town, she stopped on Main Street and went into the bakery. Only Hoefster's cream puffs could make her feel any better than she did at this moment.

Hoefster's wasn't just the type of place you went into, bought your pastry, and came out carrying a white paper bag or a box of donuts. It was a small pastry and ice cream emporium. Theresa's father used to bring her and her brother here on Saturday afternoons for a sweet treat.

Theresa smelled the sugar the moment she opened the door. The small building had been expanded since she was here last. The long counter with red stools in front of it took up one side of the room. Ice cream or a sandwich could be ordered and eaten on that side. The other side of the store held glass cases full of breads, pies, cakes, donuts, brownies, and the famous cream puffs. The back had been expanded to include tables and chairs for patrons to relax and eat the delicacies only Hoefster's could produce.

"Oh my," Everette Hoefster said as he stood over the glass counter. "I heard you were back."

Theresa clamped her teeth together, bracing herself for an off-color comment.

"You look great."

Taken by surprise, she said nothing. She'd expected him to dredge up the past. Everette had been in her class from kindergarten until she left the area.

"Never thought I'd see you in this town again." He hesitated. "I mean, after what happened."

"What happened, Everette? Do you know? Maybe you could explain it to me."

"I mean . . . I know you had nothing to do with it, but . . ." He stopped and hunched a shoulder. "Everybody talked about it."

"What did they say? That my father ran away and my mother killed herself?"

Everette looked embarrassed. "I'm sorry I brought it up. I know it wasn't your fault." He smiled an oily grin. "Can I get you anything?"

"No," she said, and turned to walk away.

"Theresa," he called after her. She continued to walk, ignoring his calls. She had reached the street before he took hold of her arm and pulled her around to face him. "I'm sorry. I shouldn't have brought that up. I don't want you to go away angry. We should be friends."

"Everette, when were we friends? In school, you were the first to start that horrible jingle. "*Terri, Terri, you're not so smart. Your daddy's gone, your mama's dead, and soon your heart will stop.*" She sang the words, wishing they had been erased from her mind but knowing they were engraved on her brain.

"I know." Everette dropped his eyes, then looked back at her. "I regretted it the moment I saw the look on your face, but the other kids had already heard it, and there was nothing I could do to stop them from singing it."

Theresa tried to move past him, but he stopped her again. "I truly am sorry, Theresa."

"Everette, I accept your apology."

"Thank you." His sigh was expelled as if her opinion of him really counted. "Won't you come back and have a cream puff? My treat."

Theresa couldn't stop her mouth from watering at the thought of the pastry. Everette took her arm, and she let him lead her back into the bakery.

"Have you seen any of the old class?" His question sounded as if she were here for a high school reunion.

"You know I left when I was in the sixth grade. Most of the old class may not even live here any longer."

"They don't, and that's a good thing for you."

She knew what he meant, and she wouldn't let it affect her mood. "I ran into Nancy the other night and at the university today."

"She teaches over there." Everette slipped half a dozen cream puffs into a small box and closed the top. "How about some coffee?"

Theresa nodded. "Black with two Equals."

"Wanna drink it in the back? I can join you for a few minutes."

"Thank you, but I have to get back. I left Chelsea with a sitter."

"Your daughter?" His eyebrows rose.

"My second cousin. You remember my cousin Meghan?"

"The one with big brown hair?" He gestured with his hands, yet there was a smile on his face. The summers Meghan had come to visit, she'd made an impression on the boys, big hair and all.

Theresa nodded. "Chelsea is her daughter."

"Is she here, too?"

"No, she died a few weeks ago."

"I'm sorry," he said. She could see the discomfort on his face. "Does this mean you're staying for good?"

"For the time being." Theresa was still not ready to believe that she'd spend the rest of her life at Collingswood.

Everette handed her the box and the coffee. "Thank you, Everette," she said. "For the cream puffs." She looked at the box. "And the offer of friendship."

"Maybe we can have that coffee one day."

"Maybe we can," she said with a smile.

Theresa had a light step in her walk as she left the bakery and walked to her car. She had cream puffs, a job, and the knowledge that most of the old guard were gone. She smiled, driving through the gates of Collingswood. Beside her on the passenger seat was the box of pastries. She thought she'd share them with Chelsea. They were going to be all right. She had a job, and when only the two of them were left on the property, they would survive.

The crew must be on a break, Theresa thought as she pulled up in front of the house. Several people spoke in groups outside the house. She wondered if it was a good day or if Dean was having more problems with the production.

As she stopped, one of the men who operated a camera opened the car door and offered his hand to help her out.

"Hi," Theresa said. "Is everything all right?"

He nodded. "Lighting is setting up."

"Have you seen Chelsea?"

"She and Robbie headed for the bubble, I believe."

Dean came out of the front door at that moment. Theresa's heart lurched. She remembered his mouth on hers and felt again the sweetness of his kiss. Quickly she turned away. She'd planned to go into the house, but she changed her mind and went toward the bubble.

She couldn't trust herself to remain distant from him. She could feel his hands on her body, even when he wasn't touching her, and in front of the cast, she didn't want to give herself away.

Theresa knew she must only be a moment behind the kids. She heard Chelsea talking ahead by the entrance to the bubble. Mrs. Abbott saw her, but Theresa motioned for her to remain where she was.

"Look at that," Chelsea said. A giant air supported structure had been constructed on the grounds. Her eyes were suddenly wide open, and her mouth held a smile of pure pleasure. Theresa had not been into the bubble before, so she was surprised and pleased at what she saw. There were rings; parallel bars, both even and uneven; beams; stationary horses—a full gym laid out like the one Chelesa had attended in Buffalo.

"This is just some stuff I have to practice on," she heard Robbie tell Chelsea. "For the movie."

Chelsea stared at the apparatuses.

"I have to do a lot of running on small ledges, jumping and swinging, things like that." Robbie shrugged his shoulders as he continued to explain in a voice dismissive of the equipment. Chelsea didn't appear to be listening. She was watching Robbie's double do giants on one of the three parallel bars in the makeshift room. Dressed in an undershirt-style leotard and white stirrup pants, his short body was straight as he went over the bars.

"Wanna see?" Robbie asked.

She nodded.

"Okay, help me put these things on." He grabbed a set of chalky white grips with red straps and tucked one under his arm. He pushed his middle and ring fingers through the small holes. Chelsea helped him secure the wrist straps. Robbie didn't notice that she knew exactly how to put the grips on him.

"These are so I won't rip my hands." He held out his unprotected hand, palm open. "See?"

Chelsea stared down. Theresa knew she was seeing the hard calluses on his hands. Theresa had seen them before and wondered how he had gotten them. The hand he was holding out had a tear in the skin that was red and angry-looking.

"Yuck," Chelsea said. "That had to hurt."

"It's not that bad." He shrugged his shoulders as if he was used to pain.

Taking the second grip from under his arm, Chelsea closed it tightly around his hand. With both hands protected, Robbie approached the parallel bar.

"Stand over there," he commanded. Then he looked at Frank Osborne, his stunt man. "All right if I show her?"

Frank nodded and moved into position to spot Robbie. Chelsea watched as Robbie's agile body went through the practice routine. After a few minutes, Robbie executed a release move, twisting in the air and coming to a stop on a rubber mat.

"Wow!" Chelsea said, stepping closer to Frank and Robbie. "That was wonderful. I want to have a turn."

She reached for his hand grips.

"Whoa!" Frank said, stopping her. "This isn't as easy as it looks, and it can be dangerous." He stared at her, even though he was almost the same height as she was.

"Aunt Theresa would say it's all right." She appealed to Mrs. Abbott.

"What's all right?" They all turned to see Theresa standing in the shade of the bubble room.

"I want to do gymnastics."

"You do?" Theresa asked as if she had not witnessed the previous scene.

Chelsea's head bobbed up and down. "It's okay, right? I'll be careful."

"You're not dressed for it," Theresa said.

"We have extra leotards," Robbie chirped in. "They are for boys, but she can wear one."

"I'll make sure she doesn't get hurt," Frank added. "And

we also have a trainer." He threw a glance at the other man standing in the small group.

"I'll be careful," Chelsea pleaded.

"All right," Theresa conceded. "Go get dressed."

Chelsea rushed off like a ball of fire was licking her heels.

"What's going on?" Dean asked, coming in behind Theresa. Her heart stopped the moment she heard his voice. The sound went through her like a bow string being plucked.

"Chelsea is going to do some gymnastics," Robbie said. "She's changing."

Dean looked in the direction of the locker room, then back at the small group. "Do you think that's wise? Training doesn't begin on this equipment."

"We won't let her do anything dangerous," Frank said.

Theresa looked at Dean and nodded. "Robbie's having a good effect on her. She's coming out of her shell."

"I'm doing what?" Robbie asked.

"You're helping Chelsea," Theresa told him.

"Helping her what?"

"She had something happen that wasn't very good, and she—"

"You mean her mom dying?" Robbie broke in.

"Yes, Robbie. Her mom died, and she needs time to get over it. You're helping her."

He smiled with a dimpled expression that could only be read as *aw, shucks*.

Chelsea came barreling out of the dressing room. Her slender body contrasted starkly with the white leotard, but there was a smile on her face. Joy suffused Theresa's cheeks. She wanted to run to the little girl and hug her close, but she stopped herself.

"I'm ready," she said.

"Here, put these on." Robbie held the grips out to her. Their hands were about the same size. Quickly, he helped her get ready, and she turned to the bar.

"We usually don't start anyone off on this," the trainer said. "I'll help you up. But all you're going to do is swing your legs."

"I can do it," she said to the man.

"I'm sure you can, but let's do it slowly. We don't want to have any accidents."

Theresa put her hand up to her face, hiding her mouth. Dean's hand cupped her elbow. Without thinking, Theresa put her other hand over it. The warmth from his touch poured over her like warm syrup.

Chelsea began to swing. Her legs came up as she pumped herself.

"Not too high," the trainer warned.

Chelsea ignored him and pushed herself higher. The trainer stepped in to stop her. Theresa moved then, leaving the comfort of Dean's touch, and put her hand on the trainer's arm. "Let her go," she whispered.

Chelsea went higher and higher until she swung herself all the way to the top and was perpendicular to the floor. Robbie's mouth dropped open as she stood still for a second, reversed her hand position, and turned completely around. She swung in a complete circle before going up and executing the same procedure again. Then she swung hard, snapping her nimble body and releasing the bar. She tumbled in the air and came down with her heels together, sticking to the mat as if she could change momentum at will.

A second of silence paralyzed Robbie and the trainer, then they both shouted at once. Dean stood dumbfounded. Theresa's eyes were fastened on Chelsea's. In a moment, she was moving, moving fast, rushing to the little girl as if she'd performed some miracle.

Theresa fell on her knees as Chelsea collided with her. They hugged and laughed. Theresa kissed her cheek and her hair and hugged her tight. Chelsea's small arms wound around her neck and into her hair.

"I did it," Chelsea said. "I did it."

Theresa pushed her back. "Yes, you did. How did it feel?"

"I loved it. I missed doing it." Chelsea's small arms hugged her again. Theresa rocked her as if she were an infant.

More was happening for them than just enjoying the moment. The two of them knew they were moving on. Chelsea had gone over that bar, and her agile little body had broken through the wall of grief. From this moment on, Chelsea could begin the trip back to the living. She could accept Meghan's death and know that she did not have to die with her mother. That she could laugh and have fun, that she could do things that made her feel good without betraying her mother's memory.

"Can I do it again, Theresa?" She spoke in Theresa's ear. Theresa pulled back and looked at her."I remember. I know how to do it."

"I know you do, but you can't start so fast. After not doing it for months, you have to build up slowly."

At that moment Robbie, Dean, Mrs. Abbott, and the trainer joined them. Theresa stood up.

"You've done this before," Robbie said. His voice was loud and excited. "Why didn't you say so?"

"I used to take lessons."

"Can she practice with me?" Robbie looked at Dean and then Theresa.

"Can I?" Chelsea pleaded. "I promise I'll do whatever they tell me."

Theresa glanced at Dean. He gave her no indication of his thoughts. "Chelsea, this is a movie set. We'll go into town and see if we can enroll you in a school."

"Ma'am?" the trainer spoke. "I don't mind training her if it's all right with Dean. Most of the time, I'm sitting around doing nothing."

Everyone turned to look at Dean. He look confused.

"I know there are insurance regulations," Theresa said, saving him from refusing. "Chelsea isn't a member of the cast, so she wouldn't be covered."

"You can hire her," Robbie stated, as if he had the answers to the universe. He pleaded with Dean. "She could be my understudy. I don't have one."

"Movies don't have understudies, Robbie," the trainer said, as if Robbie didn't already know that.

The young boy stared at Dean.

"I could," Dean finally said. "Chelsea, you're hired as Robbie's understudy."

Chelsea rushed to him, throwing her arms around his waist. Dean took a step back. Theresa could tell he wasn't expecting her show of affection.

Theresa looked at him. Every cell in her body wanted to rush to him as her niece had. But she hung back. Some remnant of logic in her brain advised her to protect her heart, but the voice was low and muffled under the need to have him hold her close.

Over Chelsea's head, Dean stared at her. Theresa had to force herself to remain still. She could feel the pull of his body and the push of her own. She wanted to go to him, to join the grateful child hugging him and tell him how important he was becoming to her life.

But that was the problem. He was becoming too important. And he was leaving. She wouldn't kid herself about that. So like the grips Chelsea had on her hands for protection, Theresa protected herself by remaining in place.

But she couldn't keep her eyes from melting or her heart from hurting.

Chapter 6

As much as Theresa knew she couldn't avoid Dean forever, she'd done it for several days. With the reintroduction of gymnastics into her cousin's life, a new routine had been established. Chelsea bounded out of bed each morning and rushed to the bubble, delighted to be going through her old routines and learning some new ones. Whenever Robbie was free, the two competed, showing what they could do. Theresa looked at them with happy eyes. Chelsea was doing better. While Meghan's photo sat by her bed, her young cousin's eyes no longer filled with tears when she looked at it.

Yesterday, another milestone in her recovery had occurred. Theresa sat on a chair in the bubble watching Chelsea learn a release movement. During a break, she came over and looked at what Theresa was doing.

"You know, Aunt Theresa, you don't have to watch me every second. I'm all right coming here by myself."

Theresa smiled. During their before time, before their lives were altered, she'd drive Chelsea to the gymnastics school, drop her off, and pick her up later. Since they had come to Collingswood, the two had been together, for the most part. She wondered if the child, with wisdom beyond her years, was letting her know that she was growing and coping.

Looking through the window of the library, which Theresa was converting into her office, she stared in the direction of the bubble and remembered Chelsea's good-bye comment this morning. She was carrying a gym bag with water bottles in the mesh pockets and her grips and shoes inside.

"I can go by myself," she said when Theresa walked her to the door. Theresa's intention had been to go with her, but Chelsea's words had changed her mind.

"Call me if you need me," she said and waved as her cousin went out the door and crossed the lawn toward the gymnastics bubble.

Going back to her desk, she sat in front of the computer and continued making plans and notes for the forthcoming school year. It was July, giving her little more than a month to familiarize herself with everything that needed to be done. She was exhilarated to have something to occupy her mind, if it could get in between the thoughts of Dean that crept in when she awoke and stayed until she slept. Even then, her dreams were of him.

After her interview in the Economics Department, the secretary had sent Theresa the required textbook and testing packages. The books had arrived a few days later and had again been delivered to Dean. She found them on the kitchen table one morning when she came down to breakfast. There was no note, and she'd been mildly disappointed that Dean hadn't tried to see her, but then thought that after her explosion when her other boxes were sent to him, he probably didn't want a confrontation.

Thinking about that brought Dean back to the front of her mind. She'd forced herself to avoid him, but knowing he was only a few yards away, she wanted steal through the rooms and watch him work. Even though that wasn't an option, it didn't stop her from wanting to make it happen.

Pushing the thought aside, she went back to the text for Introduction to Economics. The information was extremely basic, and she knew it. What she tried to do was find current examples that were relevant to today's college students and use them to reinforce her points. Most students thought of economics as a dry subject. Her goal was to make it alive to them, so pointing to relevant uses of the principles was important.

She'd been typing steadily for several minutes when a soft knock came on the door. Without looking up, she said, "Come in." She expected Chelsea was back. She always knocked unless she was in a crisis.

"Hello."

The deep baritone voice paralyzed her for a moment. Theresa heard the smile in his voice. She swallowed, gathered herself together, and turned around.

"I haven't seen you around for a couple of days." He had that lazy smile on his face that drained her of her ability to think rationally, but Theresa was determined to keep her head.

"I've been keeping busy."

Coming further into the room, he looked at the books lining the shelves. They had been there for years. Some of them Theresa had read, but most were her father's books.

Taking a chair next to the desk where her papers and books were spread out as if she was a college student cramming for final exams, he lifted one and asked, "What are you doing?"

"Preparing."

"For what?"

Theresa pushed herself back, sinking into the worn leather of the chair. For a moment, she had a feeling reminiscent of sitting on her father's lap as she'd done in childhood. The thought gave her added strength to hold on to her wits and not dissolve into the place her heart wanted to go. One she knew would leave her grieving.

"I got a job," she told him. "At the university. I start this fall in the Economics Department."

Dean nodded as if he remembered her telling him she had taught before. "I didn't know you needed a job."

The statement summed up their relationship. There were too many things he didn't know about her and vice versa, but what she did know was that time was not on their side. He had a deadline to finish his filming. The actors and actresses had contracts for other projects as soon as this one ended. The crew wanted to return to their families for some downtime before setting off on another production.

"You're not going to be here forever. When the company packs up and moves, I have to support this place." She knew she would be hard pressed to do that on a professor's salary, and she wasn't going to get into her finances with Dean. She did, however, see a wistful look flit across his face. It was there and gone so fast she had to convince herself she'd seen it.

"Why are you preparing now?" he asked.

"I'm gathering supporting information." She glanced at the computer. "Econ is usually very dry. I want to present some relevant, current examples in class."

Dean mulled this over. He looked at her, then glanced past her shoulder and out the windows behind her. "What happened the other night?" he finally asked.

Theresa tensed but tried to keep her reaction to herself. Consciously, she dropped her shoulders and slowed her breathing. "Nothing," she finally said, although her definition of nothing was a monumental change in the order of the universe.

Dean got up. His six-foot-plus frame towered over her. Even the high ceilings of the room didn't dwarf him. He walked to the fireplace on the opposite wall and turned back to her. He stood wide-legged, as if he was bracing himself for a hard blow. "I wouldn't say it was nothing."

Theresa wanted to stay behind the desk, protected by its solid presence, by the computer sitting on the end and the green-shaded banker's lamp spilling light on the new economics text.

But she got up and walked between the leather sofas flanking the unlit fire.

Dean pushed away from his position and took a step toward her. Instinctively, she retreated.

"What's wrong?" he asked. "I thought something was happening between us."

"It was." She looked down, then immediately raised her eyes to meet his. "But it's not anymore."

His eyes narrowed, and the tiny lines in his brow dominated his face. "So what happened between the kiss and the books?"

"Nothing happened," she said. "I did some thinking, and I can see that the more time we spend together, the worse things will get."

"What does that mean?"

Theresa took a deep breath. "Sit down," she said, taking a seat on the tufted leather sofa opposite the one he stood next to. Dean sat across from her. Theresa wished she had something to do with her hands. The urge to wring them was strong. Steadying herself, she folded them on her knees. "When will the film be done?"

"What?"

"It won't be forever." She answered her own question. "You'll be leaving to go back to California or Texas. I'm going to be here. I have to think about myself and Chelsea. We'll have to survive after you're gone." She paused to swallow. "And becoming more involved with you isn't going to be healthy for me in the long run."

"So, you decided this?"

She nodded.

"Without thinking of talking to me about it?"

She nodded. "Dean, it's not like we have a relationship. I'm not required to talk to you. We've shared two kisses and some intense moments of friendship. I appreciate you protecting me, your understanding of how I feel, and you taking care of Chelsea."

"But," he prompted.

"But I don't think we should let our friendship pass the point of no return."

Dean got up and switched sofas. He did it so fast Theresa didn't have time to move away. Before she knew he'd moved, he was right next to her, his knees pressed against hers.

"Theresa, our friendship is already past the point of no return. It went past that point the first night I kissed you. And you kissed me."

His words had finality to them such that she could brook no argument against them.

"Well, it can't go any further. You're leaving, and I'll be here." She calmed herself, adjusting her position so she wasn't touching him. "I can offer you friendship, nothing more."

Another of his lightning moves had him on his feet with her pressed against him. If Theresa hasn't seen him do it, she wouldn't have believed anyone could move that fast, or that she could be wrenched from her seat without feeling herself being pulled.

"I am not your friend," he ground out.

She tried to pull away, but he held her steady. They stared tensely at each other. After a long moment, Theresa relaxed against him. His arms immediately tightened around her. His head dropped to her neck, and the two of them stood together.

"Don't you understand?" Theresa asked in a muffled voice.

She felt his head nodding.

"You're a director. Your career is on the rise. There are many places you have to go and many women you'll meet along the way."

Dean's body went as taut as hard plastic. He eased her away from him and stared into her eyes. "Is that what this is about?

Other women? Invisible women? People I haven't met and aren't likely to meet?"

"It's common knowledge that relationships don't last in your business." Theresa stepped away from him, and he let her go. "Groupies follow the stars, and that includes directors."

"Famous directors," he said.

"Any directors," she shouted, then realized someone might hear them and lowered her voice. "You're going to be famous soon. Remember, I've seen some of the dailies." In fact, she'd seen a lot of them. And they were brilliant. Dean might be unknown now, but when this movie was released, his name would head the list of the newest hot and sought after directors in Hollywood. It would also make other lists, including those of starlets willing to do anything for their lucky break.

"Theresa, I know there's something between us. I have the feeling it could be something good. Why are you shutting the door on it?"

"I'm not shutting the door. I'm protecting myself."

"From me?"

For the space of a full minute, they stared at each other. Like two predators readying to strike, each assessed the other for the weakness that would be most advantageous. Theresa was finding his stare hard to bear, but she didn't want to be the first to look away.

"Can you tell me, honestly, that you've thought of an us past the time when you pack up and return to Hollywood?" Theresa asked. She stared straight at Dean, wanting to know his reaction. She could see it in the way his body went from taut hunter to defeated suitor.

"You haven't," she stated, answering her own question. "Then I suppose there's nothing else for us to talk about."

Dean came toward her. Theresa wanted to move, to step back from him, find a safer place than where she stood, but she remained in place. "There's plenty for us to talk about, beginning with what's already happened between us."

Theresa stood in the bath of heat that enveloped them whenever they were near each other. She knew she had to stand firm. If she were to survive when he was gone, she had to make him believe she was sincere now.

"We're both adults, Dean. Let's act like it. We're not drowning in the deep end of the pool. We can walk away from this, and be stronger for our efforts."

Dean stared at her as if coming to a decision. After a lifetime, he stepped back, acknowledged her with a slight tilt of his head, and walked out of the room. Theresa followed him to the door, pushing it closed before slipping down it to the floor and covering her face with her hands, sitting in numbed silence.

I'm right, she told herself. And Dean had proven it. He didn't see any relationship between them lasting past the end of the film. She was right to halt it now before either of them was so emotionally committed that heartbreak was waiting to enter the moment the last car pulled away from her gate.

It might already be too late. Theresa put her arms around herself, hugging her waist, trying to close the vast hole she felt widening there. *I'm right,* she told herself again, but being right didn't make her feel as if she'd won anything.

The truth was she'd lost.

Dean hooked his leg over the barstool and ordered a beer. The last time he'd been in this bar, Theresa had been with him. He glanced at the table where they'd sat. A man sat alone there nursing a shot of whiskey.

Filming has gone well after Dean's encounter with Theresa, although he hadn't expected it to. It was an intense scene, and the actors must have picked up on the rage that was churning inside him, for they did exactly what he'd hoped for. Yet hours later, here he was putting distance between Theresa and himself, so he wouldn't go up to the house and try to talk some sense into her.

What bothered him more was what she'd made him see in himself. Beyond the film, he did see them together. This had never happened to him before. He wasn't one to string along starlets, taking advantage of his position as a director as he knew he could. Like his brother Owen, Dean had always ended a relationship before it got too serious. But Owen had found Stephanie last year, and the two of them couldn't be happier. In fact, in three years, three of his brothers had married. Was that the reason he was looking for something more permanent with a woman? And Theresa fit the bill. But she didn't. She came with baggage, just as he did.

She had a child who might need years of therapy. She had that huge estate that would drain her finances and . . . he stopped. He really liked the house and grounds. Even when he'd first seen it with the overgrown weeds, peeling paint, broken windows, and uneven floors, he'd fallen for the place as if it was his own home. The home he didn't have and couldn't remember.

Lifting his glass, he took a drink and glanced around the bar. People looked at him curiously, but he ignored them. He was used to it from the other towns he'd visited as a member of a film crew. At least these people weren't approaching him, making veiled conversation before pitching themselves as actors for one of his movies.

Theresa had accused him of flings with starlets. He hadn't denied it, but it wasn't true. On site, he was too busy working to find time for women, and he wasn't interested in anyone in the crew. But when she'd burst into the house that first day and knocked him off his feet, he'd known he wanted her. But he'd pushed the thought aside. Now he wasn't sure he could continue doing that.

"Hey, aren't you one of those guys working up at Collingswood?"

Dean looked up to see the barmaid who'd served him the beer speaking to him. He nodded.

"That must be some film."

She was about forty, but looked older. If he'd been casting a boozy mother figure, she'd be perfect.

"It's coming along," he said noncommittally.

"I'm surprised anyone wanted to film in Collingswood."

"Why's that?"

"The place must be haunted. What with what happened up there."

Dean frowned. Theresa jumped into his mind. Had something happened to her? He usually didn't go for local folklore, but he had a vested interest in this one. "What happened?" he asked.

"You mean you've been up there all this time, and you don't know what happened?"

Dean gripped his glass harder. He wanted to shout at her to get on with it, but he forced himself to relax and wait.

"Hey, Lacey, can I get another one?" Someone from the other end of the bar called her, and she walked away.

Disappointed, Dean waited for her to return.

"There was a disappearance. No one ever proved murder, but he was murdered. You mark my words."

Dean turned and found the man who'd been sitting at the table where he and Theresa had sat last time perched on the barstool next to him. His appearance had been so quiet that he startled Dean. The man spun his now empty glass around in a circle between his two hands. His knuckles were gnarled and swollen, and his three-day beard growth was spiky and peppery grey. Unlike Lacey, his age was indeterminable. He could have been anywhere from fifty to eighty years old.

"The man who owned the house disappeared one night," he said, picking up the story Lacey had begun. "There were no signs of a struggle, and nothing was missing. His body was never found. Suspicion was levied against the wife, but without a body, no charges were ever filed. He remains 'missing' to this day." He lifted the glass and drained a single drop into his mouth. "Eventually, the talk got to her, the way people stared when she walked down the street or went into any of the stores. She was left with debts and no way of paying them. Committed suicide, leaving the two children—boy named Kevin who was in and out of mental hospitals for ten years. He owns a small grocery store about 100 miles from here."

"What about the other kid?"

"That would be Theresa. Poor little girl. She took on a lot of responsibility at an early age. And now she's come back with another kid who needs help. I guess some people are just magnets for that kind of thing."

Dean was stunned. It was Theresa's parents the man was talking about. Initially, when Lacey mentioned the story, Dean thought it had happened a hundred years ago, had been told and retold and embellished with each rendition like a folktale. Now he partially understood the reaction of the crowd the last time he'd been here. And Theresa's reluctance to explain anything when they'd gone to Lover's Lane afterward. This was a small town, and small towns lived on scandal and gossip. Everybody around must have their own version of what happened to Theresa's father and why.

Dean realized most believed his wife killed him. What had that done to Theresa? Did she believe it, too?

"Small children," Dean said. "How old was Theresa when this happened?"

"'Bout ten or eleven. Kids teased her. They even had a little song they sang to taunt her."

"Why?"

"No reason, just kids being kids. They didn't know how much hurt they could inflict. Then her aunt came and took the kids away. Never thought she'd come back."

"What about the house? It's been empty all this time?"

"For the most part. I guess one of them is holding out hope that their father will come back."

"But you don't think so."

"Nope," he said with finality. "Had no reason to leave. Janine and Alex Ramsey were the happiest married couple in America. They had two beautiful kids, the old house had been in their family for generations, his business was thriving—what was there to tear him away?"

"It may have been different from the inside," Dean commented. "Often people on the outside don't see the cracks that can tear a family apart."

The older man was shaking his head. "Not this one." He sighed as if remembering the past. "The investigation found nothing out of the ordinary. No girlfriend stashed away in a city apartment. No illegal dealings in his business. Not even an outstanding parking ticket."

"Then why would his wife commit suicide?"

"Good question," he said. "Been trying to figure that one out for the last fourteen years." He glanced at the barmaid. "Lacey?" he called and tapped his glass twice. She picked up a bottle on the way to him and automatically filled his glass.

"Another one?" she asked Dean, gesturing toward his beer glass.

He shook his head. Reaching for his wallet, he indicated the drink she'd just poured. "Let me get this one, too." Paying for both his beer and the drink for the man who'd told him the story of Collingswood, Dean slid off the stool. "Thank you for the company," he said, offering his hand. "We never exchanged names. I'm Dean Clayton."

"August," he said, taking Dean's hand in a surprisingly strong grip. "August Coleman. Call me Auggie."

"Auggie," Dean repeated. "Good night."

Dean's drive back to Collingswood wasn't the same as it had been on the previous occasion, but he found Theresa more of an enigma now than he had then. How had her father's disappearance affected her? She'd spent time in England, she'd told him. Was she running away? Apparently, they had more in common than he'd thought. Dean didn't know who his parents were. The Claytons had taken him in and made him part of their family, but he didn't remember anything earlier than from when he was seven years old. In fact, he had no real birthday, only one that he'd been arbitrarily given.

Theresa had lived with love, a lot of love, for a short period of her life. Then it had been yanked away from her. Could that be the reason she'd rejected him? His sister was a child psychologist, and how many times had he heard her say that children craved love? If they didn't get it, they built defenses to protect themselves. Was this what Theresa was doing?

Pulling the car in front of the restored carriage house, Dean got out and looked toward the fieldstone mansion gleaming in the moonlight. None of the windows were lighted, but he was sure Theresa was there and that she was awake.

Well, he thought, turning and running up the steps to the front door of the carriage house, she might think things were settled between the two of them, but they weren't and he'd make sure she knew that—sooner rather than later.

Dean, who was often up before sunrise, was showered and dressed in time to see the parallel bars that Robbie's double would swing on being set up and concealed from the camera. There was plenty of activity going on and much noise. He wondered how Theresa could sleep through it, yet there was no sign of her when Dean poured himself a cup of coffee from the urn in the kitchen.

He'd hoped she'd be up, but didn't think that would happen. Even if she was, she'd made it clear that she didn't want him in her life, so she would go out of her way to avoid him. Chelsea's sleepwalking hadn't brought her back to his house so her aunt could follow and he'd get the chance to see her, talk to her, and maybe resolve the issue that was keeping him up nights.

Pushing the back door open, he walked outside. The morning was misty, dew covering the ground and fog up to his knees so he looked like he was walking through a cloud. His feet stirred the air as he looked toward the bench where he and Theresa had sat. Turning away from it, he headed toward the light and noise of the bubble.

Dean stood right inside the door and watched. Robbie's voice filled the cavernous space with his laughter after he tried a new routine and missed.

"I'll do it again," he told his trainer before the man had a chance to reply.

"Let me show it to you again first," Frank said. The stunt double jumped up and caught the pole. Dean wouldn't have thought he could do it since he was only four feet tall, but Frank had surprised him more than once with his athletic abilities. Frank executed the move perfectly. Then Robbie moved into position, the trainer lifted him up, and he grabbed the bar. Frank and the trainer moved back as Robbie began to swing.

Dean envied his agile body as the young boy turned and twisted in the air. Dean was sure his six-foot-plus frame would never do those moves again. Then it happened. In a space of time too short to measure, Dean saw it happening.

"No-o-o-o!" The word sprang into his mind and out of his mouth before his brain registered speech. The moment Robbie let go of the parallel bar to execute a release move, Dean knew the child wasn't going to make it. His own rudimentary foray into the sport had given him just enough knowledge to recognize an accident in the making. Before it even registered, Dean's feet were already moving. He was rushing, sprinting toward the boy in the air. He prayed he'd get to Robbie in time, but a detached portion of his mind told him it was unlikely. He ran across the ground. His feet pounded into the grass as he tried to defy the forces of gravity, inertia, and momentum. Robbie was spinning through the air. He'd overrotated, gone beyond the safety zone. His trainer and spotter were out of range as centrifugal forces pushed Robbie higher and further than any practice session had taken him before. None of the three reached Robbie in time.

Robbie hit the padded floor with a thud. His body seemed to both crumple and bounce at the same time. With all the stories his brothers had told him of their exploits before they had come to the Claytons' household, Dean had never imagined anything as terrible as what he heard when Robbie hit the mat. His legs smacked the padded plastic, but the sound of bone snapping was unmistakable.

Robbie squealed in agony as several people reached him at the same time.

"Don't touch him," the trainer shouted.

Frank caught Mrs. Abbott as she was about to grab her son. Although she was much taller than he was, his strength overcame her, and he tackled her to the floor like a wrestler pinning his opponent.

"Call 9-1-1, and get the nurse over here," Dean commanded a man in the gathering crowd. The crew member turned and ran without a word.

Robbie's screams continued, bringing the entire crew to the bubble. Dean searched the group for the one of the security guards. When he saw John Willis, he shouted to him. "Keep the crowd back."

The ambulance seemed to take a year to get there. Tears streamed from Robbie's eyes as he continued to cry and reach for his leg. Dean and the trainer held his arms to prevent him from touching his leg, while the nurse did what she could to keep him comfortable until the paramedics got there. Their arrival sped the action up, as if a film had suddenly gone from slow motion to Keystone Cop fast.

Robbie's screams stopped with the increased action. Before long, he was loaded into the ambulance, and the paramedics slammed the back door closed.

As the red and silver unit sped away, the crowd dispersed. Dean planned to follow the ambulance to the hospital, along with Frank and the trainer. Someone would have to drive Mrs. Abbott back, if they could get her to leave her son's side. He'd only taken two steps toward his car when he stopped. His heart hammered in his chest. Theresa stood staring at him, her arms around Chelsea, who stood in front of her. Both looked frightened.

He went to her. Her eyes were shiny in the misty morning light. It took everything he'd ever learned, ever been taught, ever instinctively knew to be right not to take her in his arms and hold her close.

"He'll be all right," he assured her, even though he didn't know the truth of the statement. He believed it, and both of them looked as if they needed to hear it.

Then he reached down and hugged Chelsea. She tightened her arms around his neck as he lifted her off her feet. Theresa hadn't moved. She looked up at him, and suddenly, she was moving toward him. His arm reached out for her, the movement as natural as breathing. He hugged her over Chelsea, taking in her scent, reveling in the clean smell of her hair and the feel of her soft body close to his.

"We have to talk," he whispered as he turned his mouth and kissed the skin below her ear. He heard her sudden intake of air and felt her body relax against his. He wanted nothing more than to stay with her, to tell her how he felt and sort out the numerous feelings confusing him about their relationship. But he needed to go to the hospital. Frank and the trainer waited near his car.

He wanted to ask Theresa to come with him, but the hospital was no place for Chelsea. Both of them had eyes as large as saucers. Dean knew they were afraid for Robbie, and he understood their fear. Pushing the two women away from him, he hunkered down to Chelsea's level. "Don't worry; he's going to be all right," he told her.

"Promise?" she asked.

"I promise." Dean smiled at her and waited for her to return it. After a long moment, the corners of her lips turned up. Dean hugged her again, lifting her up and holding her for a moment before setting her on her feet.

"If I find out anything more, I'll call and let you know," he said to Theresa. She silently watched him go to the car and drive away. She didn't wave or move. She held Chelsea's hand and watched as the car passed them and headed toward the open gate.

It was past time for them to talk. And they *would* talk. And that wasn't all he had in mind for them to do when he got back.

Chapter 7

"Will Robbie be all right?"

Theresa yanked the door open, asking her question before Dean reached the porch. It was well after dark, and the ambulance had driven away at sunrise. Dean's expression was grave and an ache seized Theresa's heart.

"He'll be fine in time," Dean said. "His leg is broken in two places, but he's out of surgery. The doctors expect him to recover fully."

"How's Mrs. Abbott?"

"She stayed with Robbie. She was calmer than any of the rest of us."

Theresa remembered her own hospital vigils, sitting close to Meghan. She may have appeared calm on the outside, but she shook on the inside like someone with a nervous tic. Mrs. Abbott might be feeling the same. Theresa hoped Robbie would recover soon so his mother wouldn't have to spend months watching him as Theresa had with her cousin.

Theresa's shoulders dropped in relief. "Thank goodness," she said. Then, noticing the expression on Dean's face, she understood how long his day must have been. "You look terrible," she said.

"I was up before sunrise . . . then the whole day in the emergency room. I'm beat."

"Can I get you something?" She turned toward the door and the kitchen beyond. "Something to eat?"

"No," Dean shook his head. His hand reached out to stop her. It landed on her arm. A jolt went through her where his hand touched her. Dean must have felt it, too. He dropped his hand quickly. She moved further into the house, and he followed. The look on his face changed from an expression of concern over Robbie to one that reflected the reined-in passion that existed between them.

He looked worn out. She took a step toward him, another of those natural things. "Maybe you should get some sleep." The band Dean often wore to keep his hair out of his face was gone. Long tendrils flowed down his back and over his shoulders, teasing her with a searing need to reach up and push her hands through the hair extensions.

"I will," he said. "How's Chelsea?"

Theresa walked toward the living room. She'd been waiting for Dean in there. When she'd seen the lights of his car flash against the wall, she had rushed to the front door. "She fretted most of the day. I couldn't get her interested in anything. Your phone calls helped her settle down." Dean had called twice from the hospital. Once while Robbie was in surgery and again when he came out.

"It's the first time anyone has gone to the hospital since her mother died, isn't it. She might feel that anyone who goes there will die."

"I never thought of that. I'll take her to see Robbie tomorrow. Make sure she know he's going to be all right."

Theresa was astounded by Dean's understanding of the psychology of grief and death. Despite him being so tired from the day's activities, he still thought of Chelsea.

"My sister explained it to me."

"Did she lose her mother, too?"

He nodded. “She’s a child psychologist, and not only does she deal with children, but the family reaps the benefits of her knowledge and experience, too.”

Theresa smiled. “It must be nice having a big family. There’s only myself and my brother.” She stopped short of mentioning Meghan.

In the living room, Theresa sat down on the sofa. She’d brought in a pitcher of iced tea and two glasses, anticipating that Dean might spend a few minutes with her before going off to bed. Her glass was only half full. The ice had melted, making the liquid several shades lighter at the top than the bottom.

Without asking, she poured him a glass and handed it to him. Dean took it, dropping down on the sofa. He sighed heavily and drank the liquid in one long gulp. He leaned back, holding the empty glass, and closed his eyes. Theresa understood he needed time to decompress, to get over the day’s events, the long hours of wondering how the child was doing.

Theresa closed her eyes and leaned back, putting all other thoughts out of her mind, except for Dean. He was impossible to ignore, impossible to tuck away in some safe corner only to be opened when she felt the need.

They sat that way for several quiet moments. Theresa leaned over and took the empty glass from Dean’s hands. She sat it on the tray. Dean took her hand as she moved back. She stopped in surprise. Without opening his eyes, he pulled her closer to him, his arm slipping around her shoulder, aligning her body next to his as if they had sat like this many times before.

Theresa closed her eyes, reveling in the strength of the arm holding her. She was sure Dean would fall asleep if she didn’t move. She didn’t want to. She never wanted to move again. She was content to be with him, sitting quietly in this room. She’d never felt this way before. The need to fill the air with conversation, like a radio announcer constantly talking, had always characterized Theresa's interactions with men. But with Dean, that wasn't necessary. She could be quiet with him, yet never feel she was alone.

Then she remembered the phone call. "Your sister called earlier."

Dean sat up.

"She said there was nothing wrong, only that she was trying to reach you."

"Rosa?"

Theresa nodded.

"She called here?" He sat up even straighter, still keeping his arm around her. "How'd she get the number?"

"I didn't think to ask her. I thought you'd given it to her. Anyway, she said you didn't answer the house phone or your cell."

"I had to turn the cell off in the hospital."

"She said it wasn't an emergency."

"How long did she grill you?"

"Grill me?"

"Rosa is known for being nosy."

Theresa smiled. "She only left the message and hung up."

"But she called here."

"You think she was checking up on you?"

"No, I believe she was checking up on us."

"What does that mean?"

"It means Rosa is not only a busybody, she's also trying her hand at matchmaking. And from a distance at that."

"She's harmless," Theresa said.

"Yes," he admitted, his voice losing any censure that had been there. "She's harmless, but she can be irritating at times."

Theresa laughed. "Tell me about them."

"Who?"

"Your family."

"Oh, them?" His laugh was a grunt. "You met a few of them."

"On the television."

"They called about the production, but when we talked later, they had more questions about you than about how the film was going."

"What did you tell them?" Her voice was a soft murmur. She didn't want to crack the mood, and she felt normal tones would disturb the fragile curtain that enveloped them.

"That you owned the property."

"That's all?" What had she wanted him to say? She didn't know, but she wanted him to say something more personal than that she was the landlady. Theresa pushed the thought aside. Maybe she didn't want to know what he'd said about her. To prevent him answering, she asked another question. "Where do the six of you live again?"

"Three live in Texas. Brad and his wife live in Philadelphia, and Rosa and I fly around the world. Rosa's the fashion model."

Theresa remembered seeing that beautiful face staring at her from magazine covers.

"Rosa has an apartment in New York, but she spends more time in Texas than the city. My permanent address is Dallas, yet I spend most of my time in L.A."

"What do the others do again?"

"Digger is a carpenter. He used to build skyscrapers, but he now owns a small construction company near Austin. He's married to a nursery school teacher named Erin. They have a beautiful, precocious little girl that we fuss over and spoil every time we're near her."

Theresa knew how Dean was with Chelsea. She was sure he'd be a wonderful father.

"Brad and his wife Mallory are both medical doctors. He's a pediatrician and the moody one in the family. You can never figure out what he's thinking. Although he is a lot different since he and Owen found their biological mother."

"That's wonderful."

"It was. Brad had been looking for her since her disappearance."

The conversation made Theresa think of her father. What had happened to him? Why had he left them? "Was it a joyful reunion?" She held her breath, not wanting him to know how much she craved a positive response.

"It was. But she wasn't the only secret in the family."

"All families have them," Theresa said before realizing she'd spoken aloud.

"Our secret came in the form of Owen's wife. Of course, she wasn't his wife when we discovered the secret. She is now."

"I'm waiting," Theresa said. "This isn't a movie where you have to draw out the suspense."

"Sorry," Dean said. "Our parents had never mentioned any biological children. After our mother died and we were cleaning out her things, we discovered she had a daughter named Cynthia. Owen searched for her, and eventually, he found her and fell in love. They married last year."

"What a wonderful story. You have a very lucky family."

"We considered it a miracle that everything came together. Owen is the ladies' man in the group. He never wanted to marry, but Stephanie changed all that."

Brad, Digger, and Owen were married. He hadn't mentioned a husband for Rosa.

"The last of the bunch is my sister Luanne, the child psychologist. She also lives near Austin and is married to a geologist."

"Any children?"

He shook his head. "Only Digger has an adopted daughter, but I wouldn't be surprised if a family meeting is called soon with news of that type."

"And then there is you."

He hunched his shoulders. "With three weddings in the family in the last three years, I think Rosa has her sights set on me next."

"Why?" Theresa wondered if there was a girl back home, or one in L.A.

"Because of all the questions she asked about you."

Theresa waited, wondering what the strikingly beautiful woman had wanted to know. "What did she want to know?"

"If you and I were lovers."

"Are we?"

Dean's eyes snapped wide open at her question. He stared at her. Slowly, he shifted in the seat, coming forward but never taking his eyes off her.

"Are we?" He repeated her question. Both of them knew it was rhetorical.

Theresa thought about what she'd asked, but she wasn't backing down from the question. She'd known they would get to this point. Even though she'd set rules only days ago. She was going to stay out of his world, away from the heartache he'd leave behind when he packed up and left. But tonight, she was no longer a member of that separate world. It had ceased to exist, like a film reaching the end of the roll after the credits had run and the music had swollen to an ending crescendo.

She was entering a new world, a place as foreign to her as life on the moon. But this was exactly where she wanted to be. It felt right, like nothing had ever felt right before. Theresa pushed back any thoughts of standing by the rules she'd set. This was her life. She had to live it her way, and apparently, both her mind and body wanted to join with Dean's.

Theresa leaned against Dean. Neither spoke. Apparently, they were both lost in their own thoughts. After a while, Theresa drifted. Her eyelids grew heavy, and sleep stole over her. Then Dean moved. Waking instantly, sitting up as if she'd never fallen into the web of light dreams in which she held her arms around the man she loved, Theresa blinked. Her head turned, and she stared at Dean as she came to the realization she was in love with him. The knowledge came with surprising clarity. She didn't have time to think of what she looked like, to worry about the feelings that could be in her eyes, reflected on her face. The sensation was new, deep within her, like a spring bubbling to life. One she hadn't known was empty.

She was in love with Dean Clayton.

Dean leaned forward, still holding her hand. He stood up, pulling her with him. Theresa's legs were wobbly, and her body was infused with a heat that accompanied her new-found knowledge, but she stood.

"I'd better go now," he said, his voice weary and tired. He rubbed his hand across his face and headed for the door. Theresa walked with him, as he hadn't let go of her hand. In the hall he turned to her. "Good night."

Although he'd said it and the natural thing to do would be to drop hands and step back, neither of them moved. Theresa looked at their linked hands. Then she looked up. Dean was looking down at her.

"Don't go," she heard herself whisper.

"What?"

Her voice stuck in her throat. "I mean, I know you're tired. You must be. It's just that . . ." She stopped, feeling awkward, and looked down, unable to go on.

Dean closed the space between them, dropping her hand and lifting her chin so she looked up at him.

"Don't go," she said again.

"Are you sure?" Dean asked. "A few days ago—"

She covered his mouth with her fingers, feeling the end of his sentence kissing the pads of her hand. "A lifetime ago," she said. Then, moving her hand, she went up on her toes and replaced it with her mouth. Sensation she thought she was ready for spiraled through her, shocking her with its voracity, but it also had her leaning closer and closer to him, wanting more, craving his mouth, his tongue.

His arms slipped around her waist, drawing her to him,

cradling her as his tongue dipped into her mouth and he deepened the kiss. Theresa's arms went around his neck, and her body, as if it were equipped with a homing device, found the places in Dean's where men and women fit in the most intimately. She felt everything from his broad shoulders to the locks of hair that brushed against her face as the two of them mated. He lifted her off the floor, all tiredness seemingly gone from his body. She straddled her legs around him, folding her arms about his neck and letting herself go.

Pent up emotion burst the gates holding it back. Theresa put everything into the kiss. Her hands plunged inside the neck of his shirt. She felt his skin, damp and warm. She wanted to run her hands all over him, kiss him from head to foot.

Dean lifted his head. His dark and smoky eyes were filled with need.

"I need you, too," she answered. Without discussion, Dean set her on her feet. Keeping their arms around each other as if nothing could separate them, they went to her bedroom. Theresa closed the door and turned in his arms. She pushed her hands over his hair, down his arms, feeling free to do so.

"Where's Chelsea?" Dean asked.

"Across the hall in her room. I checked on her a few minutes before you arrived."

Dean's hands cupped each side of her face. He looked deeply into her eyes. Theresa didn't try to hide her feelings. Then his mouth took hers, and she surrendered to all the feelings that had been going through her since she walked into the house that first day. Her hands suddenly tore at his clothes. She wanted to touch his naked skin. She wanted to run her hands over the powerful muscles of his forearms and chest. To kiss his nipples and feel the shudder pass through him as it flowed through her.

His shirt gave way, and she pushed it over his head. She'd seen him before without his shirt, but she gasped again at the power of him. Wondering that someone so strong could also be so tender.

He found the hem of her shirt and slipped his hands up her torso. Theresa let out a satisfied sigh when Dean's hands slid over her, his palms brushing her nipples and sending rapture so pure through her that she felt the pain and pleasure of it with equal measure. Her stomach tightened involuntarily, and she arched herself closer to him.

"You don't know how much I've dreamed of this," he said, his voice barely audible.

"Me, too," she whispered as her blouse joined his shirt on the floor.

Dean backed her up to the bed. His hands reached behind her and unhooked her bra. He pushed it off her shoulders and looked at her. Theresa felt no shame as his eyes caressed her. She wanted him to see her, wanted him to know what she looked like. His fingers touched her, palms opening and smoothing over her skin. It was hard not to melt completely away under his touch.

Then things began to speed up between them. Their need for each other overwhelmed them both, and they couldn't touch each other enough. The remainder of their clothes flew off, and they were together on the bed. Dean's hands glossed over her from neck to hip. He didn't rush her as they had a moment ago. He knew instinctively what she needed. That this time, this first time, they needed to slow the pace, to hold back and savor the moment.

Dean brushed her hair back from her face and kissed her. His mouth was tender, teasing at first, then becoming more insistent. Need built inside Theresa like a pot boiling. An inner heat roiled higher and higher until she thought she'd burst if he didn't take her. His mouth devoured hers, and Theresa gave as good as she got. Her hands raked over him, touching skin that burned under her fingers.

The room filled with grunts and forced breathing. His hair

teased her shoulders like tiny sparks hitting her skin. His hand reached out, and suddenly, he had a condom in it. She didn't know where it had come from, but she took it, ripped the silver foil, and sheathed him. He smiled at her. Finally, she pushed him on his back and took control.

She lowered her body onto him slowly. It had been a while since anyone had touched her, and even though she wanted to take him whole inside her, she pulled back. Dean's eyes rolled in his head as if he were tasting the most delicious food ever. The lower she moved over him, the more intensely he held her. His hands came up and grasped her around the waist, working the rhythm she'd set. Their bodies thrust together. Rapturous sensation flowed within her, building until she wanted to scream at the pleasure of it, until she felt she'd explode if Dean didn't release the pressure building within her.

Dean rolled her over, his powerful body joined to hers. Hands as fiery as molten lava skirted down her, leaving a trail as bold and visible as a fault line. Her breasts burned where he touched her, and the twin peaks of her nipples hardened and screamed for more attention. He rounded her hips, lifting her into his thrusts, pumping into her with each labored breath saying her name in a language that was understandable only by her.

She wanted it to go on. The fever pitch of pleasure growing inside her mounted a tremendous wall and went over it, higher still, building. Dean continued his torture, this torture she welcomed, mixed with pleasure so great she never wanted it to end. She could feel it in him. He sounded almost animalistic, his body working at a passionate fervor beyond his ability to stop it.

And then the explosion happened. It built fast and hard, like a pleasure wave catching her and forcing her toward the beach. Dean dropped down on her, both of them sated and spent. Theresa's ragged breath matched Dean's. She hugged him to her, raining light kisses on his shoulders.

She'd never been made love to like this before, and she wanted him to know it. Theresa communicated this with her mouth, not her voice. She was afraid she'd reveal her true feelings if she spoke.

Dean slipped off her, but kept her close. She turned so they lay spoon-style, the heat around them receding, the smell of love filling the air.

"Go to sleep," he whispered, kissing her ear. "Because of Chelsea, I won't be here when you wake."

Theresa felt the loss of him already. She turned back, stretching out beside him, her arms wrapped around his neck as she kissed him long and hard.

And maybe for the last time. What would happen with the movie now that Robbie was hurt?

With sleep evading her, Theresa tried to remain still. She didn't want to disturb Dean. She listened to his steady breathing and the strong beat of his heart. It was comforting. She was ensconced in a fairy tale, and in her happiness, she wanted to dance around the room in ever increasing circles. When she'd returned to Collingswood, she never expected to find any kind of happiness here. Now she would have this. The cloak of sadness had been lifted. For the rest of her life, she would have this memory to paint over the hardships that she'd faced with the disappearance of her family.

She raised her head and looked at Dean. She felt him smile and knew he was awake.

"Did I wake you?"

"No," he said.

"You were so tired. I thought you'd fallen asleep immediately."

"I suppose the power you hold over me is greater than that of the sleep fairy."

She smiled, snuggling closer to him, wishing she *did* hold the power to keep him with her forever. Yet even in the afterglow of their lovemaking, she knew he was here temporarily. Refusing to think of that now, she ran her hand along his arm, loving the silky feel of his skin, the quiet strength of him.

"You're probably overtired," she suggested.

"Maybe," he said. She heard him yawn. "Although I'm used to functioning on little sleep. There was a time, when I was a teenager and the nightmares had come back, that I couldn't sleep for weeks."

Theresa stroked his arm, calmingly, comfortingly, hoping she could smooth the pain away, even pain that was years old. She knew better. She had her own nightmares that no amount of stroking could remove. Yet she did it anyway.

"My sister said it was my own fear of facing the problem."

Theresa lifted her head and stared at him. "That's not very reassuring for a psychologist."

"She wasn't a psychologist then. She was a know-it-all." He chuckled, taking the sting out of his words.

"I know Robbie's accident only happened this morning, but have you thought about what you're going to do?" Theresa asked, changing the subject.

He shook his head. "But I know what I'm going to do right now." His eyes were dark with desire when she looked into them. Instantly, her body responded. Everything turned hot at the same time. Anticipation overwhelmed her. His mouth teased, his lips brushing across hers in light, feathery kisses. Theresa raised her arm and slid it up to his neck. At the same time, his hand swept across her breast. The shock of ecstasy that went through her was faster and stronger than a meteor plummeting to earth. It reverberated inside her, making her bones turn to water. Her arms dropped to the bed as his mouth replaced his hand. Theresa couldn't control her muscles. His touch reduced her to a mass of sensation.

Soft moans came involuntarily from her throat. Nothing had ever felt so good as his hands on her, as the delicious feelings that spun through her like a narcotic. As Dean's mouth covered her in kisses, it brought her to life. She found the strength to hug him close, to join him in the pleasure palace of their sexual dance. He pushed her back onto the bed. She melted into the covers beneath her. Dean found a second condom and put it on. Then their bodies merged.

Theresa had never been so aware of anyone. As she celebrated Dean's body, she learned everything about him, from the smoothness of the skin on his arms to the hunger they shared for each other. Their breathing merged. Their hearts beat in unison. Their bodies moved in a concerted rhythm. Thoughts. Reason. Logic. It all evaporated in the inferno they created. Only mutual pleasure remained, solid and firm in their minds and bodies.

Her back arched instinctively as Dean raised her hips and filled her deep inside. He set the rhythm higher, faster, their love burning, their need increasing to a feverish point, passing that point, and reaching for something greater. Theresa's throat was scorching. Dry. Guttural sounds were forced from her as she rocked back and forth, holding on to Dean, intimately joined in both body and spirit. She knew this for the first time, the only time—no one else could ever be this in tune with her. No one could ever replace this feeling.

She was truly in love. She'd known it before, but now she knew it tangibly as she learned how life began with the commingling of a man and a woman.

Chapter 8

"Dean, wake up. Wake up. You're dreaming." He heard the insistent voice all of a sudden. It was low, far away, and he couldn't make out the words. Opening his eyes, he wasn't sure who was calling him. His heart thudded in his ears, and he fought his attacker, grabbing the arms leveling blows at him.

"Dean, it's me. Stop!"

He heard the panic. Hands fought with him. He fought back. His eyes focused. It took a second, but then he saw *her.*

"Theresa?"

She was breathing hard. Fear made her chest rise and fall rapidly. He'd pinned her to the bed. His knee held her in place, and his hands were manacles around her wrists.

"Please let me go," she said, her voice laced with panic.

"I'm sorry," he said, loosening his grip and unshackling her.

She sat up, moved away from him, covering herself with the sheet. Dean felt as if she'd cut his heart out. He'd never intended to hurt her.

"What were you dreaming?" Her voice was breathy. Dean didn't know how long he'd fought with Theresa inside his nightmare. She'd somehow become part of the dream, and he'd unconsciously hurt her.

"What did I do to you?"

She rubbed her wrists. "I won't have a black eye, but I'll need a long-sleeve shirt tomorrow." She tried to make a joke of it, but he knew he'd done something terrible.

Moving toward her, he gathered her close, held her to him. She was shaking. He kissed her forehead and cradled her against him, holding her lightly in case she wanted to free herself. He could feel her breath against his chest. After a moment, she relaxed. Dean released a breath he didn't know he was holding.

"I didn't mean to hurt you, Theresa," he apologized.

She leaned forward and kissed his shoulder, accepting his apology.

"What was the dream?" she asked.

He was quiet for a long time, trying to remember. It was always like this. He wanted to remember what it was, but his mind kept the details hidden. A smoky cloud formed a wall in front of him. While it scared him to death, he also wanted to know what was on the other side, but he could never see through it.

"It hasn't been easy, has it?" Theresa asked.

"I suppose you know how hard it can be." Chelsea had nightmares, but at least Theresa understood the child's reason for having them. Dean didn't know the reason for his.

"I don't know what my dreams are about," he continued. "I don't remember much. Only the running. It's wet, raining, storming. I'm scared, more scared than I've ever been. I can hear my breath in the silence. It's almost tangible, but everything around me is black, smoky, a fog too thick to see through. I want to see through it, but I know . . ." He stopped, fearful of saying the words. Of giving them life.

"What do you know?" Theresa prompted.

"I know there's death on the other side of that blackness. And if I ever get through it, I'll die."

Theresa reacted immediately. “Dean, how long has this been going on?”

“It started when I was found.”

“Found?”

“I was barely in school,” he said. “In the dream, I’m exhausted, but I run and keep running. Something is behind me, chasing me toward that black curtain. It’s a dark, ugly presence that bites at my heels and matches my steps. No matter how hard I run, it’s right behind me, close to my back. I can almost feel its cold hands reaching out for me. My breath is as dry as paste, and my mouth is devoid of moisture although everything around me is wet. And I keep going. My chest burns with the need for air. I push on, knowing if I stop, if I turn and look back, even for a second, it will be the end. It will devour me, rip me apart, tear my body into fragments that could never be pieced together again. I have no choice. It is my life or his. So I go on, helplessly on. And then I wake up. Sometimes screaming, sometimes . . .” He left the sentence hanging. Sometimes, he woke up fighting the bed sheets or one of his brothers. This was the first time he’d woken with his knee in the a woman’s stomach.

Theresa’s arms encircled him. Her movements were slow and quiet so as not to interrupt him. Unconsciously, he tightened his arms around her, squeezing until the two of them merged into a solitary figure.

“The first time I woke from the dream, I was shivering, screaming, fighting to get away from the hands that were holding me down. I was in a hospital, a mental ward. I was seven years old and already psychotic.”

Theresa had never been good at the morning after thing. Technically, this was not the morning after. It was still the same morning, but Theresa had awakened alone. She and Dean had never spent the whole night together, at least not as lovers. Even so, She didn't like waking without him. She wanted him there, so she could caress him, put her arms around him, and take in his scent, perfume to her.

Shooting had been canceled for today, and once Dean left and she'd fallen asleep, she didn't wake until the sun was high in the sky. Jumping out of bed, she ran to Chelsea's room only to find it empty. She found her niece sitting in a director's chair in the room where Robbie would have worked that day.

"Chelsea." Theresa approached her cautiously. Chelsea didn't move. Theresa knew what she would find as she made a wide circle around her niece. Her eyes would be staring blankly. She was retreating from hurt, going inside herself again. She was looking for that safe place.

Theresa knelt in front of her. "I know you think Robbie is going to die, but he's not," she said. "When Dean came back last night, he told me Robbie is going to be all right."

If there was such a thing as dry tears, they were in Chelsea's eyes. The little girl stared almost catatonically toward the gymnastic set-up that Robbie would have used.

Theresa heard something and looked up. Dean stepped through the door. Her body immediately overheated. The look he gave her said he also remembered every moment of their lovemaking the night before. Theresa tamped down her body temperature as he approached them.

"She thinks Robbie is going to die."

Dean hunkered down to her level. "Would you like to go to the hospital and see for yourself that he's okay?"

Her eyes focused then. She looked at Theresa and nodded slightly.

"Come on."

Robbie was sitting up in bed when they entered his room. He was alone. As they passed, they had seen his mother talking to the doctor in a glass-walled room. Theresa hadn't been in a hospital since Meghan had died, and entering the building brought back all the old memories of spending nights at her cousin's side. She glanced at Chelsea, wondering if her feelings were along the same line.

Dean took Theresa's hand as if he understood what she was going through. Chelsea looked questioningly down the hallways and at doors, searching for Robbie.

"Hi," he chirped as if he hadn't been in surgery the day before when they entered his room. His leg was encased in plaster, and there was a purplish bruise on his right temple. Other than that, he was his ole self.

"Are you okay?" Chelsea asked.

"Except for my leg."

"And you can go home?"

"Sure. My mom—"

Theresa and Dean stepped back, allowing Chelsea to ask all the questions. She needed to make sure in her mind that he was going to be all right. Dean opened the door, and they went out, leaving the two kids alone.

"Is he really going to be all right?" Theresa asked.

"You saw for yourself." He looked intently at her as if there was something else he wanted to ask but wouldn't.

"The doctor said there would be no residual effects. He won't limp or even be prevented from playing any sports. Of course, competitive gymnastics is out, but that wasn't one of his goals."

Theresa smiled briefly. "I'm glad."

"Do you need to get out of here?"

She glanced at the door to Robbie's room, then back at Dean. She ran her hands up and down his arms before dropping them to her side. "I'm all right."

Laughter drifted from Robbie's door. Both of them looked toward it. "I think she's convinced he's going to be all right," Dean said.

Theresa nodded. She sat down on a bench near Robbie's

door. Dean joined her. She was nervous. Now that she knew she was in love with him, she didn't know what to say, afraid her voice or her eyes would somehow give her away.

Dean took her hand and held it. She looked at their entwined fingers. Her life was already entwined with his, even if he didn't know it. For a moment she allowed herself to think of what it might be like to tell him she loved him, to have him return her love. Unconsciously, she squeezed her fingers. Dean lifted her hand and kissed her knuckles.

They looked at each other. Theresa couldn't hide what was in her eyes. She no longer wanted to. Dean's were dark with desire. Unconsciously, they leaned toward each other. The opening of a door down the hall halted the impending kiss before it had even begun. Moving apart as if they'd been caught, they saw Mrs. Abbott shaking hands with the doctor.

They stood up as she approached them. "Hello," she smiled.

"Is everything going to be all right?" Theresa asked.

"Yes," she said. Her smile faltered, and she looked up at Dean. "I'm afraid Robbie's going to be in the cast for eight weeks or more. Then he'll have physical therapy to go through. I'm sorry, Dean."

"Don't worry about it," Dean said. "As long as he's going to be fine."

"I've called my husband and told him we'd be home by the end of the week."

Dean said all the usual and expected things about giving her anything she needed. Then they went in to tell Robbie.

Chelsea was sitting on the bed, and she and Robbie were playing a video game with cordless controllers. Two race cars vied for dominance on the track displayed on the television screen hanging from the ceiling. They glanced up at the adults but kept playing, their concentration focused on their cars.

No one spoke until the game ended. Chelsea threw her hands up in the air in the traditional victory sign.

"Mom, she's really good. She's beat me three times."

"Four," Chelsea corrected.

"I won the first game."

"No, you didn't," Chelsea contradicted.

"Robbie," his mom cautioned. "We'll be going home as soon as you get out of here."

"I can't do the movie?"

His face fell.

"It's going to take some time for your leg to heal," Dean said.

"Who's gonna do it?"

"No one," Dean stated after a moment. His voice quavered as if he hadn't thought about it.

"Chelsea could do it," he offered, then turned and looked at her. "Course you'd have to dress like me." They all laughed.

Robbie's expression turned serious, and he looked at Dean. "Are you going to be able to finish the movie?"

"I'm not sure, Robbie," Dean answered honestly. "But you concentrate on getting that leg better."

They stayed another few minutes before Dean shuttled them out. They promised Robbie they would come back the next day.

"What are you going to do about the movie?" Theresa asked Dean as they reached his SUV.

"There's nothing I can do. I've called a meeting of the cast and crew later this afternoon. I'm sure they already know the decision."

"What's that?"

"We're going to have to shut down."

"Oh, Dean." Theresa moved into his arms. If she'd thought about it, she wouldn't have, but there were things that were natural for people in love. Even if only one person was in love. "Isn't there another alternative?"

"Robbie was a large part of the movie. Without him, there is no movie."

"What about all the effort you and everyone else have put into it so far?"

"A complete and utter waste of time and money."

Theresa could tell he was upset. She wished she could help, but there was nothing she could do. She knew nothing about the film business, except what she'd learned watching them over the last few weeks.

Dean turned and walked toward his vehicle. She made sure Chelsea was strapped in before getting behind the wheel. She didn't immediately start the engine.

"Aunt Theresa?" Chelsea called. Instinctively, children knew when things were going wrong.

"Why is Dean angry?"

"It's the movie, honey. With Robbie in the hospital, they don't have anyone to play his part."

Theresa started the car and backed out of the parking space. Robbie's accident had done more than cut short the movie. It had altered her life. Robbie would be gone by the end of the week. Dean would follow soon after. By this time next week, all that would be left of Dean's presence would be an empty carriage house and one glowing memory she would never be able to completely shelve.

Through the window, Theresa watched Dean go into the bubble. It was the only place the entire cast and crew could gather at one time. She didn't envy him. She'd never fired anyone or been fired from a job. Dean was about to put fifty people out of work, and from what he'd told her, there were also contracts for post-filming services that would have to be paid cancellation fees.

But the worst part was he'd lose his chance for his own production. And she'd never see him again.

Theresa didn't know how long she paced the room, but it didn't seem like a long time. She saw Dean walking back toward the house. She thought he was going to turn down the path and go to the carriage house, but he headed for the kitchen door.

He was coming through the kitchen door when she reached it.

"How did it go?" she asked.

"They're still waiting. I told them I needed to talk to you before I made a decision." He poured himself a cup of coffee and faced her.

"Why me? Is something else wrong? You look as if the world's about to cave in."

"Maybe," he said. "I told you Robbie was a big part of the film. We're all glad he's not badly hurt, but he can't go on."

"And that means the film will shut down," Theresa finished for him. She leaned against a counter across from him, but his magnetism reached out to her.

He nodded. "The film can't go on without him," Dean repeated.

"Can't you find a replacement?" she suggested. "There must be several child actors who can replace Robbie."

"There aren't." Dean sipped his coffee. "Robbie had specific skills. It took months to find him. We'd need someone who can do what he does. Frank can do the stunts, but he can't do the acting segments. Robbie has a lot of face time on the screen."

"Have you tried to get a replacement?"

"It's all I've done since we returned from the hospital. A couple of actors are busy with other projects, but even if they weren't, they don't know the lines and they're not physically up to the role. It would take months to train them. And in the meantime, I'd have to send the rest of the cast and crew home, some with pay, some without. Frankly, the budget can't support that. And there's no telling who would be available when we resumed."

"So your only alternative is to close down production?" Theresa's eyebrows went up at the thought of him disappearing from her life so suddenly. She'd gotten used to the crew being around and to Dean being there. She looked away from him, fearful that he would see her thoughts reflected in her eyes.

"It's not my only option. There's one other solution."

She looked back, hopeful that he could keep working.

"What is it?"

"Not what. Whom."

"All right, whom?"

"Chelsea can do it."

Theresa bolted up. "Absolutely not!"

"Theresa, don't object so quickly. She's perfect. She knows the lines or can learn them quickly. She's physically fit, and Robbie has taught her a lot of the routine. She's fascinated by the process. I see her face when she's watching. She wants to be up there." He gestured toward the other part of the house where cameras and lights were set up for a scene. "In front of the lights."

"Dean." Theresa kept her voice low intentionally. "The child is still grieving. And she's not an actor."

Dean weighed this for a second, then seemed to dismiss it. "We could let her try."

"Doesn't she need to be a member of the Actors Guild or something? Aren't there rules regarding children? Aren't there . . ." She groped for words.

"I'll have someone get all the proper papers, and you'll be informed of all the conditions and safety regulations. There will be a contract. You can have your attorney go over it."

Dean stopped and watched her silently for a moment. He sipped his coffee, waiting.

"It's been a long time since Chelsea did any hard gymnastics," she finally said. "She could get hurt, too."

He took a step toward Theresa. "I won't lie to you and say there is no danger. Gymnastics is the cause of a lot of sports injuries, but we'll do everything we can to keep her safe."

Theresa had seen them spotting for Robbie. They were

conscientious and attentive. Robbie's accident hasn't been anyone's fault.

"If you're thinking about Robbie, it was—"

"It's not that I don't trust the spotters. They're very good. It's that I think if Chelsea fails at this, it could set her back in her recovery."

"On the flip side of that, it could be just what she needs. Something to give her another focus. Something to occupy her mind and concentrate on instead of grieving."

Theresa thought about it. He could be right. It could be good for Chelsea. She wanted to jump at the chance to keep him here, but she wouldn't sacrifice her cousin's health for it.

"Chelsea is a girl. The part calls for a young boy. You can't just switch them."

"Not as quickly as that," Dean agreed. "We've shot a lot of scenes that will have to be redone, but I think we can redo the footage with Chelsea."

Theresa sighed. She didn't know how long this was going to take. Chelsea could begin the process and then get tired of it.

"I'll have to talk to Chelsea," Theresa stated. "See how she feels about it."

"Can I do it?" Chelsea came barreling into the kitchen. She ran to Theresa. Obviously, she'd been listening at the door. "Theresa, I can do it."

"Are you sure?" Theresa took her hands and looked at her.

"I'm sure. Robbie showed me how to do all the flying." She stopped then and looked at her aunt. "I was careful," she explained.

"Chelsea, it isn't just the gymnastics. The script calls for a lot of acting, many of the sequences have you in a tight, dark place. You have to cry on the spur of the moment."

"I know. Robbie told me all about it. He showed me how to do it. He even said if I didn't ask Dean to let me, he was going to ask." Her words gushed out like a faucet had been turned on.

Theresa's eyes flew to Dean.

"I didn't know," he said.

"It was in the hospital this morning. You were in the hall," Chelsea explained.

"She can work with the coach who worked with Robbie," Dean said.

Both pairs of eyes stared at Theresa. She looked from one to the other.

"Please," Chelsea prompted.

Theresa smiled at her. "Well, sweetheart, if you're up to it, it's all right with me."

Chelsea shouted her happiness and hugged Theresa, her tiny hands closing around Theresa's thighs.

"Remember you'll have to get up early in the morning to meet the deadlines that the other actors have," Theresa warned her.

"I can do it," she said, emphatically shaking her head up and down.

She looked over Chelsea's head. Dean tried not to smile. He covered his mouth by sipping from the coffee cup, but Theresa could see behind the ruse. He was pleased, and secretly, so was she. She'd get to keep him around for a little while longer.

She smiled, too. And got her own cup of coffee.

Two weeks later, production went back into full swing. True to her word, Chelsea never fretted about early morning calls. Theresa was on site for her first day. The planned scene was a crucial one. Theresa wondered why Dean had chosen such a difficult initiation for Chelsea, but she decided not to question his decision. She had to assume he knew what he was doing. In the scene, the child has seen a murder, and the villain doesn't know about her. She hides in an attic closet, terrified that she'll be discovered. Chelsea would have to play to the camera with no dialogue and no one to support her. The sequence took acting skills Theresa was apprehensive about, but she tried to keep this from Chelsea by encouraging her.

Chelsea surprised her. When Dean yelled, "Cut," there was a momentary pause before anyone moved. Including Theresa.

At first, Chelsea was stiff and scared. They redid the scene four times. Then Dean talked to her, and she practiced what he wanted her to do. From then on, she let him direct her, doing what he told her.

Dean told Theresa how pleased he was after they'd watched the dailies that night.

"She's a natural." His smile was wide, and he couldn't stop pacing back and forth. This pacing was the excited kind. He'd tried something to save the film, and it had worked. She could tell he was as excited as a small boy on Christmas morning. As soon as everyone left the room and the door closed, he grabbed her and covered her mouth with his. It was a zealous kiss filled with pent-up emotion and happiness. Both of them came away laughing.

"Chelsea feels the same way," Theresa said when he released her. "Her expression is different. She said she's never had as much fun in her whole life." Theresa spread her hands the way Chelsea had.

Dean kissed her again. This time, his lips were serious. His arms encircled her, cherishing her as no one had ever before. His hands moved over her curves, trailing fire as they moved from her waist, down her hips, and over her buttocks. He drew her into that world, the one where they had the knowledge of the ages. Theresa let herself go. Not that she had a choice. Whenever Dean took her in his arms, her heart redirected her will to the need to be held, comforted—loved.

Theresa slid her mouth free and took in a shuddering breath. Laying her head on his shoulder, she'd never been so happy. She wanted to curl her legs up and let him lift her into his arms as if she were Chelsea.

Instead of Dean complying with her unspoken wish, he turned her toward the door, keeping his arm around her waist.

"How about something to eat?" Theresa suggested.

The house was quiet. Chelsea was in bed. The "child police," a couple of women who made sure all the child labor rules were followed to the letter, had schooled Theresa in her new duties and made sure Chelsea got enough food and sleep.

"There's food in the dining room."

"Not that food," she said dismissively. "Oh, there's nothing wrong with it. It's great, but I feel like cooking something."

"You can cook?"

She punched him lovingly in the side. "Of course I can cook. When I was in London, I had to do for myself on very little income, at least to start. Then, when I came back, Meghan had a diet to follow."

"You miss her, don't you?"

They were in the kitchen. Dean sat down at the table while Theresa looked in the refrigerator.

"Meghan?"

He nodded.

"Other than my brother, she was the only family I had. We were inseparable as children." Closing the refrigerator, she looked at Dean. "If it wasn't for her, I don't think I would have survived my mother's death. My aunt was certainly no help. And I didn't want to spend my life in mental institutions."

"I can't imagine anyone being so unfeeling to a child, especially one who is grieving."

She went to the cabinet and began pulling down the ingredients for a country breakfast. "I thought you said you and your brothers were unadoptable. Didn't people do terrible things to them?"

"Yes."

It was a solitary word, yet Theresa understood. "You'd forgotten."

"How could I?" he questioned.

"How long has it been since they told you their stories?"

"Years and years."

"That's why," she said. "Those things didn't happen to you. And you have your own demons."

She saw Dean look at his hands. Theresa knew something caused his nightmares, but she didn't know what and she wasn't sure he knew either.

Giving him a moment, she opened the refrigerator again and pulled out more ingredients.

"What are you making?" he asking, obviously changing the subject.

"A country breakfast."

"It's nearly midnight. And you grew up in Buffalo, New York. What do you know of a country breakfast?"

She smiled, remembering the guy who'd taught her the finer points of Southern cooking. A subject she would not go into with Dean. "I've learned a few methods of survival in my day." With that, she cracked an egg with one hand and expertly dropped it into a bowl.

Twenty minutes later, they were enjoying country fried steak, grits and gravy, biscuits with apple butter, and quarts of orange juice.

"My father used to cook this meal."

"He taught you well," Dean said, shoveling a forkful of steak into his mouth. "This is delicious."

Theresa smiled but didn't enlighten him with the truth. "Do you think Chelsea will be all right? She's so excited; I don't want her to find out she has no talent."

Dean poured another glass of orange juice and sat back in his chair. "I intentionally chose a difficult scene, and she came through it better than I expected. If she had no talent, I wanted to know right away. What I found out is she's good.

Really good." He punctuated the comment with raised eyebrows and a surprised look in his eyes.

So he *had* chosen the scene on purpose. "It's only been a few weeks," Theresa said. "But I can see a change in her already."

"She loves acting."

"She loves you." Theresa hadn't meant to say that, although she knew Chelsea was attached to Dean. And day by day both woman and child were more and more attracted to him.

Chapter 9

Dean sat up in bed with a scream. He was drenched in sweat, and his feet were tangled in the bedsheet. Theresa's hands were on his shoulders. She'd obviously been trying to wake him.

"Did I hit you?" he asked, remembering his last encounter.

She shook her head.

He collapsed. "Thank goodness for that." When they'd left the kitchen, their mouths fused, he hadn't expected the evening to come to this. His nightmares seemed to get worse and worse as the days passed.

"Was it bad?" she asked.

"There was an attic."

"You remember it?"

"Not all of it." He hugged her tight, burying his face in her neck. "This is the first time I can remember anything though."

"Dean, are you sure it's the same dream?"

He pushed her back and looked into her eyes. "What do you mean?"

"The scene today. It took place in an attic. Are you sure the nightmare in the attic is the same?"

He pushed her away, his shoulders dropping as if heavy weights were being added to them. "I really don't know."

Theresa smoothed her hands over him soothingly. "Dean, you're under a lot of strain, what with the Robbie's accident, a new, untried actress, and trying to stay on budget, but don't you think it's time you got some attention for these nightmares?"

"You mean medical attention?"

She nodded.

"I went through years of that. It never helped. Whatever happened to me, it's very deeply seated. They could never get me to unlock it."

Thankfully, Theresa didn't react in any way. Dean rarely told anyone his story because when he did, the looks he got made him feel either inadequate or that he was making the story up.

"I'm not a psychologist, but would you tell me about it?"

"I can't tell you about it. Something happened to me when I was small. My first memory is of waking up in a hospital when I was seven years old."

"How'd you get there?"

He shook his head. "I have no idea. No one ever reported me missing. The doctor who was with me when I opened my eyes eventually adopted me and the others."

"And you never found out where you came from?"

He shook his head. "I was a throwaway kid. There are so many. At least I found a good life." He looked at her. "Even with the nightmares." He tried to laugh, but it came out a little strangled.

"You are an incredible man," she said.

He pushed her back and looked into her eyes. "Where did that come from?"

Theresa sat up and moved away from him. She wore a white nightgown with spaghetti straps. He'd teased them off her shoulders earlier tonight.

"You haven't known what happened to you all your life, and yet look at what you're doing. Your family must be very proud of you. I know I am."

When she said that, he could have lifted the world on his own back and run it around the sun. Running his fingers through her hair, he pulled her close and looked into her eyes. "We're a pair, aren't we?"

"We are," she agreed. "And we're going to be fine."

Dean wasn't so sure, but he didn't tell her that. He just held her, taking in the sweet smell of her skin. She didn't know it, but she gave him confidence, made him feel that he could do whatever he wanted. She understood the pressure he was under, yet she was there, quietly supporting him. Was this what Owen had found in Stephanie? And Digger in Erin? Was he falling in love?

The phone rang, and Theresa looked at it as if it was a foreign object. She hadn't heard anything except a cell phone in so long that an actual ring sounded like something from a movie. It took her a moment to realize what it was and to get her feet moving toward it.

"What have you got going on up there?" Her brother's voice boomed through the white handset. "Tell these would-be cops to open this gate."

Theresa laughed. That was her brother for you. "Kevin! I'm glad you're here. Come on up."

"I'm trying to, but I have a line in front of me."

"Let me talk to Officer Willis."

"Which one of you is Willis?" Theresa heard his muffled voice as he moved the phone away from his mouth.

"Ms. Ramsey?" Theresa heard the strong voice of John Willis. "He's not on the list."

"It's all right, John. Mr. Ramsey is my brother."

As soon as she hung up the phone, Theresa ran outside. A few moments later, Kevin stopped the car at the juncture of the carriage house and the main building. He jumped out of the car with open arms that folded around Theresa as she threw herself into them.

"I never thought you'd come back to the house."

"It wasn't easy," he said. "But I have something to tell you." He opened his arm as Donna Wheaton came around the back of the car and slid to his side. "Donna and I are getting married. We want you to come to the wedding."

For a moment, Theresa couldn't talk. Then she screamed. She was so happy. Launching herself at Donna, she hugged her. "Congratulations," she said, then looked at her brother. "It's certainly about time."

"I wanted to make sure all the demons were gone."

Theresa reached over and slipped her arm around his waist, walking between the two of them. "Come on up to the house. Maybe we can find something to toast the occasion, and you can give me all the details."

"Oh my God," Donna said, looking toward the back of the property. "Is that . . ." She didn't seem able to get the name out.

"That is," Theresa said, waving to Lance Hunt.

"Do you think I could meet him?"

"Donna!" Kevin said.

"Honey, I'll spend the rest of my life with you, but when will I get another chance to meet Lance Hunt?"

He didn't argue with her logic. Lance approached them, and Theresa made the introductions. Lance congratulated them on their upcoming wedding and kissed Donna on the cheek. She gave him that I'll-never-wash-my-face-again look. For a few moments, he talked with them, asking Kevin about his grocery store and telling him that although his father had once been an investment banker in New York, he now owned a small general store in Wisconsin. In between movies, Lance enjoyed going there and hanging out with him.

Theresa watched her brother's face. She knew Lance's mention of his father would bring back memories of their own father and his disappearance. Yet Kevin didn't let that show on his face. Lance left them, and they continued toward the house.

"You see him every day?" Donna asked.

She nodded. "Mostly at meals. There's always food in the dining room for the cast and crew. But let's not dwell on them. Tell me about the wedding."

Donna looked over her shoulder at Lance and nearly missed the steps up to the porch. Kevin caught her before she fell.

Moments later, they were in the dining room. Kevin hadn't looked around when he entered the house. Bad memories die hard. She knew. It had taken her a while to get them out of her head, and she'd had help. Dean's presence had given her new memories to replace the bad ones. She no longer dreaded seeing the rooms where her parents had once sat and talked and laughed. Now, she could remember herself and Dean in those rooms.

Theresa found a bottle of sparkling wine in the refrigerator and brought it in along with three of her mother's crystal glasses. She wondered if Kevin remembered them. Men didn't usually remember things like that, and he said nothing about them, only opened the wine and poured it.

"To a wonderful life," Theresa said, holding her glass up. The perfect bell note sounded as they clinked their glasses and drank.

"Have you set a date?" Theresa asked. Excitement bubbled in her voice.

"Valentine's Day," Donna said. "We waited so long. I want to really do it up right."

Theresa looked at her brother. He put his hand on Donna's and squeezed. The two of them had been in love for years, and it showed.

"We want you to be in the wedding," Donna said. "My sister is going to be the maid of honor. You can—"

"Give the groom away."

They laughed just as Dean came in. He was heading for the

coffee urn, which, like the one in the kitchen, had coffee in it day and night. Seeing them, he turned and came into the room. Noticing the wine, he asked, "A celebration?"

"This is my brother, Kevin, and my soon to be sister-in-law."

Dean's smile widened. His face had been set as he walked toward them. Now it relaxed into the one she'd come to love. The two men reached out and shook hands. Then he shook Donna's hand.

"Dean's the director and producer of the film," she explained.

"You're the man in charge." Kevin smiled as if he genuinely liked Dean. Inside Theresa, a bubble of joy exploded.

"We met Lance Hunt," Donna said. She was clearly starstruck. "A real gentleman."

"We're not filming now. You're welcome to look around."

Theresa thought Donna was going to jump up and run to the door.

"The wedding is going to be at a small church in Swanson." Kevin continued the conversation they had started.

"And we're going to Paris on our honeymoon," Donna said. "Can you imagine it, the City of Romance?"

"You'll love it," Dean said. "There's a little restaurant right outside the city. It's hard to get into, but the food is delicious and the service is exemplary. I'll give Theresa a card for you to give them. They'll treat you well."

"That's awfully nice of you," Theresa said.

He smiled and winked at her. "When is the wedding?"

"February," Kevin said.

"Won't you come?" Donna said impulsively, inviting him. "Swanson is only a few miles from here."

As soon as she'd said it, they all realized Dean wouldn't be anywhere near Royce in February. Theresa's mood crashed as surely as if the magic carpet she was sitting on had been pulled out from under her.

"I'd love to," Dean said. "But my schedule may not allow it."

"Well," Donna said, her personality always upbeat, "if you can make it, please come. We'll get your address from Theresa."

Dean looked at Theresa. She said nothing. The nonverbal communication between them wasn't working. She didn't know what he was thinking. When he left, would he give her a way of reaching him? Or would their association end at the bottom of the hill when Security removed the barricade and Lance Hunt and the cast rolled out the main gate?

"It was nice meeting you," Dean said. "I have to get back. We won't be filming again for an hour, so please take a look around."

"Thank you," Donna cooed. "What a nice guy," she said as they watched Dean grab a cup of coffee and head out the back door.

"Would you like to see the house?" Theresa needed to change the subject from Dean's departure. "There have been a lot of changes since the film company rented it." She got up. Kevin didn't move. "Most of the rooms have been renovated."

Kevin stood. Donna followed his lead. He must have told her how he felt about the house because she seemed to take her cue from him.

"I've spent years trying to forget this place," he said.

"But you couldn't," Theresa finished for him. "I understand. It doesn't have the happiest of memories for me either, but I've acquired some new memories. And I've learned scabs can form over the old wounds."

The first room she took them to was set up for the film.

"What's this?" Kevin asked.

"It's a ballroom."

"It looks nothing like the old room," Kevin said, and seemed to relax a bit. His shoulders were straighter.

"Wouldn't you like to dance in here?" Donna asked.

"Oh, they do," Theresa told her. "There's a scene where they have a huge party in this room. Lance Hunt cuts a pretty good figure in a white tie and tails," Theresa teased.

Donna looked at Kevin. "Don't worry, honey. I'd pick you over Lance Hunt any day."

Kevin smiled and dropped a kiss on her mouth. Theresa felt a tug in her stomach. She knew what they were feeling. She also wanted the security of what they had, the openness to let the world know they were a couple, a forever and a day twosome. What did she have with Dean? Only a short-term romance and the promise of heartache when he left.

They toured the rest of the downstairs rooms. Theresa knew that was enough. She headed through the kitchen and the enclosed porch and out into the yard. Donna was awed by the actors she was introduced to, but she managed to keep her jaw from dropping open each time she came face to face with one of them.

"Where's Chelsea?" Kevin asked after they'd been shown around.

"In the bubble."

"Bubble?"

"I forgot to tell you. Chelsea is part of the movie now."

"What?" Donna said.

Theresa started walking toward the bubble where Chelsea practiced gymnastics. "There was a part for a little boy, but Robbie had an accident and broke his leg. Dean would have had to shut down the production if they couldn't get a replacement. Chelsea filled in for him."

They entered the cavernous structure, and Kevin stopped in his tracks. Chelsea laughed, her young voice tinkling.

"Wow," he said. "Who would have thought it?"

"Hey, Theresa, look at me. Hi, Kevin."

Kevin waved at her. They watched as Chelsea was lifted to the parallel bar and went through her routine.

Kevin and Donna watched the jaw-dropping exercise. "She's good," he said, his voice breathless with awe.

"Yes, it was Robbie's idea that she replace him, and Dean

agreed," Theresa said. "I think all the activity is shifting her focus and helping her get over her mother's death."

"We want Chelsea to be in the wedding, too," Donna said. "She's a little old for a flower girl, but she might want to be a junior bridesmaid."

Theresa turned to Donna with a wide smile. "She'll love that."

A few minutes later, after Chelsea had performed several additional routines, Theresa walked with Kevin and Donna toward their car.

"Won't you stay longer?" Theresa asked. "You've only just gotten here."

Kevin looked up at the house before speaking. "I have to get back to the store."

"The store must be able to survive without you for one day. After all, you're going to Paris on your honeymoon."

Theresa knew, however, it was the house that was chasing him away. When he'd been inside, he'd been uncomfortable despite the renovation of the rooms. Collingswood still held ghosts for her brother. She wouldn't push the point. Kevin had spent his life trying to resolve his feelings about the events that had taken place inside that house.

At the car door, Donna hugged her, and Kevin kissed her on the cheek before getting inside. "See ya soon," he said.

"Donna, let me know about gowns and fittings and anything else I can help with."

"I will."

Lifting her hand, Theresa waved good-bye as her brother backed the car up and turned it around to drive through the iron gates.

She turned after the car disappeared. Dean had nearly reached the point on the driveway where she stood.

"Are you all right?" he asked, a frown marring his forehead. "You look like your last friend just drove away. I thought you were happy about them getting married."

"I am." She tried to smile. "It's not the wedding. I love

Donna, and it's high time the two of them made it legal. She's been in love with him since their elementary school days."

"So what's the problem?"

Theresa looked up at the house. It gleamed in the afternoon sun. The fieldstone shone brighter in the daylight.

"It's the house."

Dean followed her gaze. "The house?"

"Kevin's spent his life trying to live down the past. He sees the house as an evil ghost. It has a pretty mask covering it, but beneath that mask, is a past ready to come back and claim another victim."

"Houses can't do that." He touched her arm. His voice was low, and Chelsea knew he was speaking to her. He wanted to banish any ghosts the house might hold for her, too.

"I don't feel that way anymore." She turned to him. "I did when I first arrived. This was the last place on earth I wanted to return to."

"And now . . ."

"I know now if I had not come here, I'd never have met you."

Her words seemed to stun him. The air between them turned solid. Dean's look was such that not one of his actors could have duplicated it. He'd impacted her life far more than he knew. He'd been the catalyst for driving her demons away. He'd removed the tinge of dread the house held for her, taken Chelsea under his wing, and brought laughter through the doors.

It was a house, four walls and a ceiling. Yet with Dean, it was more than that. More than the parts. Love had seeped into the crevices and fused the cracks in the plaster. The lights poured warmth over the residents, instead of cold, frigidity. There was life in the rooms, not the darkness of death.

Without Dean, she wondered if the past could have been banished away. On impulse, Theresa went up on her toes and kissed him on the cheek.

"What was that for?" he asked.

"For my homecoming."

* * *

With his hand, Dean drew pictures using the stars in the nighttime sky. The air was soft, and the sky was filled with points of light. His other hand played gently in Theresa's hair as they sat on the bench outside the kitchen door.

He hadn't understood her this afternoon in the driveway. What had she meant by her homecoming? He felt it was a good thing, and although her comment was the same as the title of the film he was working on, he was sure the two were unrelated. The sensible thing to do would be to simply ask her, but he didn't. He wanted to bask in theory, fantasy, make-believe for a while.

"Filming must be going well," Theresa said softly.

He turned his head and looked at her, but kept his hand in her hair. It was silky, and he liked the feel of it flowing over his hands.

"Why do you say that?"

"You're more relaxed. Less tense."

"That could be because of you," he teased. She blushed. He could see her face, lit by the moonlight, turning a deep shade of maroon. "It is going well."

Theresa no longer came to watch the filming. She viewed the dailies, but she was often absent during production. Chelsea had told her she didn't need to come. And Theresa, believing the child needed some independence, granted it. It meant Dean didn't get to see her, either. She was a distraction to him, but one he wanted. He couldn't wait to get back to her at the end of the day.

His fingers tickled her neck, and she moved her head closer to his hand. "This afternoon . . ." he began. He wanted to sound casual, but somehow, his voice held that quality of expectation he insisted actors portray in a scene set just this way—big moon coming up over the trees, stars overhead, river in the distance, and a pretty woman.

"What about this afternoon?"

"What did you mean?"

"You mean about the homecoming?"

He nodded. For a long time, she said nothing. She sat up and stared at the trees in the distance, pulling her thoughts together, ignoring him—he couldn't tell which. He stared at her profile. Her eyelashes were long, sweeping up and down as she blinked. The shape of her forehead was a perfect Roman arch, leaning to a straight nose and kissable lips.

She took him back to the days when he communicated his thoughts through pictures. Then, they were often his nightmares, but Theresa was not a nightmare. And his need to capture her likeness had nothing to do with fear. If anything, she'd helped him with his problem. He'd spoken to his sister last night about the nightmare. If Theresa hadn't been there for him to talk to, would he have remembered the attic? Did it have anything to do with the scene they'd filmed that day? Or could it be a crack in the memory that had been locked in his brain since he was seven years old?

"Kevin hasn't been back here since we left when we were young."

Theresa began to talk. Her voice was low, and Dean strained to hear her.

"He spent most of his life in and out of hospitals."

She paused and swallowed, but didn't take her eyes off the tree line. His arm still lay along the back of the bench, but he no longer touched her.

"Mental hospitals."

Dean didn't react. He'd heard the story from the locals, but he wanted her to tell it her way.

"There were lots of rumors after my father disappeared when I was twelve. The grown-ups had their version. Kevin and I didn't know it until the kids at school started repeating things they'd heard their parents say. Some claimed he was having an affair, and he ran away that night. I don't believe that. My parents were devoted to each other. Even now, after all these years and remembering them, I don't believe he would have done that to my mother."

Dean didn't contradict her, but he knew of devoted couples who had affairs. In a town this size, it wasn't uncommon for the best of families to have a skeleton or two in their closet.

"That night, when my father disappeared, it was raining. The wind was horribly strong, beating against the windows. It woke me. Storms didn't bother me, but Kevin was afraid of lightning. I got out of bed and went to his room, but his bed was empty. My parents' door was open, but they weren't inside. I found Kevin on the steps. He was huddled at the bottom holding on to the bannister. He was crying, his body shaking, his hand gripping the rails."

She stopped. Dean knew she was reliving the experience.

"The hall was dark. Lightning made it a horror movie setting every few minutes. At first, I thought Kevin was afraid. Then I heard the argument." She turned and looked at Dean. "It wasn't that our parents never argued. All couples do. But this was different. They were raging at each other. As I reached my brother and tried to hold him in my arms, my father came out of the dining room and slammed the door closed."

Theresa jumped as if the door had just slammed. Dean leaned closer to her, his hand touching her shoulder reassuringly. She reached up and took it.

"I pried Kevin's hand loose and took him back to his room. The two of us waited there. We were sure Mom would come up and see how we were doing. She never did. I woke up the next morning still in my brother's room."

She stopped talking for a long time. Crickets sang in the darkness. The air remained still and soft.

"What did your parents argue about?" Dean asked, prompting her to continue.

"I don't know. Kevin refused to tell me anything rational. He kept saying it was his fault. That if he hadn't told, they wouldn't have fought, and dad wouldn't have left. Told what, he's never said."

She looked at Dean. A tiny smile lifted the corners of her mouth. "In all the years of therapy and mental clinics, he's kept the secret to himself."

"Did anyone else leave town the same night as your father?" Dean asked.

Theresa shook her head. "You're building movie scenes in your head. But as far as I know, everyone was accounted for in the weeks and months following his disappearance."

"And you have no indication that he ever returned. He just completely disappeared?"

"What about the money?"

"What money?"

"If he didn't leave for love, then the most logical thing to do is figure out who would profit most by his disappearance."

"I suppose that would have been my mother. I was too young to know about paying bills. My mother never mentioned them. The grass was still cut, and we still had food and a couple of maids until . . ."

"Until what?"

"For months after, my mom wasted away, hurt terribly by the accusation and judgment of the town. She missed my father, and she must have blamed herself. I came home one day and found her dead in her bedroom. She'd downed a whole bottle of pills. Then my aunt came. She dismissed the maids and closed the house. Kevin was in shock after these two events happened so close together. My aunt put him in a hospital and took me back to Buffalo."

"Had you ever thought of hiring a private investigator to look into the events, possibly find out what happened to your father?"

She shook her head. "I had a teacher once in graduate school who said, 'If you don't want to know the answer, don't ask the question.' I'm afraid of the answer to that question."

"I understand," Dean said. He was also afraid of the answer to the question of his past. But his fear didn't keep him from seeking to know it. His nightmares had kept him from wanting to open the door to the past, but he wanted to now. He wanted to know where he'd come from and why no one had come forward to claim him or even report him missing.

"I'm sure Kevin's showing up today was Donna's doing. She's stood by him for years. He tried to confront the house, but I could tell he couldn't wait to leave."

"What do you think about the night your father didn't come back?"

She hesitated again. "I don't know," she finally answered. "I know he wouldn't have left without a word. Even if he and my mother were having problems, there was Kevin and me. He'd never walk away and leave us without a word."

Dean understood what she wasn't saying. If Theresa's father wouldn't have walked away without a word, then something had happened to prevent him from returning.

"So you see," she said, "we all have our demons, and we all deal with them differently. You have nightmares. I left. Kevin ran inside himself. He's out now, but the house still holds him prisoner."

"What about you?"

She shook her head. "I've forgiven it." She uttered a small laugh. "I know that sounds strange. I'm sure your psychologist sister could explain it better, but if there were terrible things that happened in this house"—she turned her head and looked up at it—"they don't have to control my life." Then she looked back at him. "When I walk down the street in town, not everyone stares at me. There are some that do, but I'm no longer self-conscious about it. I have a job come September, and you helped."

"Me? How?"

"You made me see that this is a building. It's a house, an inanimate structure made of brick and plaster. It only holds power over me if I allow it to. And I no longer will. So, in effect, this is my homecoming."

Dean put both arms around her and pulled her close. He smelled the clean scent of her hair and kissed the top of her head. It would have made the perfect ending to a movie. The camera would pan out from their silhouettes. The music would swell as the big golden moon came into view and the credits rolled.

But this was her life and his life, and there were no credits to roll. Theresa had come to grips with the forces that haunted her. She'd returned to the scene of the crime, so to speak, back to the house where the evil had entered and changed the course of her life. She'd conquered it. He was pleased that he'd been part of her reconciliation, but in his own life, that process had not taken place yet. He wondered if it would ever happen.

The dream, the nightmare had been a breakthrough. His sister Luanne thought so. She suggested he go to counseling and see if he could explore it further. For Hollywood types, counseling was part of the culture. No one would wonder why he was seeing a psychologist; they'd want to know what took him so long. But Dean was unsure if that was the route to take. Maybe it was just a nightmare, unrelated to the childhood terrors that used to plague his nights.

He kissed the top of Theresa's head again. He envied her. She'd dealt with her past. He wanted to protect her, keep her close to him, and fight off any demons that came her way. But he had his own issues. He wanted to be like her, to find his homecoming.

Chapter 10

The computer screen flicked on as Dean slipped into the chair in front of his desk. It was messy, with script changes, budgets, orders, invoices, and the many other bits of minutia he needed to perform his job.

As he prepared for the family meeting, he was still thinking about Theresa's comments from three nights ago when they were looking at the night sky and she'd told him this was her homecoming. The virtual family meeting had been a way for them to keep abreast of each other after they had grown up. In their youth, they had used it to resolve conflict. They'd sit around the dining room table back in Dallas and talk out whatever was bothering them. Dean started his therapy sessions there. Eventually, his parents took him to counseling, but nothing had unlocked his memory.

Tonight was their regularly monthly check-in. There was no issue on the table to discuss, no crisis going on that required them to come together as a family.

Unless Rosa was playing her usual matchmaking. Since Dean was the only one unmarried besides herself, she'd set her sights on him. Sights, mind you, that homed from oceans away.

"Hi, Rosa. How's Brazil?"

"It was fine. I'm no longer there."

"Where are you now?"

"My condo in New York."

He'd hoped she was someplace east of Timbuktu. The Big Apple was only a stone's throw from Royce. She could show up on his doorstep at any moment. And that was a complication he didn't need.

"Anything exciting happening to anyone?" Dean asked, hoping to deflect the attention from himself. Everyone was there—his brothers, Brad, Digger and Owen, and his sisters, Luanne and Rosa.

As the family had expanded with marriages, the spouses too joined the monthly meeting. Family *was* family, no matter how they became associated.

"How's the film coming?" Owen asked, ignoring Dean's question. "Have things settled?"

"Things are going much better. It was an adjustment we all needed to make, but we're working fine now."

"What about the replacement child?"

"Chelsea Nelson." Dean gave her name. "She's working out fine. Better than Robbie, and she's never acted before."

"It must have been something short of a miracle that you found a replacement so fast," Rosa said with an I-know-your-secret tone to her voice. "How did you find someone with the skills you needed so quickly?"

Dean smiled his best Hollywood grin. "She just dropped into my arms. She's the owner's cousin."

"Owner?" Rosa frowned. "Ah, you mean the landlady."

Dean was getting a little perturbed with his sister. He wished someone else would say something. Erin was usually good for reducing the tension.

"Her name is Theresa Ramsey, and her cousin, Chelsea, is Robbie's replacement. The child already knows gymnastics." Dean explained how Chelsea knew the routines from practicing with Robbie.

"Aren't you lucky that she just happened to be there."

"Rosa, cut the crap," Brad said. Marriage had softened Brad, but he still didn't like to waste time. Rosa cut her eyes at the side of the screen where Brad no doubt was displayed.

They had no real agenda except to talk for an hour. This usually began with someone saying what they were working on or giving the details of some event they had attended.

"We have an announcement," Luanne said. She and her husband Mark Rogers filled one of the frames on Dean's computer screen.

"We're pregnant," Mark said.

Electronic pandemonium broke out. Mark and Luanne had been trying for a baby for several years. Luanne had infertility problems.

"Are you taking off work?" Erin asked.

"Not yet, but I am going to be very careful."

"I'll see to it," Mark said. The smile on his face was beacon bright.

Thoughts of Theresa jumped into Dean's mind. He already knew she'd make great mother. She was sensitive and patient with Chelsea, giving her as much freedom as she needed while guiding her in the right direction. Then, without conscious volition, Dean thought of her pregnant, carrying his child. He blinked as someone called his name.

"How are the nightmares?" Luanne asked the question.

"I haven't had another one since we talked last. I mentioned it to Theresa, and she reminded me that the scene we were filming that day took place in an attic. It's probably unrelated."

"Don't take it lightly," Mallory said. Mallory was a doctor, and she was married to his brother Brad, also a doctor. She worked with comatose patients in her continuing studies of the brain. "It could be related."

"The dream has been the same for so many years. Most of it I can't remember, but the fear part and the fog part I always see. If this attic episode happens again, I'll know it's related."

They moved to discuss a new building Owen had just

contracted for and how his business had expanded to two offices. After a while they all signed off, except Rosa.

"How is Theresa?" she asked.

"Fine." Dean gave nothing away.

"Is she special?" She asked it quietly, keeping any confrontation out of her voice.

"Are you playing matchmaker again?"

"Me? I'd never do that."

"Then why do you ask about her all the time?"

"Just being friendly. She's seems more important to you than any other woman."

"And you can tell this over an electronic connection?" Dean raised his eyebrows.

"Body language is still readable," she told him. "And I'm good at observation." She smiled the lipstick smile, the one she usually wore when she was modeling a new lip color. "You've been on location before, but this is the first time you've been up close and personal with the owner of the location."

Dean thought of the last time he and Theresa had made love. It had been like the first time. He thought of her all day long and couldn't wait for their time together. Like him, she was a person with a crutch who was pulling her life together. He wanted to help her throw the crutch away. He wanted to be the person she leaned on.

"If we decide to marry, Rosa, you'll be the first to know."

"Is that a promise?" she quipped back, her lightning fast wit completely intact.

"That's a promise."

She signed off then. Dean sat back in his chair and stared at the blank screen. Rosa was forcing him to examine his feelings for Theresa. She knew nothing about what was going on up here. His body language couldn't be that transparent, but Theresa had moved into a place in his heart. Did he want her to have a permanent place in his life?

He got up and grabbed a bottle of water, then went outside.

The night wasn't as soft as it had been a few days ago when he'd spent time with Theresa after viewing the dailies, but there was a breeze that cooled his skin. He looked up at the big house. The full moon they'd had just a few nights ago had fled. The house was dark, no lights showing in the windows. He wondered what Theresa was doing and had the urge to go in search of her.

And that's when he heard the scream.

"Chelsea!" Theresa spoke aloud when she heard the scream. She'd been sitting at her computer, working on the coming semester's classes, when she heard the sound. Pushing her chair back, she started to run from the room.

Dean broke through the front door as she reached the stairs. Both of them ran up the steps, him taking them two and three at a time. He already had Chelsea in his arms when she reached the door and hit the light switch, flooding the room with bright light.

She saw Chelsea crying as Dean rocked her back and forth. Chelsea's arms were tightly woven about his neck. For a moment, Theresa was jealous. Then she realized they were both concerned about her cousin.

"It was a dream, Chelsea," Dean said softly. "It's over. It can't hurt you."

"I want my mama," she cried, repeating the phrase over and over like a tragic song refrain.

Theresa moved closer to them. She put her hand on Chelsea's, touching Dean's back as well. He turned to her, still speaking softly to Chelsea.

After a moment, he laid her down and sat on the edge of the bed. Theresa sat behind him, both of them leaning toward Chelsea.

"Wanna tell me about it?" Dean asked.

Chelsea's head bobbed up and down on her pillow. "Mama

died." She hiccuped. Dean stroked her arm. "They were putting her in the ground." Chelsea started to cry again.

"It's okay, sweetheart," Theresa said. "Where is Mama?'

"In heaven."

"And she wouldn't want you to cry," Dean told her. "It was a dream. They will stop."

"When?" she cried.

"I don't know," he answered honestly. "Why don't you close your eyes, and we'll stay with you until you fall asleep again."

"Okay." Complying with his suggestion, Chelsea turned over on her pillow and closed her eyes. Theresa rose and turned off the ceiling light. Dean's hand reached for her, and she came back to him, taking it and dropping down on the bed next to him. Ten minutes later, they slipped out of the room, still holding hands.

"Do you think she'll be all right?" Dean asked outside her door.

Theresa nodded. "She'll sleep the rest of the night. It's unusual for her to have more than one episode in a night."

They walked to Theresa's bedroom door. It was open. No lights were on.

"Did you hear her scream from the carriage house?" Theresa asked.

"I was walking outside. I'd just finished talking to my family."

"Your meeting was tonight?"

He nodded. "Rosa had some questions about you."

"What kind of questions?"

"The nosy variety. She said she could read my body language."

Theresa looked up at Dean. His eyes were full of desire. They stood staring at each other for a long time. Theresa didn't know which of them moved first. Her mouth suddenly seemed closer to his. Slipping her hand up, she smoothed her palm over his cheek. Her eyes focused on his lips, and she ran her thumb over them. Dean kissed the pads of her fingers.

His hands slipped to her waist and pulled her toward him. Theresa pushed his hair back and let her arms circle his neck. His mouth met hers, and lightly, they kissed.

"I missed you," Dean said against her mouth.

"I haven't been anywhere."

"I miss you every time you're out of my sight."

They went inside her room. Pushing the door closed, Dean turned her in his arms and kissed her. He lifted her off the floor, his mouth tantalizing hers. Wrapping her legs around him, she took control. Her head now above his, her mouth deepened the kiss. Her tongue tangled with his. She tasted him, savored the wine-sweet nectar of his mouth. Delving in with desert thirst, her head bobbed in circles as she drank a full measure.

His hands on her back slipped to her neck, up into her loose hair. Her nerve endings prickled, and she was carried to the soundless realm where nothing logical or rational could invade their need. The tense need for release, for going beyond any defined limits, coiled inside her. Her body sought that place, that bursting zone where desire was without borders.

Theresa slipped down his frame. Her body stretched sensually across his, the contact brisk enough to set off sparks in the darkened room. Dean groaned as she pressed against his erection. Around them, heat sprang up, a hot wind that started at their feet and engulfed them. Theresa opened her mouth to breathe. Dean cupped her face and joined his mouth with hers, taking both her breath and her essence.

She felt as if she were burning. He was the source of the heat, yet instead of fleeing from him, she wanted to get closer. Reaching for the buttons on his shirt, she undid them. Frantically, her hands touched flesh. It was hot, searing her skin, yet she loved it.

She pressed her face to his chest, kissing him, opening her

mouth and teasing his flat nipples. His hands dug into her shoulders, her body both weak and strong at the same time. Unsnapping his jeans, she lowered the zipper, her hands caressing him. She bit her lower lip as the pressure of her shudders grew stronger.

Dean accepted her ministrations. Then suddenly, he spun her around and took her to the bed. Like fighting animals, they tore their constricting clothes off, removing the offending garments and taking hold of each other. Trading kisses, their naked bodies, like magnets, aligned. Dean fit her into the juncture of his legs. She gasped at the erotic sensations that rocketed through her. His hands rubbed her skin, and she was sure it would no longer hold her within its confines.

Theresa saw the foil condom packet in Dean's hand as she lay on the bed. A moment later, he pulled back. In that instant of separation, the impact was that of a hundred years of anticipation. Their joining bound the gap in time, as if their lovemaking followed after years of absence. It was an instant in time, an initial coupling of bodies, yet she exploded inside. Her voice burst forth, and Dean absorbed it in a kiss that became a full convergence of bodies.

Could she stand it? an illogical voice whispered in her head. Ignoring it, Theresa wrapped her legs around Dean, as she'd done when he held her by the door. His body thrust inside her, once, twice, again and again. She thought she'd lose consciousness as rapture engulfed her. It lifted her up, her body acting by instinct, meeting his thrusts and delivering her own. Their rhythm coincided, mounting a step higher with each coupling. Theresa let go of every restraint that governed her daily life. She gave Dean all of her. Anything he wanted was his for the taking. She opened herself like a book, her entire being there for the reading.

Theresa didn't know how long they kept the rhythm going. It could have been a lifetime or only a moment. Finally, she fell against the pillow with a long moan. Dean collapsed on top of her, his weight a passionate blanket, their bodies remaining joined. Her blood rushed like a raging river through her, pounding in her head. Her chest heaved as she took in great gulps of air. Her nerves, still wired, set off miniature shards of electricity that kept her body in a hedonistic paralysis.

Dean's hands framed her face. Reverently, he kissed her as if he was thanking her for being part of his world. Her love for him filled her. Every crevice of her body was consumed with how she felt about him. *Nothing* would ever top this. Dean slid off her, taking her with him as he turned on his side. He kept her near, cradled her as if he couldn't bear to separate.

Theresa put her arms around his tapered waist. She breathed in the heat of him, the smell of their lovemaking filling the room, and knew that he was the masterpiece of her life.

It wasn't a smell he could identify. It was sweet, with only a hint of flowers. There was a smoothness to it, something silky and pearllike. Qualities Dean knew he couldn't translate to the sight and sound, the two-dimensionality of the screen. Yet he knew he'd recognize it until the day he died. That the mere whiff of it would turn his head and change his direction.

It was Theresa, her aura, the essence that made her who she was. It was one of the many features of her that he'd become used to, yearned for, and wanted to hold in his mind for the rest of his life. He cradled her close, his chin on her head, drinking in that smell as if it were ambrosia for his soul.

As Dean's eyelids closed, light was already peeking around the drawn shades at the windows. Contentedly, he skimmed his hands over Theresa's fair skin, the yellowish red tones golden in the half-light.

Behind his lids, Dean saw a flash of light. It was bright, blinding. He squinted and opened his eyes. The room was the same. Theresa's breathing was still even. She remained in his arms as if nothing had happened. Nothing had happened, he told himself. Then he closed his eyes again and settled down for the remaining few minutes of bliss. He had to get up soon and return to the carriage house, but he didn't want to leave Theresa until the last possible moment.

The second time he closed his eyes, nothing happened for several moments. He relaxed, and the flash came again. The light burst through like the birth of a sun. It stabbed his eyes. Pain forced him to sit up in bed. His eyes flew open, but the light was still there. He was in a room, and through the brightness, he saw something.

A book.

"A comic book," he said out loud, and then everything snapped into place. The brightness fled. He was back in Theresa's bed.

"What's wrong?" Theresa sat up, instantly awake. "Did you have a nightmare?"

She must have felt his sudden movement, Dean thought, and Chelsea's nightmares and sleepwalking caused her to sleep lightly and wake suddenly.

Theresa touched his arm, then put her hand on his cheek and turned his face to hers. They were close—only a kiss separated them.

"Tell me," she said. "What happened?"

He looked at her. Her face was full of concern. Other than his family, no one had shown real concern for him. Not his doctors or his counselors, but Theresa's eyes and her touch were those of someone who wanted the best for him while requiring nothing in return.

She kissed him. First one side of his mouth, then the other. Her lips were soft. Her hands pushed his braids back.

"What happened?" she whispered.

Dean slipped his arms around her body, her breasts against his chest, his face buried in her neck and hair.

"I remembered something."

* * *

The words were so simple. *I remembered something*. He could have written them in a script. After years of trying to force himself to pull a memory, no matter how small, from his life before his seventh birthday, nothing ever came. Yet this morning, there it was.

A memory.

"Dean." Theresa called his name. They'd dressed and left the bedroom. She'd checked on Chelsea while Dean went to the kitchen for coffee where she had joined him. She touched him, ran her hand along the curve of his back. It was more than comforting. He recognized the gesture, even if she didn't know what she was doing. His mother had done that when he was young.

The counselors and doctors had told him time and again that the nightmares would go away when he felt loved and safe. His mother and father used to hold him and rub his back. They gave therapy by touch and love. Eventually, the nightmares *had* gone away.

Dean pushed a cup into her hand and took her arm. He didn't want to talk in the kitchen. He wanted to go somewhere that he could hold on to her. In the next room, camera equipment stood silent, lights were dark, the set was prepared for the next indoor scene. Dean sat on the sofa and pulled her next to him. He put his arm around her, and she leaned into him.

"Tell me about it."

He told her about the bright flashes of light. And then about the book. "I know it's small."

"No," she interrupted him. "It's a memory. It's a beginning. Since you were seven, you've remembered nothing. This is huge."

Her arm slipped around him, and his heart filled to capacity. "You can't imagine how that makes me feel. It's only a book. It's a small thing, but you understand the significance of it."

"What kind of book is it?"

He closed his eyes and looked. "A comic book."

"Did you read comic books when you were seven?"

"I don't know." He pushed her up and sat forward. "It's got blood on it."

"That's not unusual. A lot of comic books had blood on them back then."

"I mean real blood. Red blood. Fresh blood."

"Is it your blood? Have you been cut?"

"It's not my blood." He said it with certainty.

"Do you know whose blood it is?"

He turned and looked at her, shaking his head.

"Can you see the name of the comic book?"

"Too much blood," he said. It was soaked in blood, as if it had been drenched, then picked up, and put on the . . . bench. He'd remembered something else.

"What?" Theresa asked as if she knew there was more.

"The book is on a bench."

"Is it outside?"

He shook his head.

"Can you see the room where the bench is?"

He shook his head. "That's all. There's nothing more."

She rubbed his back the same way she had in the kitchen. "It will come now," she said. "The door has been cracked. Soon you'll fill in the space."

"I'm not sure I want to," he said. "Maybe this is why I haven't been able to remember. Something terrible happened."

"You knew that. The doctors had explained that a trauma would cause you to forget, right?"

"They explained it to my parents. I was too young to know what they meant then. Later I understood."

"Something probably happened to you or someone you love."

He nodded. "I know. That's what scares me."

"Why?"

"What if I was the cause of it?"

Chapter 11

The day was perfect. The air was crisp with the anticipation of fall. It was unusual this early in August, but Theresa welcomed it. She was back on campus. And she was just as excited as she had been the day she applied for a job.

Dean had been a little tense since the night he'd remembered a detail from his past. He'd explained they were doing a lot of intense scenes, but Theresa knew part of his strain had to do with the memory. She was glad to get out of the house.

She wanted to make sure everything was ready at the school, see her classroom, check on the progress of . . . whatever needed to be checked. She was anxious. She hadn't been in a classroom since she had come home to care for Meghan, and she itched to get back to teaching.

Summer school was over, and the place was deserted. In a couple of weeks, the students would return and the campus would be overrun with activity. Theresa went to the Economics department and picked up a copy of the course bulletin. Her name wasn't in it since she had come on board only a couple of months ago. She found the name of the professor she was replacing and went to his classroom.

The smell of chalk hung in the air. For a moment, she stood

in front of the empty classroom, staring at the chairs that would be filled with students in just a little while.

Crossing campus on her way to her car, someone called her name.

"Everette Hoefster, what are you doing here?"

"I still tootle around here. I never got my degree, so I take a class or two every semester. Eventually, I'll graduate. What's your reason for being here on a deserted campus?"

"I work here."

His eyebrows went up over his clear blue eyes. He still had little boy features with dark brown, curly hair that he used to blow dry to make it straighter. Now he left it alone. It curled over his shirt collar, giving him a Hollywood bad boy look.

"At least I will work here, come September. I'm going to teach in the Economics department."

"Is that what you did in England?"

"How did you know I was in England?"

"I see Kevin every now and then. He told me you were at a university there. And you still have a trace of the accent." He smiled as if he appreciated it.

"Well, it was nice seeing you. I have to get back now."

"Theresa?" He stopped her.

She turned back to him. His face had changed. His smile was gone, and his face had a serious expression.

"What is it?"

"Do you have a few moments? I don't live far from here, and there's something I'd like to tell you."

She was perplexed, unsure of what to say.

"If you don't want to go, I'll understand. Like you said, we were never really friends. But I hope we're friends now."

"You make it sound intriguing."

"It might give you some insight."

"Into what?"

"Please, I'll explain everything I know."

Theresa *had* to go then. Her curiosity had taken over. And

she had forgiven Everette, but she was unsure whether he understood that. "Lead on," she said.

Moments later, they were sitting in Everette's living room. He no longer lived at the house his parents owned, occupying instead a small house near campus. He offered her a glass of iced tea, and she sat with it in her hand.

"Everette, what is this about?" Theresa wasn't taking time for small talk.

"I've wanted to tell you for years, but last time I saw you, I didn't know if it was the right thing to do."

"Tell me what?"

Everette swallowed. "My mother died a few years ago."

"I'm so sorry. I didn't know. You and she were very close, if I remember correctly."

He looked down and then up. "You were away. We were close, but she still had secrets that I didn't know about."

"That's normal, Everette. Everyone has secrets, and she was your mother. You can't expect she would tell you everything."

"The other day when you came into the bakery, you asked me a question."

Theresa frowned. He seemed to be jumping all over the place with this conversation. She didn't remember asking him anything in the bakery. She remembered the jingle, his apology, her acceptance, and the cream puffs.

"What was it?"

"You asked me what happened. Did I know anything."

Theresa tensed. Her blood suddenly pounded in her head. They'd been talking about her parents, about what had happened.

"Everette, what could you know about that? You were twelve years old."

"I didn't know anything. Not until my mother died, and I went through her things."

"What . . . what did you find?" Theresa was almost afraid

to ask. She wanted to know, but she was unsure if she was prepared for the answer.

"There was an envelope with my name on it. It was hidden away in a place where it might not have been found for years. I believe she didn't ever want it found, but if it was, I should be the one to read it." He paused. "Inside it was a diary."

"What was in it?" Theresa's hands had begun to shake. She put the glass on a coaster sitting in front of her. Her throat was dry, and her heart accelerated out of control. She knew Carol Hoefster as Everette's mother. She sometimes worked at the bakery. She and Theresa's aunt had been friends, but Mrs. Hoefster had rarely visited their house.

"It only has one entry." Everette got up and went to one of the bookcases that flanked the fireplace. Opening the glass door, he took a small book from the far reaches of the case. Coming back, he handed it to her.

Theresa looked at the book. Not a traditional diary, but a journal book. On the cover was a photo of Collingswood. Mrs. Hoefster used to make these books and sell them in the bakery. The pages inside were blank. They had been mainly bought by tourists. She would use photos or her own drawings of local places for the covers. Theresa had never seen one with her home on the front.

She stared at it, afraid to accept it. Like Dean, who wanted to remember his past but was afraid, she, too, was afraid of what she might find in the pages of the small rectangular diary.

"What did your mom know?"

Everette pushed the book a little closer to her. "Read it."

Theresa accepted it. She lowered it to her lap and stared at it as if it were a predator that would rip her throat open at any moment.

"Can I take it with me?" she asked in a voice almost too low for her own ears to hear.

He nodded. "I think she really wanted you to have it, but

she left the decision up to me. I can't tell you if what she's written is true or not. You'll have to decide that for yourself. What I did do was buy the land."

"What land?"

"After you read the book, you'll know."

The journal lay on the desk. Theresa sat at her desk, staring at it. She'd been that way since she returned from Everette's apartment. Her eyes never wavered. As if in a trance, she kept a steady gaze on the journal, looking at it as if it were a snake ready to strike. The photo of the house in the days of its splendor alternately blurred and crystalized before her eyes.

She wanted to know what the book said, what Everette's mother had known about her family, but she was afraid to open it. A Pandora's box holding all the evil of Theresa's life, all that she thought she'd safely hidden away, had been resurrected.

The book glared at her, daring her to lift the lid, keeping her prisoner with its siren's song. Theresa's hand reached out, but she snatched it back, the same as she would have if she was reaching toward a fire. Repeating the gesture again, she still couldn't bring herself to lift the top.

Then she heard voices. Grabbing the book, she dropped it in the desk drawer and slammed it closed.

"Theresa?" Someone called her name.

She stood up, swallowing, placing her hand over her heart to stop its racing.

"Theresa?"

She went toward the door. It opened before she got there, and the most beautiful woman she'd ever seen walked in.

"Rosa," she said. She would have known her anywhere.

Dean followed her in, along with another woman. Theresa didn't recognize the second one. She'd seen Rosa on the television screen in TV ads and in countless magazines.

"How do you do?" Rosa extended her hand as she came forward. Her smile was bright and wide. She wore a royal blue dress that followed her perfect curves. A short white jacket that ended just below her breasts picked up the blue with a thin stripe running around the neck, down the front, and along the bottom. The jacket's white sleeves ended in long blue cuffs.

"It's good to meet you in person," Theresa said, taking her hand.

"I see you recognize my sister," Dean said. His smile was proud. "This is my sister-in-law, Stephanie Clayton." He put his arm around the other woman. She was beautiful, too, but not as striking as Rosa Clayton. She was dressed just as elegantly, however. "Although I'm surprised Owen was willing to let her out of his sight."

"I'm here under a very tight deadline." She smiled, then stepped forward and shook Theresa's hand. Theresa liked her immediately. There was a warmth to her that was genuine. Her eyes held a dual touch of sincerity and concern.

"We were shopping in New York and thought we'd come up for the day and see how the movie was going," Rosa said.

"In a pig's eye," Dean shot back, but his smile was broad. "They're here to see if I've lost my mind." He looked at Theresa then and explained, "I told them about the dream. And it wouldn't have been at all out of the realm of possibility for them to bring both Mallory and Luanne along."

"Mallory is on an ICU cycle and couldn't get away," Rosa explained. "And since Luanne announced she was pregnant, Mark won't let her lift a finger."

"Mallory is the medical doctor." Dean spoke to Theresa.

"She's married to Brad," Theresa remembered, speaking aloud.

Stephanie nodded. "That's right. They're both doctors. My husband is Owen. And Luanne's husband is Mark Rogers. It's hard to get us all straight at first, but it'll come to you."

A strange jolt echoed through Theresa. Stephanie Clayton had just included her in the Clayton family. As if she and Dean were a couple. What had Dean told them about her? She remembered he'd said they had asked a lot of questions about her after they'd seen her on the teleconference. Was that enough for them to show up unannounced?

Searching for something to say to defuse the moment, she offered them something to drink.

"I'd love some mineral water," Rosa said, turning and looking directly at her brother.

"Anything for you?" he asked Stephanie, obviously being asked to leave the ladies to themselves.

"Coffee, black."

His gaze moved from his sister-in-law to Theresa. "Nothing for me." She knew what was about to happen, and she felt holding on to a glass would be a sign of weakness. She was determined to be strong in front of these Clayton women.

Theresa offered them a seat the moment Dean left the room. The two of them sat facing her. Theresa chose not to sit behind her desk; instead, she chose a chair far from it, facing the sunlight that streamed through the windows and into her eyes. But she was also far from the journal she'd hidden in the drawer. It held information that could either exonerate her family or paint the past even darker. She needed to deal with that. She struggled with irritation. She didn't want to discuss some nonexistent future between herself and Dean with his family before she'd discussed it with him, if she ever needed to, which she doubted.

"I think it's great that you two took a detour from the city to come up and see your brother. He thinks a lot of you." Theresa started with a conciliatory tone that didn't match her mood.

"We think a lot of him too," Rosa said.

"He's your favorite brother, isn't he?"

Rosa glanced at Stephanie. "They're all favorites."

"But you two are closest in age. And you came to the Clayton household about the same time."

"Dean told you this?" Her expressive eyes opened wider.

"Not everything, but I'm good at reading between the lines." The look she gave the beautiful model told her that the writing she was seeing in this interview had lines as wide as those on kindergarten paper.

"When we were younger, we tended to do a lot of things together."

"Read that as *get* into a lot of things together," Stephanie interpreted. She looked about the room. "Dean says you've only come back here a short while ago."

"I taught school in England for a while."

Theresa expected Stephanie to say something about the accent and her speech patterns, but she didn't.

"Is that what you do here?" Rosa asked.

"In the fall, I'll be teaching economics at the university."

Rosa stared at Theresa. Stephanie was still looking around the room as if she was an architect intent on redesigning the place.

"What's going on here?" Theresa asked, shifting her gaze between the two women. "Why are you here?"

"I told you—"

"And I don't buy it," Theresa interrupted the beautiful model. Her day had already been ruined by the presence of the journal in the desk drawer. These two women showing up unannounced and "looking her over" as if she was some kind of pet they were considering accepting into their family was more than she was willing to put up with. "This has all the earmarks of a royal marriage interview."

"It's not," Rosa said very quickly, just as quickly as the smile had left her red lips. "We're here to visit Dean."

"Then why are you sitting in my office and not watching the filming or being entertained in his house?"

"Mainly because I asked if I could see the house,"

Stephanie said. Her practiced smile told Theresa that she was often needed to diffuse situations. Good cop, bad cop came to mind. "I love old houses with big rooms and high ceilings," Stephanie continued, and again, Theresa felt an affinity for her. The other woman looked up at the high ceiling.

"Has Dean shown you around?"

"Only the public areas. He didn't take us upstairs."

"I'd be happy to show you the upstairs, but I believe Rosa wants to ask some more questions before we go."

"I apologize for my rudeness," Rosa said. "I'm very attached to my brothers."

"This one in particular." Theresa ended the unfinished sentence.

"Dean *is* special," she conceded.

"Your brother and I have become close in the short time I've been here, but when he leaves, he goes alone." Theresa was surprised at how much saying that hurt. "Does that tell you everything you wanted to know?"

"Yes," Rosa said.

"No," Stephanie said simultaneously.

The two women looked at each other, then back at Theresa. "Are you in love with him?" Stephanie asked candidly.

"I thought Luanne was the Clayton psychologist."

"I apologize," Stephanie said. "I didn't mean to pry. When I met Owen, I got the same kind of reception. Especially from Rosa." She looked at the younger woman. Theresa saw color bleed through Rosa's skin tone. "You see, the Claytons are all adopted, and for a long time, they only had each other, trusting no one else. When you appeared on the screen and Dean spoke of you more than he's spoken of any other woman, our curiosity was piqued. And that's why we came to visit."

Theresa leaned forward in her chair. "What did Dean have to say that piqued your curiosity?"

"It wasn't so much what he said"—Rosa spoke up—"as the way he said it."

"He's a director who knows how to instruct actors on how to speak to elicit exactly the quality he wants them to convey. Have you considered that he might be manipulating you like that? Or you could be reading more into his words than what was really there."

"That's possible, but he's been my brother a long time, and I know when he's acting."

"So what do you think you heard?"

Theresa held her breath, waiting for the answer.

"We think we heard Dean falling in love," Stephanie said.

Theresa laughed. She forced herself to do so. There was no way she'd let these two women know her true feelings. She'd practiced holding them inside for a lifetime.

"Have you watched Dean directing?" Theresa asked.

They nodded.

"You've seen how intense he is when he's working?"

Both nodded again.

"Do you think there is any place in that life for him to add a person who would demand a share of him?"

Stephanie and Rosa looked at each other as if they had never thought of that.

"Your brother is married to his work. It consumes him twenty-four/seven. When he's not with the actors, he's writing or taking care of them as if he were a father and they were all his children."

"So, how did you two become close?" Rosa's question startled her, but she remained calm and still in her chair.

"He used me to bounce his ideas off of. He was rewriting the script every day, causing the cast added stress. And, as he's told you, his nightmares have returned."

"He's told you about them," Rosa stated.

Theresa nodded. "My young cousin has nightmares, and Dean comforted her by telling her he, too, suffered from them."

"She's the little girl in the film?" Stephanie asked.

"She replaced Robbie after his accident."

"He told us about that," Rosa said. "It was quite convenient that someone with the exact qualifications he needed was only a few yards away."

"It required some rewriting and additional filming, and it set the film back a couple of weeks, but Dean was concerned about his cast and crew. He didn't want to lose his chance with this film. Didn't want to disappoint his backers." Theresa looked pointedly at Rosa, knowing she had invested money in this film.

"He's told you an awful lot," Stephanie said. "Dean is usually very closemouthed about his personal feelings. You've made more of an impact on his life than you know."

Theresa's mouth went dry. If they knew that much about their brother, what was she giving away with her voice and her body? When she looked at the two women, they were both smiling.

"What?" she asked.

"You're in love with him," Rosa stated.

Theresa said nothing.

"Don't worry. It's not obvious," Stephanie said.

Rosa got up and came over to her. Theresa instinctively stood up in preparation for defending herself. But Rosa embraced her.

"You're perfect," she said.

Stephanie took her turn.

"I don't understand," Theresa said, moving a step back after the two women let her go.

"Dean likes you, and you like him. And he's remembering his past. It has to be because he feels safe and loved. And the only person we can attribute that to is you."

"So this was a test?"

"Please don't be angry," Stephanie said. "We're very concerned about Dean. His nightmares haven't plagued him since he was fifteen, and they're back now with memories that were never there before. We just want to make sure he'll be all right when things begin to fall into place."

"As you're sure they will?" Theresa was concerned about Dean, too. She was in love with him, and his nightmares worried her. The span of time he couldn't remember asserted itself in his dreams, and while Chelsea's nightmares had grown less frequent, Dean's had increased in number and intensity.

"We can't be sure. But Dean won't go to a psychologist. He'll use excuses, like the movie, the cast, people he'd put out of work, but he's really afraid to remember. We wanted to know someone around him would be there for him if he does remember."

"So I get the Clayton Family Seal of Approval?"

Chapter 12

"Are you sure you won't stay the night? We have plenty of rooms," Theresa said. She stood next to the car Rosa had gotten out of several hours ago. At that moment, Stephanie's cell phone rang, and she instantly reached for it.

"Owen," Dean said before she got it to her ear. Stephanie took a step away from them.

"It's only three hours back to the city," Rosa said. "And as you can see, Owen can't wait for his wife to get home."

Stephanie looked over at them with a smile while she continued to talk.

"Drive safely, and call me when you get home," Dean said.

Trading hugs all around, the women got in the car and drove away. The red taillights had barely disappeared before Dean turned Theresa into his arms.

"What did they really want?" he asked.

"They're concerned about you."

"Me? Why?"

"Two reasons. The first is your nightmares. They want to be sure you'll get help if you need it."

"I'm fine, and I don't need them playing mother."

"Well, you got it, even if you don't want it."

Theresa turned and went up the porch steps to the house. Dean followed her.

"What did they ask you to do?" Dean asked.

"Keep watch over you. Make sure when your memories return, if you need help, even professional help, you get it."

"I don't—"

"They told me about that, too," she interrupted. "About your reluctance to go to a psychologist. Of course, Luanne is the exception to the rule."

Dean caught Theresa's arm and led her to a porch seat. He sat across from her. "I spent years going to counselors, psychologists, doctors—none of them helped."

"But that doesn't mean they won't in the future."

He fell silent. For a moment, he looked at his hands. Then he raised his head. "Do you think they make a difference?"

"I've never had to go to one for myself. I took Chelsea when she started to retreat into herself. I think the psychologist helped me understand what she was going through."

"But . . ." he prompted.

Theresa's shoulders dropped. "But I think her activity here with the film is better therapy."

Dean smiled.

"Not so fast," she cautioned. "I said better therapy, not that therapy wasn't working. It's coming from a differenct source. You told me that yourself when you asked me to let Chelsea take Robbie's place. Dean, you're her therapist. You work with her. You talk to her, treat her as if she's a valued member of the cast, make her feel important and loved. You represent security to her."

"What happens when I leave?"

The question hit Theresa like a bullet to the heart. "I think she'll understand that you're only leaving, you're not dying. The possibility exists that she can see you again." Theresa's voice was soft and hesitant. She recognized the double layer of meaning in her words. She wasn't only speaking about her niece. It was her own psyche she was trying to protect.

Dean bobbed his head. Theresa wanted to ask what he was thinking, but she didn't dare. She was afraid of his answer. She knew what she wanted him to say. She wanted him to say that he didn't want to leave without her, but he could be thinking something completely different and she was unprepared for the hurt that might come with his reply.

"Back to your sisters' concern," Theresa said to get her mind off her own vulnerability. "I get the impression more family will be . . . dropping in if you don't let them know you're working through this issue."

Dean nodded. "You can be sure of that."

"So what are you going to do?"

He leaned back, spreading his hands in a gesture that said he didn't know.

"I have a suggestion," she said.

"Shoot."

Theresa knew his nonchalant appearance was only a front. "Promise me that if you are unsettled, even the tiniest bit, you'll tell me, and together we can make the decision?"

"That's a lot of power to put in someone else's hands."

"True. Someone who isn't a Clayton." She pause to let him know she understood what he'd meant. "But maybe distance is what you need."

He leaned forward and took her hands in his. He looked at them, turned them over in his palms, studied them. Then he rotated them back as if he were auditioning her for a dish detergent or fingernail polish commercial. "Okay, Theresa. If I feel any need for outside help, you'll be the first person I call."

She smiled, knowing he'd chosen his words very carefully. He hadn't actually agreed to the conditions. Only to call her first.

"And now what was the second?" he continued.

"Second?"

"The second reason my sisters wanted to be alone with you this afternoon."

"Oh," she said. "They wanted to interview me."

"For what reason?"

"I'm not quite sure."

"What kind of interview was it?"

Theresa dropped his hands and sat up straight in her chair. "What I accused them of was conducting a royal wedding interview."

"I have no idea what you're talking about." Dean frowned.

Theresa was sorry she'd mentioned it, but she had to explain it now. "Remember the movies about the wedding of Prince Charles?"

"To Camilla Bowles. Of course."

"Not that wedding. His first marriage, to Diana."

"I was pretty young when she died and too involved in my own life to care."

"But you've seen the news stories, the movies about her life?"

He nodded.

"Remember what she went through before she married? The interviews with the royals? The doctors' visits?"

Light dawned in Dean's eyes. Then they widened in surprise. "They did that to you?"

"Not quite. We parted friends." She smiled at him.

"How could you?"

"Because of the shared love we all have for one person—you."

Dean loved everything about being a director, except when it interrupted something important. And there were always interruptions. Like before he'd had time to question Theresa about her statement, he'd been called away to deal with a scene that was set and ready to go.

It was two hours before he could get back to her. She was

no longer sitting on the porch where he'd left her; instead he found her in the office where she'd been when he'd brought his sisters to meet her earlier in the afternoon.

She stood at the closed French doors that looked out on the vast backyard. Her back was to him, and her shoulders were shaking. Dean immediately knew she was crying.

"What's wrong?" he asked, nearly leaping across the room. He took her shoulders and turned her. Something fell to the floor, hitting his foot. He looked down, but Theresa's body blocked his view.

She clutched him to her. "What is it?" he asked again, feeling helpless. She just held on to him, saying nothing. Dean let her cry, but his own throat got tight. He finally pushed her back and tried to look at her face, but she hid it, keeping her head down.

"Theresa, what's wrong? Why are you crying?"

"My father . . ." She hiccuped. "My fa-a-a . . ." She tried again, but her voice cracked. "My father is dead."

"How do you know?" Dean saw a box of tissues on the desk. He pulled her toward it, grabbing a handful and shoving them into Theresa's hand. She wiped the tears away and sniffed several times. "Tell me what's happened."

"The journal."

Dean looked around. Spying the book on the floor, he retrieved it. "Sit down," he told her. When she was seated, he took the seat next to her and opened the book. He flipped through the pages. Only half of it had writing in it.

"She killed him," Theresa said. She had some measure of control back. The tears had stopped, but she nervously continued to ball the wad of tissues in her hand. Her voice was slightly higher than normal. "I need to call my brother."

"Why don't you start at the beginning and tell me what happened."

She told him about her trip to campus and running into

Everette Hoefster and explained how Everette had given her his mother's journal.

"Do you want me to read it, or will you tell me what it says?"

"It says that my aunt killed my father." She stopped. Dean saw her fighting for control. She bit into her lower lip. Dean flipped the book to the first page and began to read.

As long as Patty lived, I could not commit these words to writing, but now that she's gone, my conscience will not let me die without leaving behind a record of what I know about the disappearance of Alexander Ramsey. Alex was a good man, and he loved his wife and children. But Patty was my dearest friend, and I would have sworn she could never kill anyone, least of all someone she loved. But she did. She told me so on the night it happened. And I will put it down in these notes, as well as I can remember it.

Patricia Clarkson, at the time of Alex Ramsey's disappearance, lived in Buffalo, New York. Everyone thought she was three hundred miles away that night. But she wasn't. She was here. It was raining, raining hard, but I still heard it when Patty banged on my door at three o'-clock in the morning. Hank had already left for the bakery, and Everette always slept like a log. Even the rain pounding against the windows didn't wake him.

Patty was drenched, soaked through to the skin. The front of her coat had blood on it. "I killed him," she cried as she fell into the kitchen. She was hysterical, wailing and crying. Over and over, she kept saying, "I killed him." It took a while for me to get her calm enough to speak coherently. Then she told me. She'd killed Alexander Ramsey. I felt as if my heart had been cut out. I loved Patty like a sister, and I knew of her obsession with Alex. She loved him unreasonably, to the point of lunacy. She fantasized about him, ordered her life around him, tried her best to break up Jeanine and Alex when they became engaged. After they married, I thought she'd come to her senses and leave them alone, but as the years went by, she became more and more obsessed.

She never thought of any other man, although she was known to have her share of dates and men who wanted to marry her. She got pregnant with Meghan and married Lionel Parkson. When Lionel moved them to Buffalo, I thought it was the best thing that could happen to Patty. Time and distance have been known to remedy many situations. And I prayed that Meghan and being away from Royce would give Patty a new focus.

For a while, I thought it had. Patty was good at keeping secrets, good at hiding what she thought and did. I thought I was the one person who knew everything about her, the one she confided in. But Patty knew how I felt about her love for Alex, and she concealed this side of herself from me. There was one time I caught her. I was driving along the road that passes Collingswood. It was dark, and no one walked along that road after dark. Even the kids drove cars out to Lover's Lane. I saw a figure in the road, startled by the car's headlights. She stopped, and I recognized Patty. I stopped the car and made her get in. She began telling me some story with so many holes in it that it rotted while she spoke the words. When I questioned her, she told me that she often returned to Royce. That she spied on Alex and his wife. That she knew Alex loved her and only her and that he wanted to leave Jeanine. I saw Jeanine and Alex on occasion. You can't avoid people in a town the size of Royce. I knew he worshiped his wife and that he would do nothing to destroy that love. And I knew Patty needed help. I tried to talk to her, to reason with her, and after a time, she seemed to understand, but it was all a ruse. I believed it because I wanted to believe it.

That night, when she fell through the door into my kitchen and stained the floor with rainwater mixed with the blood of the man she'd killed, she told me everything. She'd been to see Jeanine and told her a bunch of lies, lies she actually said were truths "imparted to a naive and unseeing wench." She knew that Jeanine and Alex had argued after she had left. She was at the window, watching them. Then Alex left the house. She caught him outside, and the two of them drove up to Lover's Lane. It was after the kids died up there, so the place was deserted, and it was raining.

They argued. She told him how much she loved him, that she knew he didn't love his wife, that he'd only ever loved her. She wanted to run away with him. They could leave that night, go away and not return. He refused and got out of the car. Patty was so angry she wanted to hurt him. She grabbed the first thing she saw, a screwdriver. She got out of the car and ran toward him. I've seen her in her hysterical state, and she scares me when she's like that. Alex turned as she approached him. She stabbed him through the heart.

This is where I joined her in her crime. I couldn't see her go to jail. She was sick. She needed help, not to be confined in a cell. I felt responsible. I knew she was ill. I'd known it for years, and I did nothing about it. I also felt sorry for Jeanine and her two children. If what Patty said was true, their father was dead. I couldn't bring him back. So I joined her in her crime. With my son asleep upstairs, I did the unthinkable. I left him alone in the house during the rainstorm. I got two shovels from the shed, and together, Patty and I drove back to Lover's Lane. I prayed all the way there that Patty was wrong, that Alex may have been hurt, but he would recover. As the lights of the car turned into the hollowed out ground where the teenagers congregated to pet and experiment with sex, I saw the body. Alex Ramsey lay on his back, the screwdriver protruding from his chest. He was truly dead.

We wrapped the body in some old sheets and found a place in the woods where no one was likely to go. The kids only parked in the clearing. They didn't go walking. The ground was soft because of the rain, but that also made the dirt heavy. We dug a grave and put Alex in it. Patty took the sheets so if they found the body, the sheets couldn't be traced to us. She also gathered some stones and put them on top of him. She said the gases in his body might push the dirt up. I can't tell you if that's true. I didn't care. We covered the body with dirt and stones, then found some plants we knew would grow. We stuck them in the dirt over the grave and left.

That was the last time I ever went to Lover's Lane or even passed it en route to someplace else. I would go out of my way to avoid it. It was also the last time I ever saw Patty alive.

When we left, everything about us was dirty, our clothes, our hair, our bodies. We took off our clothes and showered in the rain. Drying ourselves with paper towels and napkins, we put our clothes and the shovels in plastic bags that Patty had brought food in. Careful not to get any dirt in the car, we drove naked back to my house. The sun was just beginning to rise. I gave Patty some clothes and told her to go home. I told her I would call her in four hours as she should be home by then.

After she left, I cut up the clothes and burned them. I put the shovels in that big trash bin and the mechanical garbage collector dumped them into the truck without anyone seeing them. I bought new shovels to replace the old ones. No one ever noticed.

I'm sure I'll burn in hell for my sins, but maybe I can put my conscience to rest. I leave the rest of the burden to you.

Dean stopped reading. He closed the journal and looked at Theresa. She felt more in control of herself. "Where did you get this?"

"Everette Hoefster, the owner of Hoefster's Bakery on Main Street, gave it to me. He's Mrs. Hoefster's son. We went to school together. I met him on campus yesterday. He said he'd found it in an envelope addressed to him after his mother's death. The instructions that came with it left the decision of what to do with it up to him."

"And he kept it all these years?"

"He said he didn't know what to do. If he gave it to me, it could reopen closed wounds, or I could cause a big scandal. After all, his mother was an accessory to murder. If I chose to, my actions could destroy his mother's memory. He probably also felt guilty—he'd been one of the worst offenders to me in school, making up a little jingle everyone began to sing. He didn't know if I still harbored a grudge."

"How *do* you feel?"

"A little numb." She got up and walked back to the French doors where she'd been when Dean came in. "I've relived that night in my mind more times than I can remember. I tried to remember what they were saying, but I couldn't. My brother spent his life blaming himself for our father leaving. The entire town silently accused my mother of murdering him, eventually driving her to suicide. And I went to live with the woman who really took his life. Damn! How could I not know? How could she do something like this and never say anything, never even hint that she was the killer?"

"She did say it. You just didn't understand the language."

Theresa spun around, her hands clenched as if she was ready to do battle with him. Dean stood up.

"She said it in the way she treated you. I've never seen your father, but I'll bet between you and your brother, you're the one who favors him most."

She stared straight at him and then nodded.

"She wanted you because you reminded her of him, the man she loved, the man she killed in a fit of rage. She also wanted you because she hated him for refusing to leave your mother. You were her reminder, which explains why she treated you so badly."

Theresa stared at him for a moment. She looked as if she was processing what he'd said, deciding if it had credence, if she would accept his theory. Acceptance dawned in her eyes, and she turned around.

Dean went to her. She stood rigidly, staring into nothing. He took her shoulders and leaned her back against him. "I'm the last person who would tell you to let it go. I know you can't do that, but wait a while before you make a decision." He kissed her on the side of her head. She relaxed against him. His hands traced down her arms until he was holding her at the waist, her head leaning back against his shoulder.

"You are so good for me," she said, turning in his arms and bringing hers up to circle his neck. "I don't know what I'm going to do when you leave."

She rested her head on his chest. Dean wondered if she could hear the sudden thumping of his heart.

"We could have seen his grave," Theresa said. "The night we were at Lover's Lane. We could have been right next to it and never known."

"The journal says they walked into the woods. We were probably nowhere near it. What's strange is why that area was never developed."

"It couldn't be," Theresa said. Dean heard the pieces fall into place in her voice. Her head came up, and she looked straight into his eyes. "Everette bought the land. It was the last thing he told me. He said I'd understand why when I read the diary."

After a moment, Theresa laughed. It wasn't a happy laugh, but one that oozed with regret. "Wouldn't this make a great movie?" she said. "Husband killed for unrequited love. Wife takes her own life, leaving behind—"

"Stop it!" he shouted.

The hysteria that was about to overtake her was quickly quelled. He pulled her head back to his shoulder and held her for a long time. Leading her to a chair, he pushed her into it.

"Don't move. I'll get you something to drink."

Dean left her, taking the diary with him. He studied the picture of the house on the cover. Knowing Theresa must have a bottle of wine somewhere, he checked the cabinets before settling for a can of cola. He returned to the office and popped the top on the can before handing it to her with a glass. She drank from the can and let the glass fall in her lap. Dean took the chair across from her.

"You shouldn't stay," she said.

"It's not late," Dean told her. "And I don't believe you'll be getting much sleep tonight."

"Chelsea has an early call, and so do you. I'll be fine."

Dean put his can down. Leaving his chair, he hunkered down in front of her. "Do you think I'd leave you alone after what you just found out? I'm going to be here. Just as long as you need me."

Dean woke with a start. It wasn't the dream. He hadn't remembered having a dream since before his sisters had come and gone, but something had jerked him awake. He looked at Theresa next to him. He hadn't thought she would be able to relax enough to sleep after the revelation of the diary. But the tenseness that held her had finally unwound.

Dean had led her to bed and lain with her until they both

fell asleep. He held her close, unsure when the last time was, if ever there was a time, that he had lain in bed with a woman without making love to her. With Theresa, though, he wanted to be here for her, be here when she woke up. Be the first person she turned to and talked to about her problems and her joys.

Suddenly, he knew what had awakened him. It was exactly as he'd been told, as he'd read and directed in all the films he'd been involved with.

He was in love.

Theresa stirred and turned toward him. She opened her eyes and blinked when she saw him staring at her.

"Did you get any sleep?" she asked.

"Some." They were both still fully clothed and were lying on top of the coverlet. "How did you sleep?"

"I didn't have any bad dreams," she told him, reaching up and running her hand along his jaw. "You need a shave." She smiled and kissed his cheek.

"I didn't want to leave you."

"I'm all right. I had a lot of time to think. I haven't decided anything yet. I'll take my time, just as you suggested."

She kissed him again. Dean felt his body stir the way it did whenever he was near her. He pushed a hand in her hair, smoothing it away from her face. The room was dark, romantically lit by the moon streaming through windows with curtains they never bothered to close.

"You're very wise for one so young. I assume you learned it from your brothers."

"One brother in particular. Brad, the—"

"Philadelphia pediatrician."

"You're getting to know them." He felt her smile. For some reason, that made him feel good. He wanted his family to know her and like her as he did. She was different from the people he generally met. She didn't ask for help. She didn't wallow in pity. She did what needed to be done. And she could stand up to anyone.

"What made Brad the wise one?"

"I don't know. My mother used to say he was born old. I suppose she meant he took things more seriously than the rest of us."

"How does Mallory deal with that?"

"She can hold her own. The night they met she took down a drug addict who had a knife at her throat."

"What?"

"She had been in the emergency room when the police brought in a drug addict. He was out of his head and didn't know where he was. He took Mallory hostage, not knowing she would be his worst nemesis."

"You have a remarkable family," she said.

"I know," he said. And he was thankful for them.

Dean fell silent. Resting his chin on Theresa's head, he thought about how much she was like Mallory. Mallory could hold her own. Brad had found a perfect match in her. *Perfect match*—the words rebounded in his head. They were a description of Theresa. *She* was his perfect match.

He'd never understood what that phrase meant until now. It should scare him. As Theresa had pointed out, so many marriages in Hollywood failed. And she had Chelsea to think about, to provide a stable environment for. Dean would be gone much of time. Like now, he'd be on location. Away for months. It was a life he'd chosen, one he loved.

"You're awfully quiet." Theresa broke into his thoughts.

He gently kissed her temple. "We should be asleep."

She chuckled. "We do lose a lot of sleep."

Dean got quiet a moment. "There is something I've been thinking. It's been on my mind for a couple of days now."

"What's that?" She still appeared relaxed.

"Today my sisters came." He paused. "You said the three of you shared love for one person."

"That person is you."

"What did that mean?"

He'd expected her to stiffen, and he wasn't disappointed. Her body went completely still, as if every cell in her body had suddenly ceased movement.

"Well," she paused. "We all are concerned about you. We thought that the memory of something that happened in your dream was significant. And Rosa thought that with all the work you do, you'd rationalize that the dream had no significance. So they came to get you to promise to take it seriously."

"And you?"

"Me? I agreed with them."

She was hedging.

"You would do the same if it was me, wouldn't you?"

"Of course," he answered, recognizing her attempt to channel the discussion away from herself and onto him. "I thought that maybe there was something more in the statement than . . ." he trailed off.

She moved her head and looked up at him. "Than what?"

"Than concern for a friend. I thought there was something . . . more."

"There is something more," she said, and kissed him. Her arms slipped around him. Her mouth pressed hard. She slipped her tongue into his mouth.

And he was lost.

Chapter 13

About the only time Theresa got to see Chelsea was while her cousin was on the set. During the day, she was either acting, practicing, or sleeping. The good news was Chelsea hadn't had a bad dream or a sleepwalking episode in weeks. The bad news was Theresa didn't have any time with her.

Theresa returned to the set each day. Partly, she wanted to be there with her cousin, but the other draw was being near Dean. They had become closer since that night a week ago when she'd read the journal. He seemed more relaxed, too. The filming was going well, and Chelsea had surprised everyone by proving to be more of an actress than anyone expected.

Theresa watched as Chelsea worked through a fight scene. She had to go through many stops and starts while they repositioned cameras and relit the area, but her giants on the high bar had improved dramatically. Theresa sat mesmerized while Chelsea swung her slight body around and around and then, using all her force, pounded into a cushioned wall and landed on an air blanket. Theresa knew when the actual film was shown, she would pound into her attacker.

"How'd you like it?" Chelsea asked as she skipped over and pulled herself into a chair after she finished the scene.

"You're wonderful." Theresa hugged her. "I'm a little

concerned that since Robbie went home, you never have anyone your own age to talk to."

"I like it," she whined. "Please don't make me stop."

"Oh sweetheart, I wouldn't do that."

Chelsea smiled, springboarding with the ease of childhood back to the happy little girl she was. She'd changed so much in the last month. She was no longer the withdrawn little girl who'd sat almost catatonic in the car when they drove through the gates of Collingswood.

"Did you see me doing the giants? And hitting the wall? Dean says it will look different in the movie. He says I'll hit Mr. Tommie." She yammered on, not waiting for an answer.

"I saw how much better you are doing them. They looked great." Theresa finally got a word in edgewise.

"Dean says the filming will be finished soon. But he says that's when the real work begins."

Theresa's head came up, and she stared across the set to where Dean was working with some lighting technicians. Going soon. Gone. The words hit her like bullets. She'd known he'd leave soon, but she wasn't quite ready for it to happen yet. Tears forced their way to her eyes, but she blinked them down.

The room suddenly felt small, airless. She couldn't breathe. She wanted to run, go away somewhere so she could scream, let her emotions out.

"Are you listening to me?" Chelsea asked.

Theresa's head swung back. She had no idea what Chelsea had said, but she smiled brightly. "What is it, honey?"

"I said when they are all gone, do you think I could take acting lessons? Dean says I don't need them, but I think I do."

It was her best grown-up voice, but Theresa had to concentrate on her words. Her mind was somewhere else, and her heart was heavy and sinking.

"What about the gymnastics?"

"Oh, I want to take that, too. I can do it, can't I?"

"You know you have to go to school, too?"

She hung her head for a moment, then raised it. "Yes, but I can do it."

Theresa nodded that Chelsea could have her wish. Chelsea jumped down from her chair and shouted.

Dean saw her and came over. "What's going on?"

"Theresa said I can take acting lessons after you're gone."

Dean looked at Theresa. She was unsure of what she saw in his eyes. It looked like regret, hurt. Several emotions jetted through them. She could pin none of them down.

"Chelsea says the filming is almost over."

"That's when the real works starts, right, Dean?"

He glanced at her quickly and nodded, then back at Theresa. "If all goes right, in a couple of days."

She knew some of the actors had already gone. As their scenes were completed, they packed up and moved out. Theresa had heard them in the early morning, their trailers going through the gates to get an early start before the groupies showed up, but there were several left. Most scenes had the major actors in them, so they were still on site.

"I see," was all Theresa could say. She sat down, and someone called that they were ready. Chelsea moved first, leaving her place and going back to the set.

"We'll talk later."

"Sure," Theresa said without enthusiasm. Dean's hand came up. She was sure he intended to touch her arm, but his hand hung in the air for a moment before dropping back to his side.

Theresa left the set the moment he turned away. Dean was leaving in two days, and he hadn't told her. The two of them were more than friends. They had slept together many times. She knew he wouldn't be here forever, but she at least deserved some notice.

Walking toward the front gate, she felt numb inside, like someone had cut a hole out of her and nothing could fill it. She looked at the long driveway that wound through the foliage and led to the main road outside the estate. She should never have returned here, never allowed Dean to steal into her senses. But it was too late to think about that now. It was ground she'd already gone over. This was as much her own fault as Dean's.

Straightening her shoulders, she turned around and walked back, but she didn't go to the house. Later, they were filming in there, and she didn't want to chance running into Dean during one of the many breaks they needed to reset cameras and lights. She didn't know how long she'd walked around when she found herself back in the bubble. It was much darker inside than it was outside. She welcomed the anonymity of the subdued lighting.

Grasping the bar of one of the apparatuses, she pulled herself up until her chin cleared it. The more chin-ups she did, the more her concentration centered on the task and not on the man who'd burrowed into her life and taken up residence. She would survive his exodus. Dean wasn't her first love. She'd been through this before and knew it was survivable, but she also knew it would be a long, hard process.

And it started right now.

"That's enough," someone said.

Theresa let her feet touch the floor. She turned and saw Frank Osborne, now Chelsea's stunt double.

"If you want to begin an exercise program, you need to start slowly." Frank knew how she felt about Dean. She was sure most, if not all, of the cast and crew knew of their affair. Now that it was time to move on, they all realized she would be staying behind. Frank was a compassionate soul. She'd felt that from the first and saw it in the way he treated all those around him. "If you want to work another area, I'd be happy to help you, but too much at one time is bad for you."

"Thanks, Frank. I'm not going to try anything I'm not ready to do." She walked over to him. "When do they begin to take this down?"

"In the morning," he replied. "There's another crew scheduled to come and take everything away. Dean's given them instructions to clear and clean everything. Even the grass will be replaced with sod."

"He takes care of every detail."

Frank nodded. "He's good to work with. One of the best, in my experience."

Theresa didn't address that. "Have a good trip back, Frank. I probably won't see you before you leave."

"I hope we'll see each other again. You have a great kid in Chelsea. I enjoyed working with her."

"Thanks." Theresa left him then. She went back to the house. The kitchen was always safe to enter. The doors were oiled and made no sound when people came in and out of them. As long as she made no noise, she could get to her bedroom without disturbing anyone.

The kitchen wasn't empty. One of the child monitors was getting coffee.

"I'm going out for a while. Will you be here to take care of Chelsea?"

The woman nodded as she drank from her cup.

Theresa smiled and trudged up the back stairs. Gathering her purse and a sweater, she took the journal and headed for the door. She backed the Mustang out of the garage and drove off the property. The day was beautiful, returning to summer heat. The weather had been unpredictable, with some cool, nippy days in August, followed by a return of heat. Today was humidity-free with temperatures in the 70s. The top was down, and the wind whistled through her hair. Theresa didn't try to corral it, but let it fly.

She needed to get her mind off Dean's departure, but there was also something else she needed to do. She needed to talk to Kevin. But she didn't drive directly to Swanson. Before that, she turned off at Lover's Lane. The place was empty of cars, except for the Mustang. She parked and got out. The wind was strong enough to tighten her clothes against her body, outlining it. She looked not at the guardrail ahead of her, but turned around to stare at the trees that skirted the clearing.

Somewhere in there was a grave, the answer to a fourteen-year-old mystery. Theresa began walking. The ground was covered with moss and dirt. Trees grew close together, and sunlight only peaked through the upper reaches of the branches. Theresa walked straight back. She looked from side to side, trying to discern which patch of dirt held the remains of her father.

Nothing looked different from anything around it. There were no defined paths. People didn't come to Lover's Lane to walk. Carol Hoefster and Theresa's Aunt Patty could have taken many directions to find a spot for the final resting place of Alexander Ramsey.

Theresa spent forty minutes combing the woods, checking here and there in hopes of finding the grave. At last she gave up and returned to the Mustang.

Kevin was in the office when she got to Swanson. The room was clean and neat. He was very orderly, and everything was in its assigned place, except for the papers he was working with on his desk.

"This is a surprise," he said with a wide smile. Coming around the desk, he embraced her. "What are you doing here?"

She adjusted the purse hanging on her shoulder. "I have some news, and I need your advice."

Kevin seemed to instinctively understand the seriousness behind her statement. He stepped back and leaned against the desk.

"Could we go somewhere? Your house, perhaps."

"Sure. Just let me call Donna and tell her I'm leaving." He lifted the phone and spoke quickly.

Several minutes later, they were sitting in his living room.

The fireplace mantle was covered with photos of Theresa, Meghan, and Donna. Again, the place was neat and dust free. He brought Theresa a soft drink.

"What's this all about?" Kevin asked.

She withdrew the journal from her purse and held it. "It's about Daddy."

Kevin suddenly looked as if he were made of stone.

"Daddy's dead," she announced. "This is an account of his last night."

"Where did you get it?" Kevin's voice croaked. Although he'd been stone before, his body seemed to deflate at her words.

Theresa explained how she had come to have the book. "If you want, you can read it."

He shook his head. "Tell me what it says."

She gave him a full report, leaving nothing out, but also giving him no insight into how she felt about the details.

"What are you going to do with it?" he asked when she finished speaking.

"That's why I came. I want to know what you think."

Kevin got up and paced the room. Theresa waited. "I don't know," he finally said. "It's been fourteen years."

"The people involved are all dead," Theresa said. "But that doesn't make it any less a crime. Look what it did to you."

He turned to her, then came to the sofa and took a seat. "It changed my life. There was a time I would have said it ruined it, but that's all over now. I can't change it. Can't go back and undo what's been done."

"So you think telling someone would do no good."

"Nothing positive. Everette's family would be vilified. His business could be ruined. Tongues would wag again, bringing up all the old stories. It could affect my business. And you'll be living here. Is this what you want?"

She shook her head. "I wanted your opinion."

"Theresa, I loved Daddy, but I don't remember him as well as you do."

"I just don't want to leave him buried there. I think he should have a proper grave next to Mom's."

"Do you think we could do that without the authorities knowing?"

"Not in a town the size of Royce."

"Then what can we do? Eventually, that area will be developed."

"Not as long as Everette owns it." She told him Everette had bought the land to keep the secret safe.

"What prompted him to tell you now?"

"Conscience, I suppose. He said his mother left the decision to him. If I'd never returned to Royce, he'd probably have kept the knowledge to himself."

Kevin thought a moment. He lifted his soft drink and took a long swallow. "I don't think opening this up will help anything or anyone." He paused and leveled a long look at Theresa. "But I'm behind you. Whatever you want to do, I'll support."

Theresa stood up and put the journal back in her purse. She told Kevin what she'd done on her way to see him, how she'd scoured Lover's Lane looking for the grave.

"What would you have done had you found it?"

"I don't know." She spread her hands. "Said a prayer or something. Express my guilt for all the terrible things I've thought over the years. I know I wouldn't have had an epiphany standing there, but I thought something would happen. That somehow he would know that we now understand that it was nothing about us, about Mom or me or you, that prompted him to leave us with no word."

Together, they headed for the door. "What are you going to do now?" Kevin asked when they reached it.

"I'm going to see a lawyer."

* * *

Lunch was over by the time Theresa got back. The actors were filing out the doors and heading for a few minutes of freedom before going back to work. Theresa was suddenly hungry. She'd skipped breakfast other than coffee, and now her stomach rumbled.

Parking the car, she went through the side door into the dining room. Prepared to see Dean, she was disappointed that he wasn't there. She gathered a plate of food and sat down to eat.

"Theresa," Chelsea called as she ran into the room. "Where were you?"

"I went for a drive. Is everything all right?"

"Sure. Dean asked where you were. He gets upset when he can't find you."

Theresa almost swallowed her food without chewing. "Dean was looking for me?"

"Yep." She took a soft drink from a sideboard. Theresa replaced it with a bottle of water. Chelsea gave her a disappointed look, but she didn't argue.

"Did he say what he wanted?"

"No. I think he likes you. He's always looking at you funny."

"Funny?"

"Yeah. Funny. Like he likes you." She took a drink of her water. "You look at him like that, too."

Theresa put a forkful of food in her mouth. Even Chelsea knew how she felt about Dean.

"Dean! Dean, Theresa is in here," Chelsea called.

Dean came into the room, which was empty of diners except for Theresa and Chelsea.

"Are they ready yet?" she asked.

"Just about."

Chelsea scampered out of the room. "I don't want to be late," she called as she exited.

Dean watched her go, then looked back at Theresa. She'd

finished her meal, thankfully. She knew she wouldn't be able to eat any more anyway. Taking the soft drink can that Chelsea had brought to the table, she popped the top and poured it into her glass.

Dean took a chair and straddled it. He faced Theresa. "Chelsea missed you this morning."

"She told me it was you that missed me."

"I did," he said candidly.

"Why didn't you tell me?" Theresa asked.

"I don't know," he answered honestly, knowing what she meant by the question. "I don't want it to end. Every time I thought of saying something I'd get distracted."

Theresa faced him squarely. She placed her hands on the table and gave him her full attention. "There's nothing to stop you now."

"Dean?" They both turned to look at the figure in the doorway. "We're ready."

"In a minute." Dean looked back at Theresa.

"Go," she said. "You've said everything that needs saying."

She got up and left the room. Theresa knew it wasn't completely fair to blame Dean. He hadn't developed this relationship alone. But she was hurting inside, and she wanted him to hurt too.

She tried to focus on something else. The journal seemed so much less important now than it had the day she read it. She didn't want to do anything about it. She'd decided that on the way home, but she did want her father buried properly, even if the only people standing at his grave were her and Kevin. She'd called a lawyer on the way home and made an appointment for tomorrow.

If she was lucky, Dean would be gone when she got back. Her heart would hurt, but at least only the ghosts of their love would see it.

* * *

The stairs weren't carpeted, and Dean heard Theresa's footsteps as she descended the following morning. She could have stepped out of any fashion magazine. Her hair was curled in the front and pinned up in the back, showing off her long neck. She wore a yellow suit with a jacket that was straight on one side, with three pleats on the other. The skirt stopped at her knee, and her heels showed off those long legs he remembered pressing against his own. He wanted her right here and now.

"Good morning," he said as she reached the bottom step. "Are you on your way out?"

"I'm meeting my brother and Everette."

"I'm going with you."

"You don't know where I'm going. And I thought you were leaving. Hasn't everything been done?"

He nodded. "The final truck will finish loading today and leave early in the morning. I'm not leaving until tomorrow."

He watched her as her chin dropped. He knew this was hard for her. It was hard for him, too. He'd never wanted to stay with a woman before. But their lifestyles didn't mesh. She'd told him that. She was concerned about what could happen during his long absences. There was also Chelsea to consider.

"Your brother called this morning. He told me about the lawyer. I'm going with you."

"Moral support?"

"We all need it. How many times have you been there for me?" He didn't expect her to answer. She was always there when he needed her. This was his chance to be there for one of the times in her life when she needed someone to lean on. Although she wouldn't admit that she needed anyone.

He took her arm. She didn't resist as he led her to the car. She slid into the driver's seat, and they left. The drive was long and silent. Dean attempted to start a conversation, but Theresa's answers were short and crisp.

"You didn't need to come," she said as she pulled into a parking garage.

They'd passed a sign welcoming them to Syracuse, New York, and he understood why she'd driven so far. There were lawyers in Royce and in the neighboring towns, but Royce was small, and she wanted to make sure whatever she found out didn't make its way to the gossipmongers and rumor mill.

"Theresa." Dean stopped her as she got out of the car. "I'm here for you. For the time being, let's forget that there was anything between us, and be friends."

She didn't say anything, and Dean was uncertain about what to do. So he pulled her into his arms and held her. She remained stiff for a while, then relaxed against him. He cradled her head on his shoulder.

"Come on," he whispered. Hand in hand, they walked to the lawyer's office.

They were led into the office, and Theresa, her brother, and Everette took seats before the massive desk, with Dean sitting behind them. After the initial introductions, Theresa asked the first question.

"It is true that anything we tell you is confidential and you cannot repeat it, isn't it?"

"That depends," the man answered. About thirty-five, he wore an expensive suit, and his hair was as manicured as his fingernails. He sat straight up in his chair. "As long as it isn't illegal."

The three on the other side of the desk looked at each other.

"We haven't done anything illegal," Everette stated. "But we do know of people who have."

"Why don't you tell me about it?"

The meeting was short. The lawyer pointed out there was no legal way to remove human remains from a grave without notifying authorities. Everette Hoefster had every right to dig on land he owned, but the discovery of remains would have to be reported to the local jurisdiction and an investigation would ensue.

"Is there no other recourse?" Theresa asked.

"None that is legal," the lawyer replied.

"Have we committed any crime by not revealing what we know?"

"A case could be made for that, but I doubt it would hold up. With all the parties dead and no one to corroborate the allegations of the journal, not speaking does not make you an accessory after the fact. No fact has been established."

Theresa stood up. "Thank you," she said, and extended her hand. The lawyer stood up and shook hands. They filed out.

"I suppose the old cliché is proven," Kevin said when they reached the sidewalk.

"What is that?" Everette asked.

"Let sleeping dogs lie." He looked at his sister. She reached out, and Dean immediately took her hand. It was the first indication since earlier today that she needed him or wanted his presence.

"I agree," Theresa said. "We'll let it go. As Kevin said, it does no good to bring up the past. We can't change it."

Dean squeezed her hand, and she squeezed back. Letting his hand go, she pulled the journal from her purse and offered it to Everette. He took a step back in surprise.

"It's yours," he said. "This is what I chose to do with it. Now you must decide what you want to do with it."

Theresa looked at Kevin. He gave no indication of what she should do.

"I'll keep it safe," she said.

"There is one other thing," Everette said, stopping them from breaking up and heading to their cars.

"What's that?" Kevin asked.

Again Theresa reached for and found Dean's hand.

"The land. In my will, it goes to you. We can keep the secret for as long as we live."

"How do you feel about that decision?" Dean asked when they were back in the car and headed toward Royce. This time, he was driving.

"I can live with it. I would have liked to bring my parents together. Give my father a proper burial. But I'm sure he knows we tried."

Dean reached over and took her hand. Again Theresa had proven that she had more substance to her than any woman he'd ever known outside his family.

"I know we agreed to remain friends for the meeting, but since it's my last night here, could we be friends for a little while longer?"

She looked at him and smiled. He took that for a yes.

Chapter 14

The last day, Theresa thought to herself. Wasn't there supposed to be a happy ending? Didn't the movies know that happy endings satisfied the audience more than tragic separations? Hadn't they done studies? So why was the ending of her film leaving the lovers turning their backs and moving in opposite directions? Why wasn't there a way to rewrite the script?

She'd tried, but she wasn't the writer, and in this case, both participants needed to be writing. And they were, but only up to a point.

They stopped for lunch in a small town that looked interesting and lingered over the meal. Driving back, Dean said, "I never really got a look at the country around here. Why don't you tell me about it?"

She looked through the window. Hills rose on one side of the car, while evergreens lined the side of the road.

"I don't know much about it. I left when I was twelve, remember? I can tell you the entire history of Buffalo, but Royce is as much a mystery to me as it is to you."

"Then don't talk about Royce. What about this area?"

"It's called Canandaigua. This is the Finger Lakes region, named after all the small lakes in this area. Canandaigua has a Queen Anne-style mansion around here, the Sonnenberg Mansion. The name means 'sunny hill.' It's a red brick structure with a lot of windows. I always wanted to go there, but never did. They make wine around here, too."

Theresa scanned the area. She'd been on this road before, and she remembered something. "If we turn right up there, it will take us to an old amphitheater and lake." She pointed to an upcoming road. Dean turned.

"It's my favorite spot in the whole state. At least of the ones I've seen." Excitement shot through her in anticipation of seeing it again. It wouldn't be the same as she remembered, she knew that, but it was beautiful. She'd carried the memory of the one and only time she ever seen it all her life. "My parents brought us here. We stayed overnight."

"Where?"

"Up there, turn right and park."

Dean did as she commanded. Theresa was out of the car the moment it stopped. She ran as fast as she could in her heels and suit.

"Where are you going?" Dean called, following her.

"Here," she said when he caught up with her.

Dean looked around. Theresa took his hand and pulled it around her waist. In front of them was a small amphitheater. It was a ruin with grass growing in cracks between the concrete seats. In the distance was a lake sheltered by small hills.

"You need to see it at night with a large moon in the sky. Then you don't notice the weeds and decay."

"I can imagine it," he said.

Theresa felt him smile. She'd taken his hand automatically, as she'd done at the lawyer's office. It was natural to reach for him when she needed someone.

"I was only eleven, but I thought it was the most romantic place I'd ever seen."

She turned and looked at him. "I know it doesn't look like that now, but I always picture it as serene and beautiful."

Dean looked down at her. She saw his eyes change, saw the desire in them. His head dipped, and she knew he was going to kiss her. She wanted him to. Here, in her place.

His mouth touched hers, and a coil snapped inside her. Her arms snaked around his neck, and going up on her toes, she welded her mouth to his. The kiss was desperate, as if it was the last time they would ever see each other.

Dean held her to him, his arms strong as steel around her. She wanted to raise her legs, but her dress restricted movement. Everything she had was coming out of her. Hunger. Need. Desire. It poured out of her like water over a falls.

"I've been wanting you all day," Dean said against her mouth. "When you came down those steps this morning, I wanted to take you right there."

"I've wanted you, too," Theresa admitted.

His mouth settled back on hers with a new strength, an added need. Their heads bobbed from side to side while their mouths drank of each other. Emotions burst inside Theresa. Her skin prickled, and her body turned to liquid. She melted into Dean, joining with him as much as the limitations of her clothing would allow. She spoke to him with her mouth.

His hand dove into her hair, loosening it and letting it flow through his fingers. She felt the weight of it drop as his fingers spanned her crown and he angled her mouth against his.

Theresa was dizzy. She saw, as if on the big screen, a camera circling them and knew the bewildering rapture of what it meant to fall in love. This was her canyon, the precipice over which no net could save her. The place where her heart opened and accepted that this man owned a piece of it.

"Could we go?" Theresa asked, sliding her mouth free. She was close to tears, and with Dean holding her so close, he'd know how much his leaving would devastate her.

With his arm around her waist, they returned to the car. Theresa took one last look at the amphitheater and lake before slipping into her seat. She imagined how they must look standing there, kissing, in that setting. It wasn't lit by lights or manicured into something perfect for the cameras. It was a ruin, in need of weeding and repair. But to her, it was the most romantic setting, and there she and Dean had shared a moment she'd remember forever.

And now it was back to reality. Dean packing. The truck leaving, and Dean stealing away in the early morning mist. Maybe their kiss wasn't the proper theatrical setting, but his exit had definitely been planned and executed for CinemaScope.

The house was strangely quiet. Theresa was so used to activity on the estate, that the suddenness of its absence was eerie. She and Dean had returned and found Chelsea playing a game with the sitter. After relieving her and changing clothes, the three of them had spent the afternoon watching television and making dinner.

They'd eaten, answering Chelsea's questions and listening to her chatter. The day would be normal for a family. Theresa let the fantasy of them being one linger. Finally, Chelsea went to bed. Dean said good-bye to her, and they returned to the living room.

"Are you packed?" Theresa asked, suddenly feeling awkward after crossing the room to stand on one side of the sofa.

"Almost. I have a few things to add. Most everything went out this morning. If you find anything after we're gone that we're responsible for, send it to the studio, and I'll see it's taken care of."

"I will."

Time was short, and while the day had been happy and beautiful, Theresa felt she and Dean were tiptoeing around something that neither wanted to say. If she could, she would have stopped the clocks right now. With them standing across the room from each other. But she did not have that power. So time flowed normally across the minutes, bearing them closer and closer to the inevitable point when separation would be fact.

Theresa wasn't good at endings. She searched her mind for something to say. They'd spent the night watching television with Chelsea. Now that she was no longer there as the buffer between them, Theresa felt her need for Dean bubble to the surface. Dean must have felt it, too. He started toward her. The self-preservation instinct told her to move, step back, don't let him touch her, but the need to feel his hands all over her overruled any logic in her brain.

She studied his features, feeling a little off balance, as if the air had been suddenly ripped from the room. The vacuum was filled with an electricity that snapped about them. Theresa reached for Dean's arm, sure she would fall over if she didn't touch him.

The action was the catalyst to unleash the passion coiled inside them. Just as the kiss in the amphitheater had been desperate, this one was dangerous. Theresa felt as if she were climbing inside him. His mouth ground into hers, his tongue plunging into her mouth, scorching her teeth and throat. Instantly, her body burned. Her clothes were seared to her frame as Dean's mouth devoured hers.

An eon passed before he raised his head. Theresa gulped air into her lungs. Her cheek stayed next to Dean's as if they were attached. Her breasts heaved against his chest; her heartbeat drummed in her ears, drowning out all other sound.

"Come on," Dean said.

Theresa barely heard him. He took her hand and pulled her along behind him as they practically flew up the steps and into her bedroom. As he closed the door, he turned her into his arms. His mouth descended on hers as if the world continuing to spin on its axis depended on him kissing her. He found the hem of her shirt and ripped it over her head, only separating his mouth from hers long enough to complete the action.

His hands making contact with her skin was injecting a fever into her blood. She moaned as sensations rioted inside her. The tiny patch of bare skin wasn't enough. She wanted more, wanted to feel her naked body next to his.

Dean's hands were everywhere, in her hair, over her shoulders, down her hips. Her hands went to the snap on his jeans and popped it open. She unzipped them and nudged them over his hips. Her fingers feathered against his skin. It was hot and moist, and she had the sudden urge to taste him all over.

She felt a tremor run through Dean. His mouth moved to her neck. From one side to the other, he trailed fire across her skin. How was it possible? How could one man garner the forces of nature and make them his own? Theresa couldn't think how, but she knew he had. As his head dipped and he removed her bra, replacing the fabric with the furnace of his mouth, sensation zoomed through her, and she cried out in pleasure.

Dean had to hold her up. Her entire body weight rested on his arms, since she couldn't help melting under the onslaught of such complete joy. Dean didn't let up. His mouth continued to regale her, playing a tune as clearly as if she were an instrument. Her breasts ached for more, her body craving release.

In a mad rush, they finished undressing and went to the bed. Theresa pushed him into the mattress and began her journey of taste, traveling up and down his body. She liked the feel of him, the semisalty taste of his body. He trembled as she edged over his nipples and convulsed as her mouth dipped below his waist.

With the suddenness of an exploding star, Dean switched positions with her. His weight came as a surprise, but when his body entered hers, her eyes closed in ecstasy, her entire being filled with a sensuality that suffused her with the knowledge of the ages. Dean held a power over her. He made her feel like no one ever had. Cherished. Loved. Wanted. Empowered. With him, she could do anything, be anything.

In a moment, their dance began. His body thrust into hers. Raising her legs, she joined him in the primal performance. Power built in her, a double helix winding tighter and tighter. She could think of nothing, do nothing except concentrate on the dance, allow the sensations to mushroom to the surface of her being. To her core, rapture streamed over her like a waterfall, not cool and refreshing, but hot, burning, consuming. It had its own life. It pushed her, forced the rhythm to a fever pitch.

Sounds as deep and guttural as the dawn of time filled the room. Theresa didn't know which were hers and which were Dean's. It didn't matter. They were together, battling, working, giving and receiving as they had never done before. Tonight was new, different, more intense than any of their previous matings. Theresa arched her back, nearly lifting herself off the bed as she felt the earthquake build within her. The tsunami wave started deep and built, rumbling up and forward. It roared out of control, moving fast, gathering strength, vehement in its quest.

Finally, she exploded. The helix tore apart. The tsunami slammed into shore, the energy released, and crescendoed into a detonation as powerful as the explosion of a sun. Theresa fell back to earth with a slap against the mattress. Her breathing was erratic, ragged and loud in her ears. Dean lay on her, spent, wet with perspiration, his heart hammering fast enough for her to feel it.

She couldn't talk, couldn't do anything except wrap her arms around him. His braids covered her arms and spilled over her as they both tried to control their breathing. Dean rolled to the side. Cool air rushed in where he no longer covered her.

"Oh God," he said. "I thought you were trying to kill me."

Theresa smiled, turning toward him. Her breathing had yet to return to normal, and there was nothing she could say. She let her hands speak for her, rubbing them over his torso and around his neck until her body was aligned with his.

"You feel so good," she finally said. His body was hot, and his erection pressed into her. But she meant more than that he felt good lying next to her, that he'd felt good inside her. Never had they made love with this much abandon. Never had anyone worshiped her body so completely. And never had she wanted so much to please a man.

Whatever happened next, wherever Dean went, the heartache of his being with her would remain, but she would not regret their time together or the feeling of utter oneness with another human being that she felt at this moment.

He couldn't go to sleep. Sunrise to Dean meant he would be leaving Theresa. Every thing inside him told him he never wanted to spend another night without her. But what about his lifestyle and her belief that they had no future? They'd made love many times, mad, passionate love, yet she'd never indicated that she wanted him to stay. Even when they'd argued over him not telling her he was leaving, she hadn't indicated that she wanted their relationship to continue. And honestly, neither had he.

Could it work? He'd asked himself that many times. He knew about the groupies who followed the stars. He wasn't a star, but Theresa told him he would be. Even if the film was only a critical success, he would have others. He'd get funding and be able to make more movies. This was his life.

He hugged Theresa closer. She was asleep, but her soft body molded into his. He squeezed her closer, rubbed his hands over her breasts, and kissed her shoulder.

Closing his eyes, he thought of the last twenty-four hours. He'd slept well last night. The film was complete except for postproduction, and he was happy with what he had. He'd spent today with Theresa, and she seemed content with letting her father's secret remain within the family. Tonight, they had made love. It was hot, intense, and exhausting. He should have crashed as soon as she did.

Yet he was wide awake.

Dean didn't know how long he lay there. It started to rain. He heard the droplets hitting the windows before the door opened. His eyes clicked open like a broken shutter. He stared at the bedroom door. It was closed, but that wasn't the right door. He looked at the window. It wasn't raining. Yet Dean heard it.

Pushing back the covers, he slipped out of bed. Something was wrong. Why had he heard rain? And a door creaking open? Suddenly, there was a flash of light. It was so bright it hurt his eyes. It sliced through his head as if someone had made an incision in his brain. He held his head until the pain subsided.

Finding his jeans, he slipped them on and went toward the door. He needed to go downstairs. Whatever it was, it was down there. He knew it. How? If someone asked him, he wouldn't be able to explain. But he was sure it was downstairs.

The house was quiet, not sleeping but still. He heard breathing in his ears. It was his own breath. At the top of the stairs, another flash sliced his brain again. He grabbed the banister. There was a newel post at the top of it, and he hugged it, waiting, helpless, unable to do anything except let the light run its course. Sweat covered Dean's brow. He wiped it away and ran his hands down his pants legs. It didn't make sense, he thought.

Downstairs, he approached the room where much of the filming had taken place. He stared at the doors. They were still wrong. Pushing them inward, he stepped inside the dark room. No equipment remained. The furniture that had been there when his crew arrived had been cleaned and restored to its place. He'd had sets in here, lights, cameras that took up space and made the room feel small. Yet with all that gone, the place still felt small.

Stepping further into the room, he saw the door again. He saw it in his mind just before another flash of light incapacitated him. Grabbing his head, he attempted to stop the blinding flashes, but it didn't help.

He fell to his knees, still holding his head. The room was tiny, and rain pelted the walls. He was cold. He needed a blanket. There was no light, only a slit in the door. He looked through it.

"Dean?"

He whirled toward the sound.

"I didn't kill her," he said.

"Kill who?"

"I didn't kill her. He killed her. I saw it," Dean stated, his voice full of fear.

"Dean, it's all right." Theresa rushed to him, hugging him to her. "It's all right. I'm here. You're safe. You're safe."

He looked about the room. "Theresa, I remember." He crushed her to him. "I remember what happened to me." He squeezed her tighter as if he needed to hold on to someone.

They sat on the floor, holding each other. Theresa didn't push him to talk. She waited, letting him get used to the memories spilling into his head like an erupting volcano. She rocked him as if he were a small child having a nightmare. When he quieted, she pulled back and looked at him.

"Want to talk about it?"

He nodded.

"I was hiding in the closet. I was scared. They were fighting, screaming at each other. I hid under a blanket. I shouldn't have been there, but I was cold and scared and hungry. I saw him stab her."

Theresa didn't know what he was talking about. She stroked his face and arms, soothing him. "Dean, let's sit down, and you can start at the beginning."

He swallowed hard and took a long breath. They got up and sat on the sofa. Theresa reached to turn on one of the table lamps.

"No," Dean said quickly. "Don't turn it on."

She put her hand down, leaving the room bathed only in the moonlight coming through the windows. Dean sat forward on the sofa. Theresa pulled her feet under the nightgown she'd hastily thrown on when she woke and found him gone.

He took her hand and kissed her fingers. "He was drunk. And when he was drunk, he beat me."

Theresa bit her lower lip and tried to keep calm.

"My mother died, and I was left with him. There were days I didn't see him. Good days. When he came home, he beat me. Often, I would hide when I heard him coming. I'd keep quiet, not even moving, barely breathing. There was a closet in the basement he never looked in. That was my hiding place."

Dean grabbed his head as if he was in pain.

"Are you all right?"

"The memories come in flashes," he explained in a tight voice.

"Can I get you anything?"

"No, I don't think there's a pain killer for this." He continued his story. "That night, it was raining. He came home drunk, and I didn't hear him. The thunder was loud, and he was in the house before I knew it. The sight of me seemed to make him angry. He staggered around the room. I knew I had to get out. I couldn't go to the basement, or he'd find my hiding place and it would no longer be safe. He was blocking the door. He took off his belt. I knew I was about to be beat again."

"Dean, you were only seven, right?" she said softly. Tears had formed in her eyes, and she was grateful he'd asked her not to turn on the light.

"When he came toward me, I dropped to the floor and rolled under the table. I came out on the other side, close to the door. He'd left it open, and I went through it, out into the rain. I ran. I don't know how long I ran, but I kept going. I couldn't remember what direction I was going in. I only knew that I needed to escape because that night he would have killed me. Don't ask how I knew. I knew."

"So you ran out into the rain?" she prompted.

He nodded. "I ran for about a hundred miles or a hundred years. It felt like that. I was soaked through. My legs were tired. My lungs burned. I was crying, and I was hungry as there was no food in our house. He drank all the money away. I got free food at school, but this was summertime so there was no school."

Theresa sniffed, hoping Dean didn't know tears were streaking down her face. She used her free hand to wipe them away.

"I found a house. Some of the windows were boarded up, and there were no lights. The door was closed, but it opened when I tried the knob. I went inside. I was looking for food, and I was shivering. There was no one there. The furniture was broken like ours. There was no food so I thought no one lived there. I found an old blanket. It smelled bad, but I didn't care. I took it in the closet and wrapped myself up."

"Why the closet?"

"It was where I hid from him. I thought he'd find me, so I went in the closet. I don't know how long I was there. It was dark when I went in, and when they started arguing, it was still dark."

"They?" Theresa knew his mind was rushing now. The memories were back, and he was telling her as if she had been there, too.

"I didn't know I'd fallen asleep, but I woke up when I heard the voices. They were like his, slurred and angry. I thought of running again, but I was too afraid they would catch me. So

I stayed where I was. There was a slit in the closet door, and I could see through it. Most of the time, I could only see a broken table. They were on the other side of the room. I stayed until they stopped screaming at each other. Then the rain started again. I knew it was hot outside, but I was too scared to stay where I was."

Dean took a breath before continuing. "I opened the door. It made a sound. I was sure they could hear it. I stayed there a moment, waiting, sure someone would grab me by the collar and beat me like he did. But no one came. I had started for the door when I heard something fall. I turned toward it, afraid of it, afraid of who was there. I sneaked to a door that led into the kitchen. He was beating her. She was begging him to stop. Begging him not to hurt her. Telling him to think about the baby. He didn't listen. He kept on hitting her. She tried to fight back. That made him angrier. He grabbed something from the table. A knife. And that's when I saw him kill her."

Theresa gasped aloud. She could picture what Dean was describing. Even at seven, he'd remember the details. "What did you do?"

"I don't know. I don't remember if I screamed or not. I ran out into the rainy night, hysterical. I knew the man would come for me. He'd killed the woman, and he would kill me, too. I had nowhere to go, but I ran. I kept going until I was exhausted. Then I hid again. I found a woodpile in a deserted yard bound by warehouses, and I sat down behind it. The rain pounded down on me, making a puddle around me. I didn't move. I was too tired, too hungry, and too exhausted. I must have fallen asleep or passed out. When I woke up, I was in a hospital, thin and malnourished, with no memory. Not even of my own name."

He fell silent then. Theresa wiped away more tears. "Dean, I'm so sorry."

He turned to her then and pulled her into his arms. "Don't

cry, Theresa. If I hadn't run away that night, I'd be dead now. And my adoptive parents, my sisters and brothers are the best there are. They gave me a good life, good guidance, and the ability to love. In many ways, I'm very lucky."

Theresa smoothed the tears away. Dean was a remarkable man. To find good in what had happened to him, even with the memory of it shiny and new. "Do you remember anything else about that night?" she asked.

He thought a moment. "I don't think so."

"What about an address? Names?"

"I remember my name." He stopped, saying it as if it had only just come to him. "Stephen."

"Stephen what?"

"I don't know."

"You don't look like a Stephen. Dean suits you much better."

"I don't feel like a Stephen either."

"What about other names? Did the couple call each other by any names?"

He thought a moment. Theresa could almost hear the wheels in his head cranking, unlocking memories that had long lain dormant. Light was painting the sky over the trees and brightening the room. Outside, she heard the final truck shifting gears and chugging through the gate.

"Marge. He called her Marge. He shouted it over and over. And she called him Nate. 'Nate, the baby. Don't hurt the baby.'"

"No last names?"

"I don't remember any."

"Was she pregnant?"

He shook his head. "I don't know. I don't think so. When I saw her, she was on the floor."

"If he did kill her, we should be able to find that out by searching newspaper records in Dallas. There has to be a notice if someone was killed. We could check it out."

"I'm not sure I want to. What difference could it make? It happened so long ago."

"Dean, she could have a family. And it was murder."

Theresa's own murder secret came back to her. Her father had a family, too, and for twenty years, they hadn't known what happened to him.

"Knowing is better than not knowing," she said, speaking almost to herself.

"What?"

"My father," she said. "His disappearance changed the lives of seven people."

Dean stared at her. She saw he understood.

"Her family deserves to know. Knowing is better than not knowing," she repeated.

"What do you suggest I do?"

Theresa thought about it for a moment. She'd often searched the Internet for her father's name, hoping to find a reference to him. While there were many Alexander Ramseys listed, none of them were related to her.

"I mentioned the newspaper files. On the Internet, that would take a lot of time. If you were in Dallas, it would be easier. You could use the library. Or a private investigator. You know the approximate date this happened based on the date you were found. You could search to see if anyone named Marge was discovered or reported dead during that time period. And from that, you could find her family."

"Your sense of justice is very strong," he said.

"I'm thinking of how I felt not knowing what happened to my father. I don't know what I would have done if Aunt Patty was still alive." Theresa was glad she didn't have to make the decision of whether to have her aunt prosecuted.

Dean got up and walked to the window. He pulled the sheers apart and looked out on the dawning day. For a long time, he said nothing. Theresa got up and went to him. She slipped her arms around his waist and put her cheek on his warm back. He wore only jeans, no shirt. Touching him made her tingle all over. She didn't want them separated for a moment of the time they had left.

Theresa didn't know how much time that would be. Kissing his back, she asked. "When does your plane leave?"

Dean didn't check his watch. "I've already missed it."

The impact of Dean's words had her reeling. She went still for a moment, then moved to his side. "Is the pain that bad?" she asked.

"It's not the pain. I canceled the reservation yesterday."

Theresa could hardly breathe. "Why?"

"After last night, you have to ask?"

"Yes, I do." Her voice was small and low, barely above a whisper. The lump in her throat and the knot in her chest collaborated to squeeze her voice to nearly nothing. "Last night hadn't happened yesterday."

"There's a lot we have to discuss, none of it involving my memory as a seven-year-old."

Am I ready for this? Theresa asked herself. She'd resigned herself to him leaving today. Then her heartache could begin, and she could start the process of missing him, getting over him, not thinking of him all day, every day.

"Go on," she said.

"Us."

"Us?" She shook her head as if to clear it. "Sorry. I don't mean to repeat your comments."

"I canceled the reservation because I'm in love with you, and I couldn't leave without letting you know."

Theresa's mouth opened and closed, but no words came out. Dean smiled at her dilemma. Tears crowded in her eyes and spilled down her face.

"Good," he said. "Now you can cry."

"I love you, too."

He kissed her eyes and then her lips. "It's been a long and eventful day." He breathed against her hair.

Theresa closed her eyes. She felt as if she were floating. "It has," she hiccuped.

"I have to make another reservation today," he said, "for three."

She pushed herself back and stared up at him. "Three?"

"*Three,*" he repeated. "We're going to Dallas."

Chapter 15

A warm weather girl she was not. The change in temperature from upstate New York to Dallas, Texas had to be thirty degrees and still rising. Dean's family had whisked them out of the airport and into air-conditioned cars, but not before the heat of the Lone Star State had zapped the crispness from Theresa's suit and her body.

She rode in the back of an SUV driven by Dean's brother Owen. Behind them was a small caravan of cars and vans, carrying other family members. The entire family was waiting outside the security checkpoint at the Dallas-Fort Worth Airport as they came from the gate. They weren't carrying banners, and no band played "Hail to the Chief," but the effect was the same—overwhelming.

Rosa immediately came forward and hugged her. Theresa was grateful she had at least met her and Stephanie before.

"I know all of us showing up was unexpected," Stephanie said, sitting next to her in the SUV.

Dean was in the front seat, and Chelsea had immediately hit it off with Digger's daughter, so she was riding with them.

"You'll find out this is a very supportive family. Not only do we get together for the smallest reason, but we rally when there is a crisis."

Theresa nodded. She didn't know how to handle that. Her own background was much different. Aunt Patty was unapproachable. She and Kevin hadn't grown up together, and Meghan was gone. Even if they had to rally, it would only be the three of them. Her mother and father had some cousins that lived in other parts of New York. Theresa supposed she should try to find some of them, but they had never tried to make contact with her.

"Dean's memory is a gift, not a crisis," she said. She glanced at Dean sitting in the front seat. Dean didn't even turn around or acknowledge that he'd heard his sister-in-law. He must already know something. Theresa wondered why he'd insisted she come along. This was obviously a family issue, and she wasn't family. Regardless of whether he'd told her he loved her or that she loved him, she was not a Clayton.

"Maybe crisis is too strong a word. I only meant to explain why so many of us were at the airport."

"You're scaring her," Dean said over his shoulder.

"I don't mean to." Stephanie looked at her. Her face showed compassion, and Theresa relaxed. She'd liked Stephanie from the first. "When I first came to meet the family, I was scared out of my wits. It was a dinner, and it didn't go well."

"It went very well," Owen interjected.

"They thought I was a gold digger," Stephanie smiled and ignored Owen's comment. The two men laughed.

"It's a long story. We'll tell you the whole thing one day," Stephanie said.

When they pulled into the driveway of a house in a modest section of Dallas, the number of car doors opening and closing created a music of its own. Theresa looked at the people spilling out of them, thinking it seemed like a traditional potluck and that they should be holding covered dishes.

She braced herself. For what she didn't know. At the airport, they had descended on her. She wasn't used to it, nor had she expected so many people hugging and kissing, smiling and talking over each other. They acted as if Dean had been missing for twenty years and had just been found. Theresa stepped back from the fray, but the sisters surrounded her, pulling her into the mix. Chelsea bathed in the glory of so much attention, but she'd just come off a movie set where she had an entire crew doting on her. The Claytons were just an extension of the support she'd become used to.

To Theresa, they were claustrophobia-inducing.

Dean slipped his arm around her waist. She looked at him and smiled. He knew what she needed, and he was always there for her. "They won't eat you."

"I know."

"Even if it seems like they will."

"They love you. I've never known that kind of love."

"You will," he said.

Theresa didn't get to explore that statement. Chelsea ran up to them and pulled on Theresa's arm. Next to her was Digger's daughter. Theresa couldn't remember her name.

"Theresa, Sam says I can go swimming. Did we bring a swimming suit?"

Samantha, that was her name, Theresa thought. "I'm sorry, honey. I didn't pack one."

Chelsea's face fell, but Sam saved the day. "She can use one of mine. Uncle Owen keeps some here for me."

"Is it okay?"

"Only if an adult is acting as lifeguard."

"My dad's going to watch us," Sam said.

Theresa nodded at Chelsea, and with a whoop, the two girls ran toward the house. The rest of the group had gone in that direction, too. Dean nudged her forward, and the two of them walked toward the steps leading to the front door.

Inside, the air was cooler, and already there was the activity surrounding the preparation of a meal. The rooms were large and airy, and Theresa loved the way they were decorated.

"This is beautiful," she said. "You can tell Owen is an architect."

"Stephanie is a decorator as well. Together, they redid the house. It has the same feel of the place we grew up, but it has evolved the way a house should with families living in it, growing up and older and making room for a new generation." There was pride in his voice.

"Come on in," Stephanie called from the kitchen. "We love to gather in here."

Theresa looked from Dean to his sister-in-law. She'd already turned around and walked into the kitchen. "Aren't you curious about what they know?"

"I'm dying to find out. We'll talk over the meal. We all like to eat."

They moved away from the front door. As Theresa passed the steps, she noticed the newel post. "This is different. It's not part of the renovation. It has been here for years. Who is she?"

Dean smiled at the carving and rubbed her head. "This is Clare. Digger carved it. We don't know who the model was. He said he didn't know, that he just made up the face, but we suspect it was his biological mother."

A pang of understanding surged through Theresa. She knew how he felt. She had lost her mother, too.

"Digger came when he was thirteen. Before that, he lived on the streets. Our dad saw his aptitude for woodwork, and suggested he sculpt. After Clare, he gave up the effort. Digger wouldn't name her, so the rest of them decided on Clare. I hadn't come here yet. We all rub her for good luck each time we leave the house." Dean reached out and rubbed Clare's head.

Theresa did the same on her way to the kitchen.

* * *

The kitchen was a cook's dream, double ovens, extra large refrigerator, copper pots hanging from a ceiling rack, and a counter large enough to service a family this size.

"You must entertain a lot," Theresa said.

"We do," Owen answered, reaching over his wife's shoulder to grab a carrot stick from the vegetable tray she was arranging.

"Most of the arrangement was already in place," Luanne said. She sat in a chair at the kitchen table. Theresa remembered Dean telling her that Luanne was pregnant and her husband was taking no chances that anything would happen to her or the baby. "Our parents took in a lot of kids, and meals required a lot of equipment and coordination to get enough food hot and ready for everyone at the same time." She looked over the assembly, taking them all in.

"Can I help with anything?"

"Not on your first time here," Erin, Digger's wife, stated. Digger was in the pool with the kids. Theresa could hear the girls screaming outside. "Take a seat. Dinner's almost ready."

Dean went outside. Theresa felt deserted. She took a seat next to Luanne and a woman she hadn't been introduced to.

"Hello," the woman said. "I'm Mariette Randall, Owen and Brad's mother." She had a tentative smile, and her face reminded Theresa of someone who'd been extremely ill for a long time.

She was also confused. Dean had said all his brothers were adopted and that their parents were both dead.

"It's another long story," Luanne furnished. "In time, you'll learn all about us."

Theresa didn't know if she should bring up the subject of her longevity with this family. They were hospitable in including her, but they were making an assumption that hadn't been discussed between her and Dean.

"Dean tells us you have a gorgeous house in New York," Mariette said.

She nodded. "It's in the Finger Lakes region. Mountains and lakes all around us."

"He's using it in the movie," Rosa explained from across the room.

Theresa understood that she had been discussed at length with the various members of Dean's family. She didn't know how often he talked to his family on that electronic connection, but clearly, she'd been discussed.

"I hope it looks as good in the film as it does in the dailies," Theresa said.

"Dean's very good," Rosa continued. "I'm sure he'll show it off beautifully."

Whatever they were cooking smelled delicious, Theresa thought. She hadn't had anything since breakfast, and that was hours ago. They provided a snack on the plane, but she had been too nervous about meeting Dean's family to eat.

"I hope Simon gets here soon," Owen said. "I'm ready to eat."

Who was Simon, Theresa wondered. She thought she had all the brothers straight in her mind. Mentally, she went through them, Owen, Brad, Digger, and Dean. Then the two sisters, Luanne and Rosa. Simon must be a friend. Maybe he was Rosa's boyfriend. She was too beautiful not to have dozens of men vying for her attention.

"We're waiting for Simon because he has some of the information Dean requested," Owen said for her benefit.

"I didn't know," she said. "Is he a policeman?"

Dean came through the door at that moment. His smile was broad.

"Simon's not a cop," Brad said. He hadn't spoken since they'd left the airport. He'd sat on a stool between the table and the window and watched what was going on both inside and outside. His eyes were hooded except when they lighted on his wife, Mallory.

"Simon's the family investigator," Mariette said. "He found me after more than twenty years."

"Your family has its own investigator?" Theresa asked, unable to keep the incredulity out of her voice.

Everyone stopped and stared at her. The second was long and uncomfortable. Then, like a song continued after a pause, they all burst into simultaneous laughter.

"I suppose he is," Stephanie said when the laughter subsided. "He found me, too."

"Owen had already found you," Dean contradicted.

"Yeah," Owen agreed. "Simon only confirmed your true identity."

Theresa was completely lost. "What do you mean, he found you?"

At that moment, the doorbell rang. "There he is now," Owen said, pushing his large frame up from a chair. "As usual, right on time."

He left the kitchen. As if on cue, the three women grabbed bowls and trays and marched into the dining room. Theresa could see a set table through the doorway.

"Get the kids out of the pool," Luanne ordered.

Brad got up from the stool and went outside.

With remarkable coordination, they began a choreographed parade of people with food or kids. It seemed like only moments later, they were all seated around the big dining room table. Theresa noticed how they were all paired off, husbands with their wives. Simon Thalberg sat at one end where all could see him. The kids ate in another room with Mariette.

No one mentioned Dean's memory during the meal, but when the plates were removed and coffee had been served, Simon pulled out a folder that could have laid on his lap for the entire meal. Theresa never saw him move to retrieve it. However, she did notice then that he was missing a thumb on his left hand.

On the plane, Dean had explained that he'd called the family and told them of his newfound knowledge. Owen, who was very well-connected in Dallas, had agreed to confirm what he could of Dean's story. Theresa surmised that what he couldn't verify, he'd had Simon Thalberg look into.

Theresa pushed her chair back and stood up. Everyone looked at her, and she felt like a lab specimen on display.

"Do you need something?" Stephanie asked.

"No. You all are about to begin a family meeting. I thought I should leave."

Dean took her hand. "I'd like you to stay. You were there for the worst part. You should see it through to the end."

She sat back down, and Dean pulled her chair both in to the table and closer to his. Attention was focused back to Simon, and Theresa let out a slow breath. Dean's hand took hers, letting her know she could relax.

"I checked for violent crimes that occurred two weeks on either side of the date Dean was admitted to the Children's Medical Center of Dallas."

While he had the folder lying on the table, he did not open it to refer to anything inside it.

"The woman's name was Marjean Harris. She was Marjean Lincoln before she married Grover Harris. They would have been married twenty-eight years if she were still alive today." He opened the folder and handed a photo to Dean.

He looked at it. "This is her."

"It's a morgue shot," Simon said. "And she's pretty banged up."

Dean offered the photo to Theresa, and even though Simon's statement implied they shouldn't look at it, she did. She wanted to understand what had hurt Dean all these years, and if the two of them had a future, she wanted to have familiarity with anything that affected him.

She passed it to Digger, who sat on her right. The photo

made its way around the table. Only Erin turned away from the brutally beaten face.

"Mrs. Harris was found four miles from the warehouse district where Dean was found. Nine miles from where Dean lived with his stepfather. She'd left her children with a teenage babysitter. Told her she was going to the movies."

Simon gave nothing away by his demeanor or body language. He neither approved nor condemned the behavior of the people he talked about.

"The house was rented by Helen Serra. At the time, she was working the streets along Crown Street."

Dean swung around and explained to Theresa, "It's a poor section of town."

"She's no longer there. Today, she owns a bar on Amigo Road." Owen supplied that bit of information.

"The bar is strictly legitimate," Simon went on. "She's streetwise, a been there, done that personality. Her clientele aren't the elite of the city, but she allows nothing underhanded to take place there."

"I suppose the aftermath of discovering Marjean Harris scared her straight," Digger said.

"You remember this?" Erin asked.

"It happened during one of those periods when we were forced by a school project to listen to the news every night and read the newspaper. It was the current event of the day."

"It did cause a sensation," Simon said. "Ms. Serra was having an affair with Mr. Harris. The way she told it to the police, she was supposed to meet Grover that night at her house. When she got there, Grover was missing, and Mrs. Harris was dead in the kitchen. At the time, she didn't know who Mrs. Harris was, but she called 9-1-1 and the whole story played out in the papers and on television."

"No one connected the death of Mrs. Harris with Dean's discovery," Luanne said. "And since you couldn't remember anything, no one ever put two and two together."

"Of course not," Erin added. "You were seven years old. You were found miles away from that house. I'm amazed you even got that far."

"Fear is a powerful thing," Dean said.

Theresa's heart hurt. She imagined him at Chelsea's age, traumatized, afraid of being killed by his stepfather and then seeing a murder. No wonder he'd blocked it out.

"What happened to Mr. Harris?" she asked before she realized she'd spoken aloud. She'd planned to sit quietly and let the Claytons do what they did. They were a family. She was not part of it.

"He disappeared that night. He's never been found, although he's still wanted for questioning in connection with her death."

"Any idea where he is?" Dean asked.

Simon shook his head. "I haven't had enough time for a thorough search. From what I could discover, he ceased to exist the night she died. No tax returns, no credit cards, no loans, no driver's license renewals, no speeding tickets, no encounters with any local law enforcement agency, not even a library card. He just vanished."

"Isn't that hard to do?" Brad asked, speaking for the first time. "For someone who knows how to falsify records, forge new ones, it's difficult. For a someone like Grover Harris, it should be impossible."

"I agree," Simon Thalberg said. "But he *did* disappear, and if he is still alive, he's the exception to the rule."

"You believe he's alive." Theresa stated it. She was sure Simon wanted to find him.

Thalberg looked directly at her. "I do," he said simply.

"Dean, do you want him to try and find Harris?" Brad asked.

Theresa stared at Dean.

"What would be the point?" he said. "It's been twenty

years. I was seven years old. A good lawyer will have this thrown out before it even gets near a court."

"He's right," Simon said. Practically every head in the room dropped in defeat.

"What happened to the children?" Erin asked. She owned a nursery school, and Sam was her adopted daughter.

"They went into foster care. I have no other information on them at this time."

"Do we know what kind of father he was?" Again, Erin asked the question.

"I'd say not a good one," Luanne answered. "I checked this out. From what the neighbors and the school had to say, he was rarely home. Always drunk and arguing when he was there."

"So he probably wouldn't try to contact his children." Brad stated.

"Then follow the woman, Serra." Mallory spoke for the first time.

They all looked at her.

"I don't mean literally follow her," she explained. "I mean follow how she got where she is. She's a legitimate businesswoman. Where did the money come from to start her bar? Even if it isn't the best in town, capital was still needed to get it started. A prostitute isn't likely to have start up money."

Several people nodded.

"It's up to Dean," Owen said. "You know we support you in whatever decision you make."

Theresa was impressed with this family. They talked to each other regularly even if they had no reason. And they were all here, disrupting whatever plans they might have had, to be with Dean after he called to tell them his memory had returned. While their presence was a little cloying to her, they dearly loved their brother, and since she loved him too, she couldn't fault them. They didn't know her circumstances. Unless Dean had told them. And she was sure he hadn't.

Dean looked at her. "What would you do?"

"I don't think I should voice an opinion. Owen said this is your decision. Although you don't have to make it now. You can take some time to think about what you want to do."

"That makes sense," Rosa agreed. "Why don't we all get a good night's sleep, and let Dean have some time to think about it. He knows we'll stand with him."

General agreement seemed to think this the best way to proceed.

"I'll leave this with you." Simon pushed the small folder he had across the table to Dean. "Along with the photo of Mrs. Harris, there is one of her husband. It's old and grainy. I found it in a newspaper morgue."

Dean accepted the folder, but didn't open it.

"I also found something else. Something you didn't ask me to look for."

Theresa took his arm. She felt his muscles contract under his shirt sleeve.

"My stepfather." It wasn't a question.

Simon nodded. "He's alive."

The news couldn't have been worse, Dean thought. His stepfather was alive. He didn't want to see him again—ever. Simon's departure was the impetus for everyone to stand up and clear the table. While Simon had held the floor, very few of the Claytons had touched the coffee sitting before them. As they took the cups and filed into the kitchen, Dean and Theresa remained where they were.

Closing his eyes, he leaned back against the chair. What was he going to do? Theresa continued to hold on to his arm. He was glad she was there. He liked the feel of her hands on him.

He'd told Simon to wait, that he would call him if there was anything further he wanted him to do. When Simon had left, no one had asked Dean what he planned. They'd left him with Theresa and that damn folder lying on the table.

"What are you thinking?" Dean spoke without opening his eyes.

"I'm thinking of you," Theresa responded. He could hear the worry in her voice.

"What would you do?"

"About opening that folder?"

He sat up and opened his eyes, looking directly at her. "Yeah."

Reaching over, she picked it up. "I don't think I could resist."

"Wouldn't that be a little perverse?"

"Dean, you're human. Even abused children want the love of their parents."

He thought about that. The person who came to mind when he thought of Dad was Reuben Clayton. With him, he'd received love, understanding, guidance and hope.

"He wasn't my real father. I never knew my real father, my biological father. My mother showed me a picture of him once, but I don't remember what he looked like."

"What happened to him?"

"He died. At least she told me he died. Right now, I don't know what to think." His voice held defeat. He could hear it. So much of his life had been explained, but the effect was to unravel him. The only person holding him together was Theresa.

"If he'd been alive, don't you think he would have tried to find you, reported you missing?"

"I don't know. I never saw him. If he was alive, he didn't want me."

Theresa put the folder down and moved from her seat to his. She sat on his lap and hugged him, pulling his head to her breasts. "But you found people who loved you and cared for you."

"They did," he said, pushing back to look at her. "I am

grateful to them. I love them as much as any biological child can love his parents. But I also feel . . ."

"What?" she asked, oh so softly, as if he might not tell her if she used a normal voice.

"Abandoned. Unwanted."

"Dean, you have a large family. Look how they dote on you. That welcome at the airport was such an outpouring of love."

"I know. I understand. My logical mind knows my family loves me. I am lucky they found me, but I can't help the other feelings. I'm thinking it might have been better if I never remembered." He smiled, but he didn't feel it, and he was sure Theresa knew it. "After all, people who eavesdrop never find out anything good about themselves. And I've been trying to eavesdrop on my life since I was seven years old. Look what I found out."

"I know you don't mean that."

The trouble was, he did.

"No one mentioned a missing person's report," Theresa went on. "Why didn't your stepfather report you missing?"

"I don't know. I suppose he was glad to be rid of me. He only used me as a punching bag."

Theresa leaned forward and kissed him lovingly on the mouth. "I wish I'd known you then."

"You were busy with your own life thousands of miles away."

"I know, but maybe we could have supported each other."

"I think I'd have liked that."

She ran her hand down his face. It was soft. He grabbed it and kissed it.

"What about school? Someone had to miss you."

"My parents told me they searched the missing children's data bank, but I was never listed."

"They didn't know your name. How could they search for you?"

"They looked every month and only viewed the photos of

the male children who were added since the last time they searched."

Stephanie came in at that moment carrying a tray. "I thought you might like some coffee."

Theresa stood up, and Dean immediately got up and took the tray from his sister-in-law. "Why don't we all have coffee in the other room and let this subject rest for a while?"

Theresa nodded. He knew running away from his problems wouldn't solve them. And he'd been running for twenty years. But he was exhausted now and wanted to think about something else.

"Uncle Dean. Uncle Dean," Sam whined as she skidded around Stephanie and came into the room. "She says you put her in your movie. *I* want to be in your movie." She pointed at Chelsea, who had run in after Sam.

Dean was suddenly relieved at the change in subject. He stared at them for a moment. Sam had a pout on her face that he'd seen before. He tried not to laugh, but all the pent-up emotion he'd been holding in since Simon Thalberg had entered the house came bursting out in the form of laughter.

"Stop laughing," Sam commanded, folding her little arms across her chest. She stuck out her lip.

"I'm not laughing at you, sweetheart." He picked her up and swung her around. "You've already been in one of my movies. You were in the first movie." She'd been the subject of one of his class projects. She was probably too young to remember it. She was nine now, but at the time, she'd just turned five.

He set her on the floor. She turned to Chelsea and, pointing to herself, said, "*I* was in the first movie."

"So?" Chelsea said. "He told me they're going to put my name on the screen. It'll say *Introducing Chelsea Nelson*." She gestured with her hands the way Dean had done it.

"Girls," Stephanie stopped the argument, "remember, you're friends. Now go back into the other room."

Sam, showing a flair for the dramatic, swished her little body from side to side as she went out of the room.

Dean heard her saying, "But I was still first," as they walked toward the room with a big screen television.

"She's going to be a handful," Dean told his sister-in-law.

"She's already a handful," Stephanie agreed. "But she's all ours."

Dean nodded.

"The guys are in the den. Don't ask me what they're doing," Stephanie said.

"Mind if I join them?" he asked Theresa. She shook her head.

"She'll be fine with us," Stephanie said.

Dean picked up the folder. It should at least be hot in his hand, he thought. It wasn't very thick, but it held part of his life. On his way out of the room, he slipped it on top of the china cabinet. If he was lucky, it would fall into a crevice and not be found for the next twenty years.

Chapter 16

The women had gathered in a great room at the back of the house. It had a vaulted ceiling with three fans twirling above, pulling the hot air up and away from the occupied space.

"What would you like to drink?" Rosa asked almost the moment Theresa and Stephanie came in. "We have a wide assortment, coffee, water, or something cold."

"What are you having?"

"A margarita."

"I'll take one of those, with the salt."

Rosa poured it and handed it to her. "We all want to know," she said.

"Know what?" Even though they were Dean's family, she thought he should tell them what he decided.

"Are you two getting married or what?"

Theresa nearly choked. She set the glass down. Tears came to her eyes as she tried to cough the liquid out of her windpipe.

Mallory started for her. "Talk to me," she said.

"I'm all right, Dr. Clayton," she wheezed. "I wasn't expecting that question." Slowly, her passages cleared, and she could speak normally. Wiping her eyes, she looked at the assembly. "Dean and I aren't getting married."

"We thought . . . I mean . . . from what Rosa said," Erin began but stuttered over her words.

"Dean's never brought anyone home with him before," Rosa said. "Women follow him around, but there's never been anyone he was really serious about."

"Until you," Stephanie said.

"I think you're reading too much into this."

"I don't think so." Mallory spoke. Everyone looked at her as she didn't speak often, but when she did, people listened. "I know how I felt and how I tried to hide how I looked at Brad when I fell in love with him. You've got that same look."

"Yeah," Stephanie agreed. "You positively glow."

Theresa felt the blood rush to her face. Her feelings were readable. These women knew she was in love with their brother. But they weren't getting married. Dean hadn't asked her to marry him. And Theresa was a logical person. She dealt in supply and demand. She understood the groupies in Dean's chosen profession and knew that she couldn't keep up with what was to come in his future.

"You know," Theresa said. "You all are a little overwhelming." She tried to keep her voice from sounding perturbed or snotty.

"We are," Stephanie said. She looked at the four other women. "The first time I met them, I felt like they gave me the third degree."

"And you continue to do it. Didn't you learned from prior experience?"

They laughed.

"Sorry," Stephanie said. "We're just concerned for Dean."

"I am, too, but that doesn't mean we're engaged."

"Would you like to be?" Rosa asked.

She pulled no punches, Theresa decided. When she was on a course, she didn't take detours.

"That's between the two of us."

"Don't get us wrong." Luanne, who'd said nothing yet,

spoke. "Dean is kind of special. He's our baby brother, and we've gone through a lot with him."

"Haven't I already had this interview?" she asked. Their concern for their brother was bordering on obsessive. "And in case you haven't noticed, your baby brother isn't a baby anymore."

"Just answer me one question," Rosa said. "Are you in love with him?"

Dean came in at that moment. Every eye had been on her. They shifted to him. He looked at all the faces. Theresa didn't know if he'd heard the discussion or not. Her body grew even hotter than it had been under the scrutiny of his family.

He took in the tension in the room.

"Who died in here?" he asked.

Dallas was a vast network of broad boulevards and tall buildings. Dean negotiated them with ease. Immediately after he'd come into the room where Theresa was being grilled, she had gotten up and left. Her intention was to get as far away from the Claytons as possible.

Dean stopped her as she was heading for Chelsea. "What happened?" he asked.

Theresa said nothing. She called for Chelsea.

"She'll be all right," Dean said. "What happened?"

"I'm leaving," Theresa told him. She reached the stairs. Clare seemed to glare at her. So much for good luck, Theresa thought.

"Why?"

"I'm not comfortable here."

Dean's brothers came out of the den, obviously investigating the commotion going on in the hall.

"Keys," Dean said, holding his hand up. Instantly, four sets of keys were produced. Owen tossed his across the room. Dean caught the set and took her arm. Together they went to Owen's SUV.

Dean didn't say anything as he drove. She needed time to calm down, and Dean was giving it to her. He finally pulled into the parking lot of a big sand-colored building.

"What is this?" Theresa asked when he opened the door on her side and took her hand.

"A place where we can talk without being interrupted."

The walkway to the building was long and impressive. The sign outside said *The Women's Museum.*

"Do you mean someplace I can shout and scream?"

"You want to shout and scream?" he asked in jest. "We can go to Texas Stadium."

Some of her anger dissipated. "No, I don't want to cause a scene."

"Good." He led her up the multilevel staircase to a quiet place. "Now tell me what happened."

"They started grilling me."

"About what?"

"You, of course. What is with your family? First, two of your sisters come to Collingswood and scope me out. Now the entire clan is on my case. Haven't they ever heard of hospitality? Maybe I should leave my social security number so the family investigator can check me out, too."

"That's not fair," Dean said.

"Maybe it isn't," she conceded. "But they are overpowering. I don't know if I can handle this. I don't know if I want to."

"What do you mean by that?"

Her heart hurt. She wanted to be with Dean. Nothing would make her happier, but she couldn't stay here. "I think I should go home."

"Why?"

"You don't need me here. You have your family. They love you. I know that. I can't imagine my brother or even Meghan running to my aid if my nightmares suddenly had meaning."

"Yet you flew all the way from London the moment she called you. And you've committed to rearing her child. Don't you think they would do the same for you? Or is the real reason you think they wouldn't come because you wouldn't ask them?"

He rendered her silent. It had been a long time since anyone had read Theresa so clearly. Dean was right. She would have done anything for Meghan or Kevin. But for herself, she wouldn't consider asking them.

"This is how my family is. We don't have to ask. We're there because we know it means something to us."

Theresa turned to him, and he opened his arms and hugged her close. She loved being in Dean's arms. Her body came alive when he held her like it had never done with anyone else.

"I know you want me to like them. I want to, too, but they're so . . ."

"Close?"

She looked up at him. He understood. Dean dropped a kiss on her lips and pulled her back to him. She felt as if a warm coat had been placed over her.

"They're very touchy-feely."

"They only want to welcome you." He pushed her back. "I understand that you didn't grow up in that kind of atmosphere. Because we were the throwaways, we were like you, standoffish, wary of relationships, loners. Our parents constantly held us, hugged us, encouraged us to talk, made us feel wanted, and gave us a place to belong."

"And you all do belong. But I don't. I used to think Collingswood was the worst place on earth. It had taken everything I loved. But I understand now that it's where *I* belong."

Dean spun her around. "You don't," he said, his voice harsher than she'd ever heard it directed at her. "People don't belong to places. We're mobile for a reason. We can go where we want. And we adapt."

"So you think I could learn to adapt to large groups of loving people? Like your family?"

"I'd like that."

"Why?"

"I love you."

"Are you sure?" she asked. He'd said it before, but she was afraid to believe it. So much of her life hadn't turned out the way she dreamed it. Dean was the pinnacle of dreams. He was loving, sensitive, attentive, a great lover; he adored Chelsea, and she could spend the rest of her life with him.

"Absolutely," he said. "I want you to—"

"Don't say it," she stopped him.

"You don't know what I was going to say."

"It doesn't matter. Just don't say anything else. You have other things to deal with first."

"You're talking about my stepfather."

She nodded. "And Mrs. Harris."

He kissed her. "But not now. Now it's just us."

"I like that." Theresa looked around for the first time. "What is this place?"

"The Women's Museum is a history of the female—art, sports, there's always a special exhibit. They have many openings here. In fact, Owen practically met Stephanie on this very spot."

"Really," she smiled. "She's the only one I like."

He laughed. "Funny you should say that."

"Why?"

"She's the only real Clayton in the bunch."

"I don't understand."

"Stephanie is the biological child of our adoptive parents. We didn't know about her until two years ago when we discovered some papers. Owen was obsessed with finding her. We hired Simon Thalberg."

"He also found Mariette?" Theresa remembered.

Dean nodded.

"Now I understand what they meant by the family investigator."

"Yes, and if you ever try running away from me, we'll have him find you, too." He laughed in her ear, but Theresa knew he was serious.

The sun had set by the time they got back to the house. Although the lights were burning in several rooms, several of the cars were missing. He rang the doorbell, even though this was his permanent address. Since Owen and Stephanie had married, he never just barged in anymore. Using the key on the ring Owen had tossed him, he opened the door. Dean held Theresa's hand as they entered the foyer. The house was quiet, empty of his brothers and sisters.

"Where is everyone?" she asked as they walked down the hall toward the great room.

"Probably at Jake's. It's a local restaurant. They probably thought you might need less Claytons around," he said.

Theresa glanced at him. "I know they didn't mean to come on so strong. I was rather unappreciative, too."

"I'm sure both sides will get the chance to apologize."

Dean walked into kitchen and looked for a note on the refrigerator. It was there. He snapped it down and handed it to Theresa.

"Do you want to go and join them?" she asked. "The note says they had a reservation for nine. That was only half an hour ago."

Dean shook his head. Opening the refrigerator, he pulled a pitcher of iced tea out and got glasses for the two of them.

"Why don't we just relax a bit. We can meet them for dessert."

Theresa took the iced tea and went into the great room. This was one of Owen's renovations. Dean liked it. Although it was cavernous, it was also intimate and roomy. No doubt Owen designed it for the growing family that they had become. In the last three years, there had been three weddings, and now with Luanne pregnant, there would be even more family members.

He looked at Theresa and wondered if she'd join the family if he asked her to marry him.

"What about dinner?" Theresa asked. "Aren't you hungry?"

"Only for you," he smiled, but he was only half joking. She turned to look at him, and he was definitely not joking. "Come here."

"Dean, your brothers could come back at any time."

"No, they won't." He walked toward her. She backed away. He kept going until she reached the middle of the room. Dean placed his hands on her waist and pulled her into him. "Thank you for coming with me." His mouth touched hers, and the fire between them roared. Dean wondered if it would be like this every time. So far, each time he got near her it was like a raging fire was ignited. When they made love, nothing short of a nuclear explosion could describe it. No one had ever made him feel this way before.

Dean felt Theresa's hands on his shoulders. Her arms moved under his braids, and her fingers spread into his hair. Volcanic tremors raced in his blood. Her long body was soft against his, and her mouth was as eager as his. Dean wanted to tear her clothes off and take her right on the floor, but he slipped his mouth from hers and held her close. His breath was ragged as he gasped for air.

Together, they walked to one of the sofas and sat down. Dean immediately got up, remembering the folder Simon had left. He picked up his iced tea from the table where he'd set it. Retrieving the folder from the high shelf, he came back and dropped down next to her.

"Are you sure you want to go through that now?" Theresa asked. "It's been a long day with flying here from Rochester."

"I think now is a good time. Before the house fills up."

"Oh," she smiled. "You mean you need less Claytons around, too."

He leaned over and kissed her as an answer. But it was true. With the family around, he was both on display and expected to discuss his decisions. He hadn't made a decision yet. Theresa would understand that.

"Would you like me to leave?" Theresa asked.

He searched her face. She could easily have been one of his parents' adopted children. She was so in tune with their values. Dean thanked God she wasn't. He had no brotherly feelings toward her at all.

"Stay," he said. "I want you to share this with me." She'd shared the terrible revelation of her father's situation with him. But he wasn't sharing with her as payback. He needed to be with someone, and he wanted no one other than Theresa with him while he sorted his life out.

Opening the folder, he found a picture of himself on top. He'd seen it many times. It had been taken in the hospital and had gone out to services for missing children. He wasn't a match, and had never been. When Simon replaced the photo of Marjean Harris, he'd put it on the bottom. The next picture was that of his stepfather. Fear sliced through him the moment he saw the picture. It had been over twenty years, all but a few days of it without a single memory of the man, yet the face of his tormentor still had the ability to breed fear in him.

Theresa put her hand on his arm. She sat directly next to him, their bodies touching. Dean was sure she was communicating her love bodily.

"Do you want to face him?" She knew without him explaining whose picture he was looking at. Dean's stepfather didn't look as mean as he had when Dean was a child. He was an old man, craggy-faced, bald on top, with the gray whiskers of at least a three-day growth. His eyes, however, still looked hard.

"I don't know."

"What would you like to ask him if you could?"

Dean didn't have to think. He knew exactly what he wanted

to know. But like Theresa had once told him about her father, he didn't know if he really wanted the answer.

"I'd want to know why he never reported me missing."

"Maybe it says something in the report."

Theresa took the typed papers from the folder and looked at the inventory. Simon Thalberg was very precise and neat. He cataloged everything that was in the file by page number. She found the page. At the top was an address.

"Do you recognize the address?"

Dean didn't. He shook his head.

"Do you remember where you lived when you were seven?"

Again he shook his head. "I know you're old enough to memorize your address and phone number at seven, but I don't remember that. I can only picture the house we lived in and the closet in the basement."

Theresa rubbed his arm again. She read more of the report. "He's dying, Dean."

"Alcoholism?"

"Yes."

"I guess he never changed."

Her fingers tightened on his arm as she continued to read.

"What?" he asked.

"Apparently, Simon interviewed him." She looked up. "I see why he's the family investigator. You only remembered everything three days before we left Royce, and he got all this information in that short period of time."

"He's very good. We had Stephanie's address in twenty-four hours."

Surprise showed on her face for a moment. Then she looked back down and read.

"What does it say?"

"Simon asked him what happened the night you disappeared. His answer is he doesn't remember anything about that night."

"That's probably the truth. He never remembered anything the day after one of his drunken episodes."

"Simon also asked your question. His answer is the same, he doesn't remember. But . . ."

"But what?" Dean was anxious. How could you just lose a child? And not care? He thought of Digger and how much he had gone through when his son by his first wife died. When Erin and Samantha came into his life, he'd been willing to die for his adopted daughter. But his stepfather had never wanted him. He was in the way, a burden, someone for the old man to beat on.

"Simon went to your school. He spoke to your second grade teacher. She had gone to your home to find out why you stopped coming to school. Apparently, your father told her you'd gone to live with an aunt in another state."

"She never followed up?"

"It doesn't say. But there is a note from Simon. He writes, 'Dean was only in the first grade. If any papers had come from another state, they would have gone to the office, and a secretary would have sent the requested information. But in this area where you still have itinerant workers and indigent families, kids come and go in school without much notice.'"

Dean didn't want to continue talking about his stepfather. It was painful to review his life this way. In Theresa's dark living room, when his memories had come back, he'd remembered all the pain, the fear, the feeling of helplessness, thinking that no one wanted him. Having it reinforced didn't make it any easier to accept even when logic told him it was a blessing that his stepfather hadn't reported him. Had he told authorities and Dean had been sent back, what would his life have been? How long would he have lived? He was certain he would have been beaten to death one night.

"Let's go on to another part of the report," Dean suggested. "What does it say about Mrs. Harris?"

Theresa read for several moments. "Most of this is what

Simon said after lunch today." She turned a page and read further. "Nothing more."

He was quiet for a long moment. He thought about the children Mrs. Harris had left behind. How had they grown up? Did they have the same type of loving parents that he had or were they casualties of a foster care system that didn't care?

Dean reached for the papers. He placed them in the folder and closed it.

"Enough," Theresa stated.

"I think I'll ask Simon to check out the girlfriend, Helen Serra."

Mallory had suggested this earlier, and Theresa smiled her approval. "What's your reason for doing this?"

"The children. Like you, they've lived all their lives not knowing the truth about their mother. They need closure. And my parents would have said it was the right thing to do."

"I wish I'd known your parents."

"They'd have loved you."

"What about your stepfather? Any decision on him?"

Dean shook his head. "He never wanted to see me again. I think I'll grant him his wish."

"Can you live with that?" Theresa asked.

He nodded. But he wasn't really sure. What could he say to a dying man? He'd seen enough movies, knew enough plots, and lived enough with real people to understand that twenty years could change a man, especially a dying man. He didn't want to face his stepfather. He didn't want to feel any compassion for him. He didn't even want to continue the hate he'd felt. Even if he was still the same bastard he'd been when Dean was seven, nothing would change Dean's past. Seeing him had no purpose.

Yet Dean knew that before he left Dallas, somehow he'd come face to face with the man who set him on the path to becoming who he was today. There would be no thank-you in that meeting. Dean didn't believe in destinies or set courses.

No matter what, he'd have turned out in the same place he was now. He believed that given love, even the poorest children could achieve. But living without love breeds hopelessness.

He could remember that hopelessness. It had a face. And even though the face was old and craggy with a three-day growth of gray whiskers, it was as menacing as when it had been younger, stronger, and with a terrified child within reach.

Soft piano music played in the great room when Theresa came down the next morning. She didn't see any speakers. They must be concealed in the walls. Stephanie was alone, her feet curled under her as she drank a cup of coffee.

She'd looked in the room where Dean slept, but he was gone. She thought he'd be in the kitchen eating.

"Sleep well?" Stephanie asked. She got up and came toward her.

"I did," she told her. She hadn't expected to. It was a strange bed in a house full of people, and she was concerned that Chelsea might disappear in the night. The two of them had shared the room even though Chelsea wanted to stay in the room with Samantha.

"I'll fix you something to eat." She walked toward the kitchen. Theresa smelled bacon and coffee.

"Is everyone still sleeping? I thought I was late coming down."

"Most are outside in the pool. They'll be in to eat in a while."

Theresa looked out the window. She scanned the guys for Dean. He wasn't there. "Where's Dean?"

Stephanie handed her a cup of coffee. "Cream and sugar?"

"Black," she said. "Do you have any Equal?"

Theresa sat at the table, and Stephanie got the sweetner. Theresa fixed her coffee the way she liked it and took a sip.

"Did he go to find his stepfather?"

"He wanted to go alone," Stephanie said.

"I thought he would." Theresa got up. "Yesterday was my first day here. Today I can help."

"Can you do eggs for thirteen?" Stephanie faced her. "Are you superstitious?"

"No, but aren't there fourteen, including me and Chelsea?"

"We dropped my mother-in-law off last night at her house. It's not far from here."

Theresa took the eggs and began breaking them in a bowl. "I know a little about you all, but none of the real details. Dean said you are the only real Clayton and that Simon found you in one day."

"It wasn't quite like that. I learned that I'd been adopted a short while before my biological mother died. Brad and Mallory were getting married. I crashed the wedding."

"You did?" Theresa smiled. "I wouldn't think of doing anything like that."

"I was desperate." Stephanie put a pan of biscuits in the oven. "I wanted to meet my mother, but she died almost the moment I found her."

"I'm sorry."

"I am, too, but the family has told me many stories about her. She and my father were wonderful people. And they raised some pretty wonderful children." She glanced out the window. Inevitably, she was talking about her husband, Owen.

Theresa thought of Dean. He fit under that description too. She suddenly frowned, wondering how he was doing alone with his stepfather. She'd never seen him blow up before, but she knew he had it in him. She hoped he'd contain himself.

"Stop worrying." Stephanie broke into her thoughts. "Dean

might think he's alone, but Digger is there with him. If he needs help, he'll have it."

Theresa smiled, but Stephanie had turned back to her task. The kitchen smelled warm and inviting. Just when everything was ready, it seemed the entire clan knew. They came marching in, dried and dressed and ready to eat. Food bowls were passed around, and the general happy family routine begun.

The atmosphere was much less threatening today than it had been almost twenty-four hours ago. Theresa regretted her behavior.

Digger came in as everyone was taking their seat. He kissed his wife and daughter and looked at her. "He's in the hall," he whispered.

Theresa left her seat and rushed out of the room and into Dean's arms. He lifted her off the floor and kissed her hard.

"I know you had to do this alone. I wish I could have gone with you."

"I know, but it's like you reading that journal that Everette Hoefster gave you. You had to do it alone."

She understood. "I did." She pushed herself back. "How was it?" she asked.

"He looked worse than he does in the photo. He didn't recognize me. Didn't even remember me."

"How'd that make you feel?"

"It should have angered me and probably would have if he'd been able to respond, hold his own, even stand up. But he couldn't. I remember when I was seven, I thought of fighting him, getting big enough to knock him down. But fighting with him as he is now would be like beating a man who is lying on the ground."

She kissed him. His arms went around her, and he hugged her tight. She kissed him for more than being the grown-up in this situation. It was for all the things he was and had been to her. When he let her up for air, she took his hand.

"Breakfast is ready," she said.

Chapter 17

School began on an unusually warm day in September. Theresa was grateful for something to do. She'd rambled around the huge, silent house since her return to Collingswood. She had a full load of classes, and thankfully, the days went by quickly with thoughts of Dean invading her mind only during the changeover of classes and through the long nights.

She had fresh faces, the former upperclassmen of their high schools, now the lowly freshmen at college. It was a new world for them, and Theresa understood that. She was navigating her own new world, one that did not include seeing Dean on a regular basis.

Or ever again.

They had parted on good terms. He'd kissed her passionately as they separated at the airport to go down different walkways to different planes, different destinations, and different lives.

He called, often at first, but lately, the calls were less frequent. Theresa told herself she wasn't surprised. This is how things worked. In a long-distance relationship, it was easier to just let things slide.

Theresa had thought when they'd gone to Texas together, things might work out, but she was back to reality now. It was her and Chelsea. Everette Hoefster came by every now and then to see if she needed anything. Thanks to Jane Greene, the woman who'd hired Theresa in the Economics Department, the people in town had begun to invite Theresa to events. The fact that she was at the university gave her a bit of credence in their eyes. Theresa went because Chelsea needed friends, and so did she.

Her cousin still talked about all the people who'd been on the estate during the summer. For a while, she was the local celebrity at Royce Elementary.

September dissolved into October, and the small town was preparing for Halloween. Theresa eyed the small lighted pumpkin on her desk. Chelsea had given it to her after a trip to a local farm.

Theresa went back to correcting papers from the recent midterm exams. The phone on the desk in her office rang, and she nearly jumped out of the seat.

"Hello," Dean said when she answered. "I've missed you."

Theresa's heart nearly burst out of her chest. "Dean! I've missed you, too."

"I know I haven't called recently. I'm working with the editors over the film."

"I understand," Theresa said. She often said that when he called. "When do you think it will be finished?"

"It usually takes six months from can to screen. We're a little ahead of schedule, mainly due to Chelsea."

Theresa smiled. "Why is that?"

"Her footage requires almost no editing."

"I'll tell her that. She's already asked me if she can be in another movie."

She heard the hesitation on Dean's end of the phone. "That's one of the reasons I'm calling."

"You're beginning another movie?"

He laughed. "Not this fast. Word's gotten out here about

her acting ability, and a couple of friends, other directors, want to give her a screen test."

"Out there?"

"Yes. Do you think you could bring her out for a long weekend?"

Theresa's heart jumped again. She wanted to say she'd be on the next plane, but she had obligations. "Why can't they look at the dailies on your film?"

"They have seen the dailies. But they'd like her to read for something else."

"I can't leave. I have classes every day."

She listened, hoping she would hear disappointment over the airwaves. She wasn't sure it was there.

"Are you working twenty-four-hour days?"

"Mostly."

"I was thinking Chelsea could come out alone if you would pick her up and take care of her while she's there. She hasn't had a sleepwalking episode since you were here."

"Fine." He seemed to jump on that solution quicker than Theresa would have liked. "I'll have the arrangements made. One of the teachers from the set can chaperone her while she's here. Do you think it will be all right if she misses school next Friday and Monday? She can fly out on Thursday night and come back Monday."

Theresa searched her brain for a reason but couldn't find one. "Halloween is next weekend."

Dean breathed hard. "She'll need to get used to the time difference."

"I'll talk to her," Theresa continued, "but I'm sure it'll be fine." Theresa knew how excited Chelsea was about the movies. Doing a test would make her happy. She loved Dean, and he loved her, too. Halloween would take second place to a trip to see Dean.

"I'll make sure she celebrates Halloween out here."

"She'll love that." Theresa swallowed the tears in her throat.

"Good. My secretary will contact you with the details."

So that was what their relationship had come to. A secretary.

Theresa replaced the receiver a moment later. She'd asked about Dean's family, and he'd given her a short report on them.

None of the loving words she'd imagined he should say. It was a business call.

It had been the longest weekend. Chelsea had called her once when she arrived at Dean's house. Her tiny voice was excited about seeing palm trees and warm weather. Theresa knew exactly what she meant. When she'd gotten off the plane at Heathrow and gone into London, it was a different world from anything she'd known before. The pictures and movies didn't do it justice. Theresa had never been to California, but from Chelsea's enthusiasm, she would no doubt love it.

The plane was in, and Theresa stood outside the security checkpoint watching for the flight attendant to bring her niece to her.

"Theresa!"

Theresa heard the small voice and saw the ball of energy running toward her. Reaching down, she caught Chelsea and swung her around, setting her on her feet.

Chelsea starting talking immediately. "It was so much fun, Theresa. I had a great time. The test wasn't a test at all. I didn't have to write anything. I just had to say something into a camera. When it was over, Dean said I could come back. And, Theresa, you should see the pool in his yard. It was almost like the one at Uncle Owen's. And I didn't sleepwalk at all."

Chelsea prattled on, trying to crush everything that happened during her four days into one breath.

"Do you think we can go and live there, Theresa? And I could be in the movies."

"Chelsea, we have a house."

"I know." She dropped her eyes, then quickly looked up. "Can we go and visit sometime?"

"I don't know. Dean is a very busy man. He doesn't have time for us."

"That's not true."

Theresa froze at the sound of Dean's voice. She stood up, spinning around in one movement. He was there. Standing in front of her.

"Dean."

"She did a great job. And I did tell her she could come back anytime."

Theresa could hardly breathe. He was here. He was *here*. She couldn't think of anything to say. She blinked, expecting him disappear, thinking that he'd been a wish, a hoax her brain was playing on her. But when she opened her eyes, he was still there.

Dean stared at her. Around them, people moved to and fro. Children toddled after parents. Businessmen hoisted briefcases onto the security belt and removed computers from them. Planes took off and landed, but none of the sound penetrated Theresa's brain. All she could think was that Dean was here.

"God, I've missed you," he said. His voice was dark and hoarse. His emotions were visible in his eyes and on his face. Theresa watched him, her own desire evident. She made no secret of it, did not try to hide anything she was feeling.

"I love you," Theresa said. The two steps it took to reach him, she covered in a run. Their mouths met, clung; tongues danced, invaded, tasted, fused. Theresa felt as if he'd been gone for decades, centuries. She missed his smell, the feel of his hair, the solid way he held her. She missed how his mouth felt on hers and the way his body drove her crazy.

"We've got to get out of here," Dean said against her mouth.

"Are you guys going to do that all day?" Chelsea said. "We're not on a set."

Theresa laughed. Her cousin could double as comic relief, and at the exact moment, she was needed. Theresa's body was erupting. She wanted Dean. Craved him. Wanted him inside her, driving her mad with passion. She didn't know how she was going to drive with him only a touch away and her hands dying to rove all over him.

Theresa couldn't wait for Chelsea to go to bed. Her young body had quickly acclimated to West Coast time, and she was wide awake and excited when her normal bedtime came.

"Do I have to?" she whined. "I'm not sleepy."

"You will be in the morning when you have to go to school."

"No, I won't."

Theresa didn't argue with her. She pulled the covers back and intimidated her cousin with a look. The little girl got in the bed and settled on her pillow. Theresa sat on the bed and smiled at her.

"I'll tell you all the rest tomorrow," Chelsea said. She'd talked nonstop since she got off the plane.

"I'd love to hear every detail."

Dean stood over them. Theresa leaned down and kissed her on the cheek. "I missed you," she told Chelsea.

"I missed you, too."

"Good night, Chelsea," Dean said.

"You'll be here when I get up?" Her question was more a statement.

"I promise," he said.

Theresa's temperature shot up at least ten points. Dean took her hand, and they went back to the living room.

"How is the film going?" she asked when they were seated

next to each other. She felt awkward, like the two of them had no history, like they were on their first date and unsure of what the other one was thinking.

"Trailers are in theaters. We expect to release it on time."

"That's wonderful. You must be very proud seeing your dream take shape."

"Proud? I'm scared to death. Suppose they hate it? It's my first major film, and critics are quick to dismiss an untried director."

"You have nothing to be afraid of. It's a powerful story."

"You haven't seen it, at least not from beginning to end. Not the way theatergoers will."

"Ask me to the screening." Her heart pounded. She was assuming he wanted to invite her to California again. This time, she'd go. If she had to find a substitute for her classes, she would.

"Will you come?" His breath was anxious. "The whole family will be there."

She moved closer to him. "You couldn't keep me away."

He dragged her to him, pulling her across his legs until she sat on his lap. "They don't bother you anymore?" He kissed her ear. Theresa closed her eyes as her body began to tingle.

"I think I'm used to them."

"Good." He pulled her head back and kissed her neck. She moaned at how her breasts tightened, as if they anticipated Dean's hands. He didn't disappoint them. Slipping his hands under her sweater, he scorched her skin as he rubbed over her torso and released the hook on her bra. His fingers found her nipples, and she gasped at the sensation that rocketed through her with him touching only a small part of her body.

"It's been a long time," she whispered.

"Too long," he said.

"Oh Dean, I missed you so much."

His mouth covered hers. Reason was lost within her. Instinct took over. Her need of him, of this man, this one man, forced its way to the surface. Breaking through barriers of rationality, removing conscious thought, and leaving her hungry for him.

She turned her body and straddled his legs. "Do you have a condom?" she asked.

He nodded.

Her mouth went back to his. Her fingers fumbled for the buttons on his shirt. His hands found the waistband of her jeans and slipped inside the tight band. Bringing them around, he released the snap and lowered the zipper. His hands went inside. She was wet when he touched her. His finger slipped over the core of her, bringing to life rapturous feelings that spiraled inside her like a whirling top.

Dean pressed her back, sliding them both to the floor. "Did I ever tell you that I had fantasies of making love to you on this floor?"

"I had that fantasy, too," she admitted.

Slowly, they removed each other's clothes. Inch by inch, they revealed skin, kissing every square freed by the fabric. They looked at each other without shame at being naked, but with appreciation akin to worship. With the realization that they were meant to be, that something within the universe drew them together like opposite poles of a magnet. Dean completed her. He understood her moods and the subtle changes that made her happy or sad.

"Let me know you," Dean said. "Let me be the one."

He kissed her again, tenderly, softly. His mouth feathered her lips and her face. His hands drew down her arms and over her belly. Her skin felt like bubbles were boiling under the surface. She wound her arms around his neck, lifting his hair and letting it fall over her arms.

Dean deepened the kiss, and suddenly, they were spinning out of control. He found the condom and slipped it on. Then, spreading her legs, he joined with her. Pleasure balloons filled and burst inside her. They created their own world.

Mountains and hills sprang up like volcanoes, lifting the earth to form a new surface. Hot lava flowed between them, spewing up in huge displays of red and gold sparks. Rivers of emotion cut through the ground, carving out the rhythms of Dean's primal dance with her.

The drumbeat ended as they fell back to earth, exhausted and spent, but with a feeling so new, so distinct, that it defied description.

"I never want to be separated from you," Dean said. "You've got to marry me. I don't think I can go another day without you in my life."

"Dean . . ."

"I know you don't like my life, but we'll have to compromise. I can't live another three months like the last three."

"Neither can I," Theresa said.

"I want you to marry me," he said.

She stopped. Her breathing was hard. Trying to control it, she sucked in air, breathing harder and harder in her attempt to stop.

"You have to marry me," Dean whispered, his body still out of control. "I promised to go to a wedding in February."

"Whose wedding?" Theresa asked.

"Your brother's."

In the heat of the moment, she'd forgotten that Kevin and Donna were being married in February and that Donna had invited Dean.

"I won't wait," Dean said.

"For what?"

"I want to marry you now. As soon as the semester ends. Then we can go to California."

"Suppose I don't want to live in California?"

"I'll tell Chelsea on you."

She laughed. "So that's how it going to be? I get out of line, and you tell my cousin."

"Get used to it." He kissed her again, pulling her close. "You haven't answered my question."

"The one about a wedding?"

"That would be the one."

Twisting around, she faced him. "Let me do it now. Yes," she said, holding on to the consonant until Dean kissed her and began another exploration of her body.

Epilogue

A Year Later

It was a wonder that Theresa had not scraped all the fingernail polish off her newly manicured nails. She'd had them done that morning. They matched the elegant Versace gown she wore. And it was all she could do to keep them still, especially since the roving cameras seemed to alight on her and Dean each time they broke for a commercial.

Her wedding rings weighed heavily on her third finger, gleaming brightly in contrast with the bloodred nail polish. But sitting and waiting at the Academy Awards for Dean's final three categories to be called was driving her insane.

The Homecoming had been nominated for twelve Oscars. So far, the film had won nine of them. Chelsea sat on one side of her, clutching the Oscar she'd won for Best Actress in a Supporting Role.

"Wait until the kids at school see this," she'd said when she returned to her seat after the photo session backstage.

Dean sat on her other side. Seated in front of them was Opal Cooper, the film's lead actress. She'd just returned from accepting her gold statuette. Behind them, Lance Hunt held his first Oscar after three nominations.

Four categories remained. Dean was nominated in three of them. The winner of the fourth from last left the microphone. Dean caught her hand. His was ice cold.

"Don't worry—it'll be a clean sweep," Theresa whispered. Her heart was pounding. Her words held more assurance than she felt. There were five nominees. Dean had taken her to see all of the nominated movies. The crop was powerful. The decision of the voters had to have been difficult. However, Theresa knew Dean's was the best.

" . . . and the Oscar for Best Original Screenplay goes to . . . Dean Clayton for *The Homecoming*."

It was impossible to hear anything after the announcement of Dean's name. The roar of the auditorium drowned out further sound. Theresa jumped in her seat and threw her arms around him. He kissed her. Tears sprang to her eyes and rolled down her cheeks as he got up, shaking hands with those around him, and went to the stage.

Theresa couldn't remember any of the speech he gave standing at the podium. Blood rushed in her head, and she heard nothing of his words, only saw the tall, gorgeous Clayton she was married to. At home, he'd practiced different speeches if he won any of the three awards he was nominated for, but if he stuck to the script or rewrote it on the spot, she'd only know when she watched the video later.

Dean returned to his seat before the final two awards were announced. There was a break in the program as the television viewing audience went to commercial. At home, it was probably a couple of minutes' worth of visual advertising. Sitting in the plush seats of the Kodak Theatre, it felt like a lifetime.

Dean went on to win the Best Director Award and accepted as both producer and director of *The Homecoming* when it won Best Picture of the Year.

"I love you," he whispered as he kissed her and got up.

His third time that night at the acrylic podium. He looked

intelligent and sexy. Theresa considered herself the luckiest woman in the world to be married to him.

"I'd like to thank my wife and my daughter," Dean started, holding the gold statuette in his hand. On the huge screens behind him, the camera found Theresa and Chelsea. "Much of the credit for this picture . . ." He looked at the Oscar. ". . . goes to them, and only Chelsea's name is in the credits." The audience laughed.

"I'd like to thank my family, my brothers and sisters, who believed in me and this project. But they are family, and that's their job." Again, the audience laughed.

Theresa pictured the Claytons watching Dean from their seats on the second lobby level. Dean had just created history with his three Oscars. It was an event the family wouldn't have missed. Like Stephanie had said, they all got together for the tiniest reason and rallied for a crisis. This reason wasn't tiny. This rally wasn't for a crisis but a celebration.

"Seriously, they did believe in this picture enough to back it, so I thank them for not only their moral support but also their cash."

Dean continued to thank the members of the cast and crew, many of whom smiled widely from their seats, some holding Oscars of their own.

"I know we're pressed for time. Many of you want to get to the parties, especially those of you carrying the little gold guys." He paused for laughter and held up the Oscar. "But I'd like to tell you something about this labor of love. *The Homecoming* was closer to my heart than I knew when I started the project."

There was a knowing change in the audience. Theresa could only describe it as an outpouring of respect. Much of the community knew of Dean's part in bringing Marjean Harris's killer to justice. What they didn't know was how much of the film mirrored the actual events in the hidden reaches of Dean's past.

"It's won me more than this award, which I will forever treasure," he continued. "It also won me a new life and my own homecoming. Thank you."

The audience stood up, applauding as Dean left the stage. After the final joke from the host and the dismissal for this year's program, the audience began the process of emptying the 3,400-seat theater. Theresa carried two of Dean's Oscars. Chelsea carried her own. Leaving their seats quickly, they went toward the stage where they had agreed to meet Dean if he won.

Minutes later, he came from behind the stage. Theresa watched his six-foot-plus frame, dressed in black tie, descend the three steps and come toward them. His smile was broad, and although people tried to stop him to congratulate him, he walked directly to her.

Without a word, his arms went around her waist, and he kissed her. Like the perfect ending to a love story, the boy won the prize. He got the girl. And they all lived happily ever after.

Dear Reader,

While I didn't begin *On My Terms* with "Once Upon a Time," I got to end it with "Happily Ever After." I've wanted to do that for years, and Dean Clayton and Theresa Ramsey seemed the perfect couple to bestow that wonderful phrase on.

This is the fourth installment in the Claytons series. I can't tell you how much fun it was to work with the characters in this book and their wonderful house in the Finger Lakes region of New York State. I love this part of the country. The scene about the moonlight in the amphitheater is true. I went there as a budding teenager, and it was the most romantic place I'd ever seen. Setting the book there was a no brainer.

I'm about to delve into my next Clayton novel. This time, it's Rosa's story. After the way she's welcomed the last two Clayton wives, it's time for her to get the Cupid comeuppance.

I hope you'll continue with me in other Clayton adventures. If you'd like to hear more about *On My Terms*, and other books I've written or upcoming releases, please send a business-size, self-addressed, stamped envelope to me at the following address:

Shirley Hailstock
P.O. Box 513
Plainsboro, NJ 08536

You can visit my Web page at the following address: http://www.geocities.com/shailstock.

Sincerely yours,

Shirley Hailstock